EFRAIN'S SECRET

EFRAIN'S SECRET

SOFIA QUINTERO

Ember

Text copyright © 2010 by Sofia Quintero
Cover art copyright © 2010 by Veer, Inc.

All rights reserved. Published in the United States by Ember, an imprint of Random House Children's Books, a division of Random House, Inc., New York. Originally published in hardcover in the United States by Alfred A. Knopf, an imprint of Random House Children's Books, a division of Random House, Inc., New York, in 2010.

Ember and the colophon are trademarks of Random House, Inc.

Grateful acknowledgment is made to International Creative Management, Inc., for permission to reprint an excerpt from *Here Is New York* by E. B. White, copyright © 1949 by E. B. White. Reprinted by permission of International Creative Management, Inc.

www.randomhouse.com/teens

Educators and librarians, for a variety of teaching tools,
visit us at www.randomhouse.com/teachers

The Library of Congress has cataloged the hardcover edition of this work as follows:
Quintero, Sofia.
Efrain's secret / by Sofia Quintero.
     p.   cm.
Summary: Ambitious high school senior and honor student Efrain Rodriguez makes some questionable choices in pursuit of his dream to escape the South Bronx and attend an Ivy League college.
ISBN 978-0-375-84706-6 (trade) — ISBN 978-0-375-94706-3 (lib. bdg.) —
ISBN 978-0-375-89549-4 (ebook)
[1. Drug dealers—Fiction. 2. Violence—Fiction. 3. High schools—Fiction. 4. Schools—Fiction.
5. Hispanic Americans—Fiction. 6. Bronx (New York, N.Y.)—Fiction.] I. Title.
PZ7.Q44Ef 2010
[Fic]—dc22
2009008493

ISBN 978-0-440-24062-4 (tr. pbk.)

RL: 7.1

Printed in the United States of America

10 9 8 7 6 5 4 3 2 1

First Ember Edition 2011

For my nephews Juan, Alex, Josef, and Victor, outstanding young men all

Imperative ♦ (*adj.*) necessary, pressing

Application fee to Harvard University: $65
Tuition per year for a full-time student: $32,557
Annual room and board: $11,042
Average SAT score for incoming freshmen: 2235
    (although Harvard ain't trying to admit that)
My chances of getting into any Ivy League
    college with an SAT score of 1650: worthless

I type "SAT prep" into a search engine when Chingy yells, "Yes!" from the computer station next to me. "I got a 1560." The librarian puts a finger to her lips. After mouthing an apology, he asks me, "How'd you do, cuz?"

"You don't want to know, kid."

"C'mon, man." Chingy's giddy because the average SAT score of an incoming freshman at Howard is only 1530. Being senior class president and having a GPA of 3.5, he's headed to D.C. next August. That is, if his older brother Baraka doesn't convince Chingy to join him at Morehouse in the ATL. "I know you did better than me," he says, leaning over my shoulder to peek at my monitor.

"I got a 1650," I finally say.

"Yo, I think you broke the school record, man! Mrs. Colfax said that back in 1986, this girl scored 1050 on the old version of the test." Chingy activates the calculator on his computer

1

desktop and types in some numbers. "Yeah, E., you did it! A score of 1050 on the old test is only a 1515 today. Congratulations, man!" I feel like a fraud but still give Chingy a pound for being a good sport about my outscoring him. "Get a teacher to mention that in a recommendation. That way you won't sound arrogant in your essay. Stay shy, cuz."

"You don't get it, kid," I say. "I *have* to retake the damn thing." A 1650? I studied all summer. After borrowing every prep book I could from any library within walking distance—Princeton Review, Nova, Kaplan, you name it—I spent a few hours every week practicing math problems and memorizing hundreds of vocabulary words. When I took the test three weeks ago, I swore I scored much better than I did on the preliminary exam last October. But all that work did me no good.

I open up a new window in my browser to search for the next test dates. Thankfully, even the colleges with December 31 deadlines will accept scores from the test scheduled for late January. With November around the corner, however, that gives me only two months to study. As I write down the test date and registration deadline, I tell Chingy, "Harvard ain't checking for no 1650."

But Chingy's already back at his station, pimping out his class ring on the Jostens Web site. A sales representative is coming to our high school next Friday, so today all the homeroom teachers handed out catalogs and order forms. You can design your ring on the company Web site, then print out an order form to give to the rep along with a fifty-dollar deposit. As Chingy adds and subtracts features, the subtotal on his monitor rises and falls. "Yo, E., what you think?" he asks. I roll my seat over to his computer. With a tap of the mouse, Chingy rotates the ring on the screen—a bulky model from the "Champion" series in white gold—so I can see it from all sides. "Smooth?" he asks as he clicks an onyx onto his design. "Or the majestic cut?" Chingy taps the mouse again, and the black stone morphs into a polygon.

"Definitely smooth. All those cuts are too busy," I say, kicking off to roll back to my own station. "What happened to stay shy? You ain't Allen Iverson."

"Dude got jokes." Chingy clicks back to the smooth onyx. The price of his ring drops twenty-five bucks but still costs over three hundred dollars. "Yo, you know what Leti told me? Some wild child just transferred to our school."

"Yeah?" Leticia Núñez is Pedro Albizu Campos High School's one-woman news network. She provides breaking stories on public affairs and human interest along with occasional unsolicited editorials, but her specialty is—you guessed it—gossip. I suppose when your best friend is GiGi González—the hottest chick in school—a girl has to make her claim to fame some other way. I scan my search engine results and click on the link for an SAT prep company whose name I recognize from subway ads.

"This kid is from K-Ville."

"K-Ville?"

"You know . . . New Orleans. Katrina."

"Oh." At a hundred fifty bucks per hour with a minimum commitment of twenty hours, I can forget about one-on-one tutoring. But I've already tried the cheapest option—studying independently with books and software—and that ain't cutting it. "Leticia must have it twisted. Why would he transfer to a high school in New York City so many years after the hurricane? That makes no sense, kid."

"*She's* been here since Katrina, and according to Leti, home-girl got kicked out of Mott Haven High School because she threw a chair in a teacher's face."

"That's gangster." Enough with the *bochinche*. That 1650 put me in a serious bind. Even if I had a new computer with a fast

3

Internet connection at home—which I don't—my gut tells me only a live class that meets for six to eight weeks before the next test date will make a worthwhile difference in my score, but how much does that cost? Eleven hundred bucks, that's how much. Even though it means being limited to the public library's hours, I check out online courses as a last resort. The least expensive one is four hundred dollars. Even if I skip the prep course, I still have to shell out another forty-five dollars registration fee for the January test. No fee waivers for a second shot at the Ivy League for me. Plus, eighteen bucks for the answers to last month's test so I can see which ones I got wrong. And that's just the beginning because there are no scholarships for students just to apply to college.

There goes *my* class ring. As much as I want one—as much as I *deserve* one—I can't buy one now. But, really, when did I ever? Deserving a ring and being able to afford it are two different things, and a man has to set priorities and make sacrifices. It's all good. I'll get a ring in four years when I graduate from Harvard. With a crimson stone, baby, *veritas* engraved around it. Word is born.

Abet ♦ (v.) to aid, help, encourage

"Don't look so scared," I say as I lay out the financial aid forms across the kitchen table. After clearing it of all the shakers, keys, bills, bills, and more bills, my mother sits down with this apprehensive look on her face. "I just need you to give me some information and then sign them. It won't take long." The ironic thing is, if we owned a house, stocks, bonds, and things like that, we'd be drowning in financial aid forms, so for once, being broke has some benefit. My moms can actually rest on her one day off after *haciendo la compra,* washing the clothes, balancing the checkbook, and a hundred other things.

Moms places fresh batteries in the calculator. "Okay," she says, jamming a pencil into the electronic sharpener. After grinding it to the rubber as if the shavings were cash, Moms fusses over her tax returns, repeatedly tapping the forms against the table.

"It looks like a lot of paperwork, but most of it is just information, that's all."

"Well, I guess I should read it, then," she says, reaching for a random booklet from Yale. Ten seconds later, the frown lines on her forehead reappear. "Oh my God . . . Honey, the tuition at this school costs thirty-five thousand dollars."

"Yup."

My mother glances again at the page. "Per year, Efrain!"

"Lo sé."

5

Her dark eyes dart down the page. "Room and board is an *additional* eleven thousand dollars. Each year!"

Okay, I freak out a bit every time I think about it, too, but I'm determined to find a way. Holding up a batch of forms, I force a smile and say, "That's why we're doing this."

"You can get a big enough scholarship to cover everything, right?" Now my mother sounds hopeful, as if she answered her own question. "We'll do whatever we have to do. *Lo que sea*." See how she says *we*? My moms believes in me, all day, every day.

"I'll probably have to take out a student loan every year," I say. "But the interest rates are really low." It took me a long while to accept that I will have to borrow money to pay for college, but it is what it is. If Harvard is going to give a kid from the 'hood a full scholarship, it ain't going to be the valedictorian of Albizu Campos High School but the dude already getting a free ride at Exeter, Andover, or some prep school like that. Real talk.

My mother shakes her head. "That's what I should've done to finish college." My surprise must be obvious because she flashes a big grin at me and ruffles my hair. "Yes, Efrain, your mother finished two years of college. Where do you think you get all those smarts?"

I definitely knew I didn't get them from Rubio, but I just assumed that when my mother graduated from high school, she went straight to work. "Where'd you go?"

"Not Yale, that's for sure," she laughs. "I would take two trains to Jamaica, Queens, to go to York College. I was majoring in occupational therapy. Back then you only needed a bachelor's degree to qualify for a license." My mother talks with her chin on her hand and faraway eyes as if she can still see her dream play across the yellowing wallpaper of our kitchen.

I debate whether I should ask, but my curiosity gets the best of me. "Why didn't you finish?"

My mother drops her arm as if I should know. "I had you."

"Oh."

She reaches out for my hand. "Hey, once you were in school, I could've gone back to college. But your father and I didn't think we could afford it. I mean, it might've been possible had we been willing to borrow the money, but, I don't know. . . . Your father and I were both raised to either save money for the things we wanted or just accept that we couldn't afford them and learn to live without them. But we were wrong, Efrain." Moms picks up a stack of blank forms and sifts through them. "Learn from our mistakes, honey, and set the right example for your sister. Go to college first, get married if that's what you want to do, buy a home within your means, and *then* have children if you want them. In that order." She winks at me. "Your education and your home are investments in your future. They're the only things you'll ever truly own and are worth going into a reasonable amount of debt to have. If Rubio and I had done that, you wouldn't be sorting through this mound of paperwork right now wondering how you're going to pay for college."

"I don't blame you, Mami." When I turned fourteen, my moms encouraged me to get my working papers, work part-time, and make my own money so long as it didn't interfere with my schoolwork. She always held a full-time job, but truth be told, I don't put it past Rubio to have discouraged her from going back to school. Dude be *machista* like that. Moms probably worked because they needed her to, especially when Mandy came along. "You did whatever you thought was right for us."

She squints at the form in her hand. "Your father has to fill out this one." My mother hands it to me. It says, " 'Noncustodial Parent Financial Information Form. If your parents are separated or divorced, and the parent you live with has not remarried, your noncustodial parent must satisfy this additional requirement to complete your aid application. Both parents are asked to provide their financial information so we can determine their individual contributions to your college education.'"

I suck my teeth and cast the form aside. "Whatever."

My mother leaps for the form. "Look, I hate to discuss money with Rubio, but this is for your education. Remember, Efrain, whatever it takes. And I'm sure your father will want to help put you through college."

"How can he now that he has that baby?" My mother avoids my eyes by examining the form. Yeah, that's what I thought. Then she suddenly bursts into laughter. Hey, if there's anything remotely amusing about writing in intricate detail how much money your family *doesn't* have, let a brother in on the joke. "What's so funny?"

My mother reads from the form. "'In the interest of confidentiality, your noncustodial parent's information is submitted separately using this form, which is available from this office and on our Web site in printable format.'" She lets out a belly laugh, dropping the form on the table.

I don't get it, but I smile anyway. It's mad rare to see my mother cut up like that. "I guess the school wants to help a dude hide his assets."

"What assets?" Moms yells in hysterics. "They think I don't already know that Rubio doesn't have shit?" This counts as one of those laugh-to-keep-from-crying situations, so I just whoop it up with my moms. She catches her breath to say, "'Chacho, if money were that important to me, I never would've dated your father, much less married him. Unless he has another job I know nothing about, there's no secret here."

No, Rubio has no secret job. But for a long time, he did have secret expenses. And once he had assets, too. He just decided to trade the three of us in for younger models.

Pertinacious ◆ (*adj.*) stubbornly persistent

The late bell for zero period buzzes, jolting me awake. That 1650 haunted me all weekend, so I must have dozed off while waiting for Mrs. Colfax in front of her office. She turns the corner with her keys in one hand and her "Teachers have class" mug in the other. I pick myself off the floor and say, "Hi, Mrs. Colfax."

"Oh." She slows down. "Good morning, Efrain." Maybe I'm just trippin', but I think I annoy Mrs. Colfax because I make her earn her paycheck as the college advisor. She probably came to AC thinking she wouldn't have to do any work because the students here barely graduate, never mind head to college.

"So let me guess," Mrs. Colfax says as she unlocks the door to her office. "You need another fee waiver." I follow her inside, and while she opens the drawer where she keeps the manila envelope with the waivers, I reread the poster above her desk for the thousandth time. The photograph is of a basketball hoop, and under it in gold letters it says, "You'll always miss 100% of the shots you don't take."

"I need two, actually."

"Two?" she says, hugging the manila envelope like it contains her life savings.

"One is for Princeton; the other is for Yale." And please spare me the speech about how these two waivers make a total of four, and that is the maximum she can give me. I don't need Mrs. Colfax to remind me that from here forward, I have to come out of my shallow pockets for the fee to every college application I complete.

Mrs. Colfax sighs, sits down, and motions for me to take the seat across from her desk. She says, "So you're applying to Princeton, Yale, Harvard, the University of Pennsylvania, Columbia—"

"No, not Columbia." Nothing against Columbia, except that it's in New York City. I got mad love for my hometown, but isn't college about expanding your horizons, learning to be on your own, and all that? When I graduate from law school, I'll come back, no doubt. Get a good-paying job, help my mother, and give my sister a leg up. But to do for them, I first have to lift myself up, and that means I have to bounce for greener pastures.

"Are you applying to any of the CUNY schools, Efrain?"

"Oh yeah. Hunter, Lehman, and City." If push comes to shove, and I don't get into an Ivy League college, I'll just go to CUNY for a year, then transfer. But that's plan B.

"Good, Efrain, because . . ." Mrs. Colfax pauses like she's trying to deliver some tragic news. Pulling two cards out of the envelope and laying them across her desk, she says, "You have to be realistic about your chances of being admitted to an Ivy League college. They're very competitive schools, and—"

"I know." Who doesn't? Last year Harvard received almost twenty-five thousand applications for only two thousand seats. That's what makes it Harvard.

"Did you receive your SAT score yet?"

"Yeah." I hesitate to answer. "I scored 1650."

Mrs. Colfax yells, "Efrain, that's wonderful!" One minute she discourages me, the next she acts like I just won the Nobel Prize. "Now, I have to check," she says, all giddy, "but I'm almost positive you broke the school record—"

"Yeah, but I have to take the SAT again and score much

higher," I interrupt. "Plus, I'm in the honors program, and I'm probably going to be valedictorian, right? All that counts for something, doesn't it?"

"Yes, but please understand, Efrain. Even if you were to get into one of the Ivy League colleges—and the chances are very slim—I'm afraid you'd be in way over your head. The honors classes here at Albizu just don't compare to the advanced courses that your peers at other schools are taking. For example, they're taking calculus."

"I wanted to take calculus," I shout. "It's not my fault they cut it." Only five students registered for calculus, so the principal canceled the class. Mrs. Colfax explained that since calculus was an elective, a class of five was too small to justify the cost of offering it. Everybody was heated, especially me. When an admissions committee sees that you didn't take math during your senior year, it's not going to think *Maybe the school doesn't offer calculus.* No, the committee will think *This lazy kid is just doing the minimum course work necessary to graduate,* especially coming from a school like AC.

"The point remains, Efrain, that first-year course work at a Harvard or Yale would be new to you," says Mrs. Colfax. "But it'll be familiar to students who have gone to elite high schools. They'll have already read the books—"

"So I'll get a list and read them over the summer."

"Even if you get in, you're going to be so overwhelmed!"

"Why do you keeping saying that?" But I know what Mrs. Colfax means. The woman doesn't believe I can even get into any of those schools. Either she cops to it or falls back. As if a Latino kid from the Bronx who went to an "academically challenged" high school never got into, never mind graduated from, Harvard or Yale before. The damn high school's named after a Puerto Rican who did just that!

11

Mrs. Colfax tries to clean up. "You should apply to even more city colleges and a few of the state universities, too." Then she ODs again, reaching across her desk to put her hand over mine. "C'mon, Efrain, even if you were to get into Harvard, you'd be a little fish in a big bowl. But at a school like Lehman or Hunter, you'd be a big fish in a little bowl just like you are here at Albizu Campos. Don't you want to be a big fish, Efrain?"

I yank my hand away, snatch the fee waivers off her desk, and toss them into my book bag. Mrs. Colfax looks hurt, and I feel bad, but only for a second. "No disrespect, Mrs. Colfax," I say, "but I ain't no fish." I throw my backpack over my shoulder and leave.

Validate ♦ (v.) to confirm, support, corroborate

"How many of you have seen this movie?" asks Señorita Polanco. She holds up a DVD of *The Bronx Is Burning*. I wanted to see that joint, but it played on ESPN, and when Rubio left, so did the cable.

Marco raises his hand but still calls out, "Yo, Miss P., you gonna show that?"

"Yeah, Miss Polanco," yells someone in the back of the room. "Show us that movie."

Don't these clowns know by now when Señorita Polanco's set to throw flames? She only speaks English during class when she's livid about something. Last time she broke out in English, she had overheard GiGi González and Leti Núñez raving about Jennifer Lopez in *El Cantante*. Señorita Polanco went off about how stereotypical J. Lo's performance was, how the movie placed too much emphasis on Hector Lavoe's drug use instead of his musical legacy, and on and on and on. She worked herself into such a tizzy, she forgot our *Don Quixote* test. Instead, Señorita Polanco gave us a crash course on the salsa scene in New York City during the seventies, and the next day she brought in a documentary about Fania Records and some CDs from her own collection. Only on Friday did she slap us with the *Don Quixote* test with a bonus question about Lavoe at the end.

Everyone gets a kick out of Señorita Polanco's political rants yet hates the extra assignments they often lead to, especially all her extra vocabulary lessons. She detests when we use

"Anglicisms." You know, when we don't know the correct word for something in Spanish and resort to an English word with a Spanish twist. *"¡Esto no es un tro!"* she yelled one time while banging her fist against a picture of a truck. *"Esto se llama un camión. Es un camión, ¡no es un tro! ¡Díganlo bien ahora!"*

"Es un camión," we respond to her demand that we use the right word.

Since Señorita Polanco's rant about *El Cantante,* Leti is on a quest to get back on her good side. Today, she calls out, "That's the movie about all the things that happened in New York City during the summer of 1977, right?"

Stevie yells, "Yeah, there was a mayoral race, the Yankees' run for the World Series, Son of Sam, a heat wave, a blackout—"

"¡En español, Esteban, en español!"

"¡Ay, señorita!" he grumbles. *"Yo no tengo suficiente vocabulario para describir todos esos fenómenos."*

"¡Pues, aprende, chico!" Señorita Polanco walks to the board and writes the words *heat wave*. Then she translates them into Spanish. *"Ola de calor."* She writes that on the board, too. *"¡Díganlo!"*

"Ola de calor," we repeat.

Then she writes *blackout* on the board followed by *apagón*. *"¡Díganlo!"*

"Apagón."

"¿Y cómo tú no sabes eso, bro?" I yell to Stevie. "Don't you go to DR every summer, where there's a heat wave or a blackout, like, every other day?"

Everybody laughs, including Señorita Polanco. Stevie throws his hands up and asks, *"Pues, Señorita Polanco, en el verano de setenta y siete en Nueva York, ¿cómo se dice en español,* Things were poppin'*?"*

We crack up again, and I give Stevie a pound for that. Finally, Señorita Polanco hushes us. *"Quiero se preguntarles, en la miniserie* The Bronx Is Burning, *¿cuántas veces mencionó a los puertorriqueños?"* Even those who saw the miniseries can't seem to remember, so she says in Spanish, "Well, I finally watched it this weekend, and the only time it mentions Puerto Ricans is in reference to terrorism."

Everyone's amnesia disappears as they shout "Yeah, that's true" and *"Es verdad."* Marco says, "A group of Boricuas called the FLAN bombed two buildings in Manhattan."

"FLAN?" I can't help but call out—and in English, no less. "That's *flan*. What terrorist organization is going to name itself after a dessert?"

"That ain't gangster," Stevie agrees.

"Whatever," says Marco. "They just said 'Puerto Rican terrorists' and never explained why they were wilding out." Now he sounds as upset as Señorita Polanco.

"En español," she reminds us, and once again she has us politicking while getting our learn on. This is my favorite class, no doubt. It even beats my civil rights elective.

The hour sails by, and the bell rings. Everyone rushes off to their next class while I hang back. "Very nice use of the present perfect indicative," says Señorita Polanco.

"Gracias, profesora." I take a deep breath. I don't know why this is so hard to ask when I know she won't say no. "Señorita Polanco, I was wondering if you would please write a college recommendation for me."

"Of course, Efrain!" she says. "It would be my pleasure. Just give me the forms and deadlines." When I reach into my bag for the folder I created with her name on it, stuffed with the recommendation forms, a calendar of deadlines, and self-addressed stamped envelopes, Señorita Polanco laughs. "Your confidence and resourcefulness are going to get you far, Mr. Rodriguez."

I hope she's right.

Pittance ♦ (*n.*) a very small amount, especially relating to money

After my last class, I head to the school library to my job as a peer tutor. It's only ten hours per week for minimum wage, but at least I don't have to spend time or money traveling to work. When I reach the library, Chingy's outside finishing off his usual after-school snack of soda and chips. "S'up, cuz," he says.

"Gimme some of those," I say. Then I dive into his bag without his blessing, and he pretends to mind. That's just how we do.

No, Chingy's real name isn't *Chingy*. We may be 'hood, but we're not ghetto, so don't get it twisted. A few years ago, some girls started calling him Chingy because he looks just like the rapper. Hated it at first. "What about Nas?" he'd whine. "Why can't they call me Jigga?"

" 'Cause you don't look like a llama or a camel, kid," I'd say. "Take a compliment."

But then it was *Chingy, Chingy, Chingy* from the likes of GiGi González, and let's just say homeboy acclimated. This is why when he works my nerves or I'm in the mood to work his, I remind him that his mother named him Rashaan.

That's rare, though, because we've been boys since kindergarten. Even Baraka calls me his little brother, too. Not seeing Chingy every day will probably be the toughest thing about going away to college, but he wants to go to an HBCU—a historically Black college—just like Baraka. BK wants Chingy to go to

Morehouse, where he's a junior, but Chingy's leaning toward Howard. He says that he's not trying to go to no all-boys school.

"Check it," says Chingy. "GiGi said she and Leti and all her girls are headed to the Grand Concourse now to see that new horror movie. Asked us to meet her there."

"You mean she asked *you*." GiGi's official, but that girl only goes out with two kinds of guys. Pretty boys like Chingy and street cats like my other friend Nestor.

"Nuh-uh," says Chingy. "She told me straight out, 'Bring Efrain.' "

"No, she didn't." Chingy's got jokes. Don't get me wrong. I'm not a bad-looking dude. My mother's a Nuyorican who's always being described by girls around my block as "that Black lady with the 'good' hair." (Don't get mad at me. I'm just telling you what they say.) My sister Mandy, who just turned twelve, and I take after her. And Rubio? With that blondish brown hair and green eyes, they don't call him Rubio for nothing. At least, that's what the dumb chicks and ignorant jokers who admire him do. Moms claims that I favor whichever parent's standing next to me, but I don't see it. The only thing Mandy and I get from Rubio is the last name Rodriguez, but according to the U.S. Census, so do over eight hundred thousand other people. Rubio probably fathered half of them.

Anyway, when girls find out I'm an honor student, they're, like, *Oh, but you're so cute. You're mad cool, too.* Why are they so surprised that I'm smart because I don't act like an herb? I like girls as much as the next guy, but I can't be bothered with anyone stuck on stupid. Problem is a lot of smart girls try to hide it, which isn't all that smart, so what am I supposed to do with that?

"I kid you not, cuz," says Chingy. Yeah, if Chingy truly wanted to mess with me, he would tell me that we had a physics test when we didn't. "So let's skip tutoring today and go check out that movie. Maybe GiGi'll get all scared and grab onto you talking 'bout *Oh, papi!*"

"Shut up," I laugh. "For real, though. I can't, man."

"C'mon, E.! Sweren won't trip on the first day of the program. I mean, how many times can you go through the same orientation?" Chingy flings his soda can into the trash. "Besides, we're his favorites."

True. Chingy and I have been tutoring for Mr. Sweren ever since our first year at Albizu Campos, and we're the only two in our graduating class that have stayed with the program. "I don't know, Chingy."

"We're seniors now!" he whines. "You need to give into the itis, son!"

I laugh. "Bro, that itis will kill you." Not that I'm not tempted. I imagine GiGi smiling when she sees me and telling me that she's happy I decided to come. And then I see her whispering to Leti when I reach into my pockets to pay for our tickets and come up with nothing but lint. Forget the popcorn, cherry slush, and Milk Duds.

And even though there's no way I can make thirty grand between now and next August to pay for a full year's tuition at an Ivy League college, I still need every penny I can save. As hard as I came at Mrs. Colfax this morning, she's right. Once I get admitted, I'll have to run hard just to stay in place. Maybe with enough savings, loans, and grants, I can avoid having to work during my first year of college. With those twenty hours to study, maybe I can bust out a four-point-zero, make the dean's list, and win enough scholarships to stay in school for the next three years. But I don't know how much money the government will lend me or how many scholarships I can win. The only thing I can control is what I earn, so the more, the better.

Between spending money I don't have and earning the little

money I can, I make up my mind. "Sorry, man," I say to Chingy as I hold out my fist. "I have to stay here and make that paper."

He gives me a pound. "You mean those coins." Chingy and I may tease each other about our choices, but we always respect them. That's why we've been boys for so long.

"Whatever, kid." I open the door to the library. "I'll tell Sweren you came down with the itis."

Chingy laughs. "You wrong, man, you wrong."

"Tell GiGi I said hi."

"Maybe I will, maybe I won't."

Yeah, he will. "Peace out," I say as I close the library door behind me.

Officious ♦ (*adj.*) offering one's services when neither wanted nor needed

I notice her the second I walk into the library. What a banger! Her skin is just like the wooden chairs, dark and smooth. She wears her hair in neat cornrows, and I like that. Some of the Black girls in my school do the craziest things with their hair—finger waves, burgundy streaks, lopsided haircuts. But even if a girl is fine, who notices her face with all that commotion at the top of her dome?

If this girl has on any makeup other than lip gloss, I can't tell, and I like that, too. Her nails are long and plain but clean. She's what Chingy, Nestor, and I would call a Halle. The last time we hung out before those two fell out, we found this Web site that showed just how much makeup and airbrushing goes into making famous women look like "natural beauties." It's scary, man. The only woman we all agreed wakes up pretty every morning was Halle Berry. Even with crusty eyes and morning breath, Halle can get it, all day every day. So now, whenever we spot a natural beauty, we say, *Halle at three o'clock.*

I go up to her and say, "Hi, I'm Efrain. You're new, right?"

"Yeah, I'm Candace." She smiles at me, and her teeth glisten like porcelain. They match her eyes like the jewelry sets my moms used to wear when Rubio took her dancing when I was little. She would put on these pretty dresses and match her necklace and earrings. She still has them, just never wears them because she works sixty-hour weeks, Rubio's with that chick Awilda, and . . .

Let me stop thinking about that because I'm going to get upset, and I don't want Candace to think I'm a ruffneck.

"So, where are you from?" I ask her.

Candace's smile disappears. "The South." Then it hits me that she might be that transfer student Chingy mentioned last week. But "the South" is a big place, and this girl doesn't look . . . I don't know. I mean, I've seen videos of those poor people who lost everything to Hurricane Katrina, and Candace doesn't seem . . . Well, she certainly doesn't look like someone who'd throw a chair at somebody. Besides, if that were true, wouldn't she be locked up somewhere? I start to ask her if she's from New Orleans, but then I figure if she wanted me to know, she would've said so. Instead, I ask, "Are you a senior?"

Candace hesitates again. "Almost."

She seems so uncomfortable. I decide to quit asking questions and make her an offer. "Well, whatever help you need, I'm your man."

Candace scowls at me. "What do you mean?"

"You know, whatever class you're having trouble with, I can help you." Then I say a quick prayer that she's not taking physics.

"I don't need your help," she snaps.

"Whoa!" What's up with that? "I'm just saying—"

"I heard you the first time, and *I* said I don't need your help."

Before I can answer, I hear, "E., what's up?" Lefty Saldaña comes over and gives me a pound. "This is the year you finally get me out of Math B, rah?"

God, I hope not. Lefty's nineteen and in the tenth grade, I kid you not. Now you know why we call him Lefty. Every year he needs a new tutor because no one who knows better wants to be stuck with him. I've avoided Lefty so far, so I hope Mr. Sweren doesn't ruin my last year at AC by assigning him to me.

Mr. Sweren sails through the door. "Hello, everybody. Have a seat." Candace stalks clear across the library. Mr. Sweren drops the papers and books he's carrying onto the table in front of him and says, "Okay, by a show of hands, who's here to receive tutoring?" A few kids raise their hands. I look at Candace, and she's staring straight ahead as if she knows my eyes are still on her. Mr. Sweren grabs some sheets and walks from table to table. "This first session is an orientation for tutors only. If you're a tutee, take this form and fill it out. Bring it back tomorrow, and I'll have a tutor assigned to you and a meeting schedule." Then Mr. Sweren walks over to Candace. "Miss Lamb, it's wonderful to see you here. The program really needs you. We never have enough math tutors." She flashes him that porcelain smile, and he hands her another stack of forms. "Would you mind passing out those forms to the other tutors?"

"Sure, Mr. Sweren." Candace takes the stack and rises from her seat. She reaches my table, and even though I hold out my hand, she drops the form on the table in front of me and keeps it moving. All because I assumed she was a "tutee"? Maybe I should be relieved she didn't go WWE on me and smash a chair over my head. Some dudes love girls who cop attitudes, but I'm not the one. I have more important things to worry about, but, man, do I wish I did have the money to meet GiGi at the movies after all.

Insidious ♦ (*adj.*) appealing but imperceptibly harmful, seductive

Before heading to my building, I stop at the bodega for a candy bar. Nestor and his crew stand in front of the icebox as usual. Nestor, Chingy, and I, the three of us, we used to be boys. But when Nes quit school and started slinging, Chingy wasn't having it and cut him off. Me, I don't like what Nes is doing either, but we all grew up together. I just couldn't drop him like that.

Not that I hang with Nes. Ain't no secret what he's doing on that corner, so Moms would give me mad grief. Besides I don't want to get caught out there with those cats when the po does one of their sweeps 'cause they're not trying to hear that you were just chilling. As far as they're concerned, if you're hanging out with the dealers, you must be buying or selling yourself.

Nes walks up to me and holds out his hand. "What's up, E.?" Then he squints in my face. "Girl trouble?" Man, sometimes Chingy can be oblivious to my moods, but Nes still reads me like a book.

"Ha." I think about Candace and then get mad at myself for thinking about her. "Remember Mrs. Colfax?"

"The typing teacher?" asks Nestor. He claws the air, wiggling each finger from one pinky to the other. "A-S-D-F-J-K-L-semi-colon. To this day, I can't break that spell, yo."

Yeah, in addition to being the senior advisor at AC, Mrs. Colfax is assistant vice principal of the business department. That means she not only "advises" the students who want to attend college, she also provides career counseling to those who don't and teaches business classes. At least, that's what she's supposed to do.

Anyway, I tell Nes what Mrs. Colfax said to me that morning. He shakes his head and says, "That's messed up. How she gonna say that to the smartest guy in the whole school?"

"That's all I'm saying."

"Man, let Colfax bogart her little fee waivers," says Nestor. "Say the word, and I'll hook you up with a job so you can pay them fees yourself like that, no worries."

Ain't that something? We found out what Nes was up to after dropping out of AC when he tried to recruit Chingy, who was insulted that Nes stepped to him. Although I never admitted it to either one of them, it bothered me that he didn't approach me, too. I never *wanted* to sling, but did Nestor think I was soft or something?

I walk toward my building, and Nestor tags along. "Yeah, Efrain, you should definitely go to college," he says. "Go to college, become a lawyer, and be the first Hispanic mayor of New York City, you know what I'm saying."

"Shut up." But I like the way it sounds.

"For real. But college ain't cheap."

"Who you telling?"

"Sell for me, and you'll never come up short on tuition. Especially once you start college. Students be my best customers."

"Get out of here, man." I'm about to joke about how bad it would be if heads found out that the first Hispanic mayor of New York used to sling when I see Rubio come out of the hardware store across the street.

Nestor catches the look on my face and turns around. He calls out, "Rubio!" Rubio gives him a slight nod and then glares at me.

24

I glare right back, then turn around to go into my building. Nes points and says, "Your pop's the man!"

I look back across the street, and there's some girl who's *not* Awilda talking to Rubio, looking at him all lovey-dovey. Nestor laughs and punches me in the arm. "Your father's, like, Super Playa!" I head up the steps to my building and wish Nestor would just go back to his corner. But he follows me up the stairs even though he knows I can't invite him in. "Yo, speaking of playas, how's Chingy?"

"He's a'ight." That's all I can say. Once I told Nes something about what was going on with Chingy—it was so trivial, I can't even remember—and Chingy read me. He said if I wanted to stay friends with him, I'd best not tell Nestor any of his business. I thought he OD'd, and we didn't talk for a few days. Then one day he did something funny in gym, I cracked up, and we got back to normal. We never talked about our fight over Nestor, just pretended that it never happened.

Nestor waits for me to say more. When I don't, he says, "Tell 'im I said, 'What's up.' "

"Okay," I lie. Chingy won't be trying to hear that message, but Nestor doesn't need to know that. "Peace, kid."

He finally starts back down the steps. "One, bro." I watch him until he disappears around the corner, but Rubio's still scowling at me from across the street. Where does he come off judging me for the company I keep? He calls my name, but I give him a dirty look and let myself into the building.

Aberration ♦ (*n.*) something that differs from the norm

The second I walk into the kitchen the next morning, I know something's up because my moms isn't chatting up my sister, Mandy, and doesn't tell me good morning.

Moms works at Yannis's Discount on Third Avenue off 149th Street. Since she doesn't have to be there until nine, and her bus ride is only twenty minutes, she's here when Mandy and I get up for school. Usually, she talks up my sister until I walk in and then turns the interrogation on me. I shouldn't say it like that. Moms just wants to know what's going on in my life, seeing that she works ten-hour days, six days per week. It's all love.

But this morning she just steals annoyed glances at me without saying anything. I say, "Hi, Mami," and kiss her cheek. This is the first time I'm seeing her since yesterday morning. Because she gets home so late, Moms either cooks dinner in the morning so my sister and I can heat the food up later or she leaves us money for takeout, frozen dinners, or something like that. When she comes home from work, I'm usually in my room doing homework or hanging out with Chingy. Sometimes she stops by my room to ask me if I want some homemade Dominican cake baked by Yannis's wife or if I have any dirty clothes to wash. Most times, though, my moms comes home, eats dinner, maybe watches a little TV in her bedroom, and then goes to sleep. Mandy and I usually only see her over breakfast.

I grab the box of Cap'n Crunch from the top of the refrigerator and then open the door to get the milk. My moms says, "Amanda, go finish getting ready for school." Oh yeah, something's definitely up if she's calling my sister "Amanda."

"I'm ready."

"Did you put everything you need in your bag?"

"Yeah."

"Well, go make your bed."

"I made it already." Obviously, my mother has something she wants to talk to me about alone, which is why my nosy little sister is lingering.

"Go, Beyoncé," I say.

"Efrain, stop," Mandy giggles. She loves Beyoncé, although every time she sees a picture of her with Jay-Z, my sister says she doesn't like him for her. I tell her me neither.

"Then do what Mami tells you."

"Oookaaay." Mandy finally takes her bowl to the sink and leaves the kitchen.

My moms stands up and walks to the doorway, checking to see that Mandy's in her room instead of eavesdropping in the hallway. "Efrain, your father called me at the store yesterday."

In a flash, my appetite disappears. "So?"

"He told me he saw you hanging out with Nestor."

I drop my spoon into my bowl. "Man—"

"Don't *Man* me, Efrain. I'm not one of your friends. *Díme con quien andas y te diré quien eres.*"

Tell me who you run with, and I'll tell you who you are? I usually dig those Spanish *refranes,* but this ain't Señorita Polanco's class. *"Mami, yo no 'taba andando con nadie.* All I . . ." I really don't believe this. Bad enough that Rubio's got the nerve to bother my mother at work over some nonsense, but Moms is buying it, too? Without finishing my cereal, I pick up my bowl and head to the garbage. "Forget it."

"Don't tell me to forget it."

"I just bumped into Nestor at the bodega on my way home from school, and he walked me to the door. That's it, Mami. I'm not hanging out with him."

"Then why are you so defensive?"

Because, after all he's done, you believe Rubio over me. But the lump in my throat won't let me say that, so I just dump my cereal into the garbage and toss my bowl in the sink. See why I can't stand Rubio? First, he plays my moms dirty for the whole neighborhood to see, and now he has us fighting, which is something we almost never do. "What happened is what I said happened."

Moms hesitates. "Well, your father was pretty sure. He told me that he called you, and you just ignored him."

I walk past her out of the kitchen and into the hallway. "Mandy!" I pick my backpack off the chair. "Mandy, c'mon, we're leaving."

"Efrain . . ." I don't usually disrespect my moms, but I can't listen to this anymore. I walk to the door, refusing to answer when she calls my name. My sister runs out of her room with her backpack and jacket on. Knowing my mother's not going to say anything else about Rubio or Nestor in front of my sister, I open the apartment door and head to the staircase.

My sister rushes to catch up to me. When we're outside, she asks, "Efrain, why you hate Papi so much?" I don't like to lie to my sister because I know how it felt to be her age and have older people lie to my face. Exhibit A: Rubio. But I also think it isn't right to expose kids to more than they can handle. Again, refer to exhibit A. So I don't say anything.

"He be asking for you all the time," says Mandy. So now Rubio's trying to manipulate my little sister to get to me. He can't step to me man-to-man, always has to run his game through the females. Whatever. After we walk a few brisk paces in silence, Mandy finally says, "He keeps asking me when you're coming by to see Junior."

"Junior? Who's Junior?"

Mandy sucks her teeth at me. "The baby, dummy."

Figures the egomaniac named the baby after himself. "How do you know all this?" I ask. "You've been to Awilda's?"

Mandy doesn't answer, but the guilt's all over her face. She says, "The baby looks just like you, Efrain. Papi showed me your baby pictures, *y ustedes son iguales.*" She says it like it should make me feel good. "Oh my God, Efrain, when Papi holds Junior, he's so funny, talking all that goo goo ga ga." Says that like it should make me feel good, too. Like Rubio's being all fatherly with his new baby who looks just like me should count for something. Mandy laughs, and it takes my all not to sneer. I ask her, "So, Awilda doesn't have a problem with you going over there?"

Mandy just shrugs. Then she says, "Oh, Efrain, you want to hear something funny? When I left, I kissed the baby, and then I kissed Papi, and then I kissed Serenity. Awilda's looking at me like she's expecting me to kiss her, too, right? But, instead, I said, 'Bye, Wildebeest!' Get it? And she's got, like, this stupid look on her face 'cause she's not really sure what I said." And Mandy laughs like she really showed Awilda a thing or two. "Wildebeest!"

"Yeah, I get it. So let me ask you something. Why you don't like Awilda?"

"Because she's the reason why Mami and Papi don't get back together."

But does Mandy know that Awilda's the reason they split up in the first place? Not that it really matters. I mean, yeah, she's a big ol' smut who knew that Rubio had a wife and kids and got with him anyway. The bottom line, though, is that, smut or not, Awilda doesn't owe my moms anything. Rubio's the one who stood before the priest and made the vows. He's the one who broke his promise. Even if Awilda was throwing it at him, he had no business catching it. Word is born.

"Mandy, how can you be mad at Awilda but not be mad at him?" I ask. "If Rubio really wanted to be with Mami—if he really wanted to be with us—he would just come back, and nothing Awilda could do would stop him."

"She went and had a baby, dummy. He can't leave her there all alone with the baby."

"But he could leave Mami with the two of us, right?"

At first, Mandy doesn't answer. Then she suddenly punches me in the arm, and thanks to Chingy, who taught her how to ball her fist and swing her arm just right, my sister does not hit like a girl. "Ow!"

"Shut up, Efrain," she yells. "Just shut up, okay!" Then Mandy flies up the block toward her school.

Rancor ◆ (n.) deep, bitter resentment

Chingy and I always meet on the corner of St. Ann's Avenue and 141st Street after I drop off my sister and walk together to school. But when I arrive, he's nowhere to be found. I check my watch, and I'm right on time. Always am. Chingy, too. The first time Nestor made us late for first period was the last. I insisted that we give him a few minutes, and the next thing we knew, Chingy and I were running to beat the bell. After that, Chingy would bop through the intersection at exactly eight o'clock without breaking his stride. Whoever showed up just jumped in alongside him, and usually it was just me. Sometimes when we were halfway to AC, Nestor would come huffing and puffing behind us, yelling "Y'all niggas left me." Eventually, he stopped appearing altogether, but it took Chingy and me a few weeks to realize that he had dropped out of high school.

Suddenly a man calls my name. It's none other than Rubio sidling up to me in his Civic, and it's too late to pretend that I don't see or hear him. "You need ride to school?" he asks. I barely shake my head. Damn, Chingy, where you at? "Come on. I take you."

"I'm waiting for somebody."

"¿A quién? ¿A Nestor?" I just suck my teeth and give him my back. "I have question about the paper you mother give me."

Chingy finally races around the corner. "Thanks for waiting, cuz. If you had bounced, I wouldn't've been mad at you." Without noticing Rubio, he steps and rambles.

I fall in beside him as if nothing is unusual. "What happened, kid?"

"Man, I overslept. The Giants-Cowboys game went into overtime, yo. You know a brother had to stay up and watch it."

Rubio creeps the Civic alongside us like a stalker. When we reach the corner, he turns right and blocks our path. A woman with a shopping cart curses at him in patois for blocking the curb cut. He ignores her and unlocks the car doors.

Chingy peers through the passenger window. "Yo, E., it's your pops." He throws open the back door and jumps inside. "*¿Cómo está, Señor Rodriguez?*"

But Rubio's eyes are only on me as I slide into the front passenger seat and slam the door behind me. "*Estoy bien. ¿Y tú . . . ?*"

This is mad embarrassing. "His name is Rashaan," I bark. The guy has only been my best friend for twelve years. "Get it right already."

"Chill, E. It's cool. *Estoy muy chévere, señor. Gracias por preguntar.*"

Rubio isn't here to help Chingy practice his Spanish, so I finally turn to ask him what he wants with me. "*¿Y qué quiere conmigo?*"

"*¿Qué quiero yo contigo?*" he repeats sarcastically. "*Eres tú que m'está buscando sin venir a verme, mandando a tu mai.*" Me looking for him? Yeah, right. If I wanted to see him, I know where Awilda lives. I know where all his jump-offs live. And this is why I didn't want my mother to call Rubio about the financial aid form in the first place.

"Don't you know it's rude to speak Spanish in front of people who don't know it?" Of course, that's Rubio's point. He doesn't want Chingy to understand what we're talking about. On the real? Neither do I. I'd rather not have this conversation at all.

"Speak for yourself, son," says Chingy. "I'm fluent."

We arrive at AC, and I fly out of the Civic. "You come by my work," says Rubio. "We talk about you papers for school."

As Chingy thanks Rubio for the ride, I bound toward the school building. He double-times to catch up with me. "What's up with you, man?"

"I told my moms to leave that alone." As Chingy walks me to Spanish class, I explain how Rubio created static between my mother and me by blowing my chat with Nestor out of proportion. I can tell that Chingy doesn't like the fact that I was parlaying with Nes, but he bites his tongue. "Then she calls him about some forms he needs to fill out so I can apply for financial aid, and he got it in his head that she used that as an excuse to talk to him, freakin' narcissist. And now he's trying to bypass her and come to me, fronting like he doesn't understand the paperwork."

"So?"

"So?"

"Even if he thinks that about your moms, what difference does it make?" says Chingy. "You know the truth; your moms knows the truth. Besides, your pops probably really doesn't understand the forms. It's not like English is his first language."

"Don't defend him."

"I'm not trying to defend him. I'm trying to look out for you." We reach my classroom. "Look, E., I know your pops did some foul stuff, and I understand how you feel about him, you know, using you to hide his dirt. But if the guy wants to step up and help you with your grind, let him. Maybe that's his way of making it up to you. Don't get in your own way just to spite him, cuz. That's mad stupid."

That's what I mean about Chingy being oblivious. I don't question that he's trying to look out for me, but, obviously, he doesn't understand at all to say something like that. The bell rings, and I tell Chingy to peace out and go into my classroom.

Giving in to Stevie's incessant reminders that she hasn't shown us a movie all month, Señorita Polanco plays a documentary about the Young Lords called *¡Palante, Siempre Palante!* As she dims the lights and the credits roll, my mind is still on Chingy's advice. If I were anything like Rubio, I'd do exactly what Chingy says. I'd use him to get what I needed regardless of how it might make anyone feel. But just because Rubio's my father doesn't make me his son. I'm my own man. A man unlike him.

Brazen ◆ (*adj.*) excessively bold, brash

Ten minutes into physics class, Chingy throws a folded piece of pink paper on my desk. I look at him like he's crazy, and he tilts his head toward the front of the room. GiGi González waves to me from where she sits in the first seat in the same row as Chingy. Her French manicure is hot. Way better than all the colors and hardware Leti likes to pile on her nails. I unfold her note.

> Hi, Efrain!
> Why you didn't come with us to the movies yesterday?
>
> Love,
> GG

I look up and mouth *Work*. She mouths back *Oh*. Then she pouts and rubs a fist over her eye like she's crying. I drop my head behind my notebook before she can catch me smiling. But Chingy throws a peanut or raisin or whatever they gave out at lunch at me, so I flip him the bird.

A few minutes later he throws another piece of whatever at me. When Mr. Harris turns his back to write the work-energy theorem on the board, I jump up from my desk, chop Chingy in the neck, and rush to sit back down. The other kids in the class snicker at us, and Mr. Harris whirls around. "What the heck's going on here?"

"Nothing," a few people mumble.

"I guarantee you this will be on the Regents, so I'd stop messing around and pay attention if I were you."

When I look down to copy the notes from the board, I find another folded pink note on my desk. I hesitate to open it. GiGi's the business, but I have to bust my ass for my measly seventy-two average in physics. Leti is the current salutatorian and is only five points behind me. I know homegirl's gunning for me, and I'm not mad at her for that, but I *have* to be valedictorian if I want to go to any Ivy League school, especially if I don't score a 2100 or more when I retake the SAT in January. No either/or, man. I have to do both, which means finding a way to take that prep class at Fordham that starts in a few weeks.

Chingy lets out a big *ahem* to remind me that GiGi awaits. I can't resist anymore and open her note. Under what she had already written in blue, she wrote in red:

> You don't have to lie, Efrain! If you had to
> go meet your girlfriend, just say so. Lying
> just makes me even more jealous.

She drew a bunch of lines under the word *more* and drew a face with the tongue sticking out.

"Efrain Rodriguez?" I snap up my head. "If a skier glides from the top of mountain A down the slope and back up to the top of mountain B, and there is no friction in the ice," says Mr. Harris, "is that potential energy to kinetic energy or vice versa?"

I can't even front. "I don't know."

"Georgina González?"

The whole class snickers again, and someone starts squealing *Georgina* like a farmer calling his pig. GiGi's never liked her real name, and that's why she's had everybody calling her "GiGi" since

36

elementary school. These herbs are only laughing at her now because they could never get a hottie like GiGi.

She says, "It's PE to KE."

"Why?"

"Because as he's going down mountain A, the skier's losing height and gaining speed. Gravity's changing the energy from the height, which is stored energy—potential energy—into energy from the speed, which is motion or kinetic energy. So it's PE to KE."

The funky look on Mr. Harris's face tells us that GiGi's right, and some of the kids clown him. So what does Mr. Harris do? He says, "Since you didn't know that, Mr. Rodriguez, you can answer all the questions at the end of the chapter in addition to the homework assignment."

When the bell rings, I grab my books and race out of the classroom. Chingy chases me as I run down the steps to the school library. "You're trippin', cuz," he says to me. "Not a dude in this school that wouldn't give up ten years of his life to get with GiGi González, and you go and dis her."

I say, "That chick's nothing but trouble." What does GiGi want with me all of a sudden anyway? I fling open the library door. Some of the kids who need tutoring are already there.

"E., I know this is gonna sound bugged out, but you gotta listen to me." Chingy puts his hand on my shoulder like he's my favorite uncle. "There's just some kind of trouble that does the body good."

I laugh. "Man, that's just, like, the stupidest—"

"Yo, who's the Halle, son?" Chingy interrupts, his eyes following Candace as she walks from the door to a table. "And why were you keeping her a secret from a brother?"

"Candace?" I say it with the same attitude she gave me yesterday.

"Damn, it's like that?" Chingy puts his hand to his heart as if he's trying to hold the pieces together.

"Just like that." At least GiGi's got a smile for you. All Candace has is a chip on her shoulder. She can keep that. "Remember what Leti told you about that transfer student? The one from K-Ville?"

GiGi walks into the library. All the guys—even the ones who weren't checking for Candace—turn to watch her strut. "Hey, Efrain." She comes toward Chingy and me, and I can feel the hate swarm us like a biblical plague. "Can I speak to you?" She slides her arm through mine and pulls me aside.

Lefty yells out, "Yo, GiGi, you work here now?" GiGi rolls her eyes at him. "Aw, man."

Chingy says, "Sorry, bro. That was your last chance to graduate before 2020." Everyone laughs, no one harder than me. When Mr. Sweren assigned Lefty to Candace, I thought, *That's what you call justice.*

GiGi tugs at my sleeve to get my attention. "Look, Efrain, I didn't mean to get you in trouble with Mr. Harris." I wouldn't have minded so much if it were English or some other class I'm killing. But physics is killing me, and possibly my chances of attending an elite college. "Let me make it up to you." Now she smooths her hand over my collar. "I'll do your physics homework for you."

"Yeah, right." For a second, I thought GiGi was going to suggest something else, and if she had not got me caught out there in physics, I would have been disappointed that she didn't. Thank God Chingy's obtuse because he would never let me hear the end of it.

GiGi punches me in the arm. "I'm serious. Drop by my house around eight tonight to come get it." She winks at me and starts to walk to the door. She yells over her shoulder, "Just call me first when you're on the way 'cause a lady likes to prepare for her visitors."

The millisecond the door taps the frame, Chingy starts. "That's what's up, player! You heard that? She said, *Come get IT*. My boy Efrain's, like, the pimp of the honor roll." He laughs at his own joke until he catches the look on my face. Then he immediately stops. "You know what I mean."

"Whatever," I say. This is why we're boys. Once he has a clue, Chingy always does the right thing.

"Better not do nothing until I get there 'cause clearly you're going to need my help," he says, popping his collar. "I'll be the Cyrano to your Christian, cuz."

I may not take French, but I know damn well how that tragedy ends. Chingy's first "tutee" walks into the library, so I point and say, "Go help somebody who actually needs it." Mine is late, so I wander over to the rack where the librarian keeps her recommendations. I get caught up in a directory of college scholarships when I overhear Lefty giving Candace a hard time.

She says, "Focus, Dominic, please. Let's break the problem down using smaller numbers to make sure we understand it." If it were anyone else, I'd feel sorry for her, but since it's Ms. Like That, I just snicker to myself. "It says the jeweler charges double the amount it costs him to get the merchandise. So let's pretend that he gets a diamond ring for five thousand dollars. How much does it mean he would sell it for?"

"You like diamonds, boo?" says Lefty the Lamest. "I can get you a diamond ring if you want one."

Fool can't get himself out of high school, but he's going to buy Candace a diamond ring? I laugh until I realize that maybe Lefty *can* buy her a diamond because plenty of "students" at AC just come to ply trade in the locker room, stairwells, and cafeteria. Kids go to class to avoid them as much as to learn. Who knows what Lefty keeps in that bag besides the books he never cracks open?

I give it to Candace, though. She runs with it. "Okay, so you go to the jeweler to buy me a diamond ring that he got for five thousand," she says. "How much is he going to sell it to you for, Dominic?"

"Hold up now, mami," says Lefty. "If I give you this diamond ring, what are you going to give me?"

Okay, dude just OD'd, and I can't abide that. I head over there. "Yo, Lefty," I say, leaning over him and jabbing him in the shoulder. "Answer me this. How many times do you have to repeat the tenth grade before you realize that girls don't think it's cute?"

Lefty juts up his chin and scowls at me from the corner of his eye. "Yo, Efrain, I know you didn't just dis me, 'cause then I'd have to tutor *you*, know what I'm sayin'?"

Mr. Sweren shushes us from the front of the room. "The school day may be over, but the library's rules still apply. Lower your voices."

"Yo, Sweren, you'd better check Efrain or there's going to be a whole lot more rule breaking up in here."

"What's going on over there?"

"Nothing, Mr. Sweren," says Candace. "Efrain and Dominic are messing around, but I have it under control."

Mr. Sweren says, "Rodriguez, why are you over there fooling with Saldaña when you have someone waiting for you over here?" He points to a table at the back of the room where the tenth grader I'm supposed to be tutoring in Spanish sits looking lost.

See what happens when you don't mind your own business? *That's* why chivalry is dead, man. And I wasn't even trying to check Lefty because I like Candace or anything.

As I walk back to my tutee, Candace tells Lefty, "He's right, though. You really want to impress me? Pass math for a change." Ordinarily, I would laugh, but she just irks me.

Affinity ♦ (*n.*) a spontaneous feeling of closeness

It irks me so much that I wait for Ms. Like That after the program. I tell Chingy what I have to do, but only when I convince him that I'll call him before I hook up with GiGi tonight does he finally take off. I don't know exactly what I'm going to say to Candace, but she needs to hear something so we make it through the school year without incident. Twelve years of school, and I never had any problems. Not when my old classmates at St. Gabe's discovered why I had to transfer to public school. Not when guys at IS 162 would call me a faggot because I like to read until Nestor told them we were boys, and they let me be. Not when my mother found out about Awilda and her pregnancy and my home became the second circle of hell. Just because Candace has had her troubles doesn't give her the right to create any for me. God has been known to throw a few character-building adversities a brother's way with no assists from her, you feel me?

I wait by the main entrance for twenty minutes, wondering if Candace might have left through another exit. When I head back to the library and cross Candace on her way out, I immediately let her have it. "Look, I don't know what your problem is, but save it for someone who deserves it." I expect her to roll her eyes at me, yell back, all those things that girls do, then keep it moving, but Candace stops right in front of me. "And here's a clue: I ain't the one."

41

"Okay, Efrain," she says.

"Nah, don't *okay* me. I've been nothing but nice to you, Candace, but you act like I offend you by even acknowledging that you exist."

"You're right," says Candace. "I just had a long talk with Mr. Sweren, and I told him what happened with Dominic. He said he wasn't surprised that you intervened. That you're a stand-up guy. I realize that I've been nasty to you for no reason, and I'm sorry."

It takes a moment for her sincerity to sink in. I don't think I ever had a girl say she was sorry to me and truly mean it. Girls usually whine or giggle when "apologizing," making it obvious that they really don't want to admit that they're wrong. Or they have an ulterior motive like GiGi did. Actually, GiGi never did say she was sorry, did she? I just say, "No one's nasty for no apparent reason."

We start walking toward the exit. "This is going to sound weird, Efrain, but sometimes I can't stand it when people are nice to me. Especially when things are fine. I start thinking, *Where are you going to be when I do need help?*"

But that doesn't sound weird to me at all. On some inexplicable level, I get it. I get her. "Keep doing like you do, and you won't have that problem for long," I say. "Just send those folks my way because I could use a little kindness after dealing with you."

Candace twists her mouth, trying not to laugh. That girl has some pretty lips. She notices the scholarship book in my hand. "Oh my God, a boy with a book?" Candace takes the book from me and thumbs through it. "And without pictures!"

"Whatever." I wish I were as good as she is at keeping a straight face, but I'm not. "Now, if I said something like that about you and math, I'd be wrong, right?"

"Touché."

We walk out of the school building. "Which way are you going?" She points at the bus stop for the Bx17 at the end of the block. "I'll walk you." She must live near me because that bus goes right by my building.

"Mr. Sweren says that you're probably going to be valedictorian."

I smile and shake my head. "Not if I don't ace physics." The second I say it, I want to take it back.

"Physics isn't easy."

"You're having a hard time with physics, too?"

"No," she says smirking. "I'm in advanced science."

"Scared of you," I say, and she laughs. We get to the bus stop, and Candace and I both sit down.

"What colleges are you applying to?"

"Harvard, Yale, Princeton . . ."

Candace laughs. "And you scared of me?" I shrug it off like it's no big deal, yet I'm glad she realizes that it is. Then she says, "You must've killed the SAT."

My heart sinks. I don't want to sabotage this better impression, but what if news of my record-breaking yet still unimpressive score reaches her? I settle on "I could've done better. I will do better when I take it again in January." I almost believe it. I *would* believe it if I had a seat in that prep course.

Candace asks, "So you're applying to all seven Ivies?"

"All of them except for Columbia just because, you know, it's in New York City."

"So you want to go away to college," she says. "Yeah, me too."

But the sadness in her eyes tells me that *away* for Candace means something different than it does for me. "You want to go back home?" The bus rambles down the block toward us, but I'm not ready for the conversation to end. But, damn, where did I pull out that stupid question? If she is from K-Ville, she doesn't want to be reminded of all that, and here I go and suggest that she wants to head straight back to that trauma.

The bus pulls up to the curb, and the doors open. Without saying anything, Candace walks past me and mounts the first step. Funny, I'd rather she light into me again than not talk to me at all, but what choice do I have? Just as I accept this will end where it started, Candace turns around and says, "Dillard."

"Huh?" Then I correct myself. "I mean, excuse me?"

"My first-choice college is Dillard University. Back home in New Orleans." All I can do is nod, but Candace smiles at me like it's more than enough. "See you tomorrow, Efrain."

"Bye, Candace." She climbs into the bus and takes a seat by the window. We wave to each other as the bus pulls away and down the street. I still wish the conversation did not have to end, but then I remember it's all good. She still has the book I borrowed from the school library.

Obdurate ♦ (*adj.*) unyielding to persuasion or moral influence

When Nestor sees me, he runs across the street. "What's her name, bro?"

"Man, get away from me with all that." I hope he's bluffing. Either I'm walking around with a pathetic expression on my face, or he's mad intuitive for a dude. Either way, it's not a good look.

Nestor catches up to me and punches me in the shoulder. "So, what's up?" he asks. "Talk to me."

I feel good, so I decide to give him a bone. Just not the T. "You know GiGi González?"

"Do I know GiGi? She was my first kiss, bro. Set the bar mad high!" Nestor takes a second to reminisce. " 'Member how we were playing seven minutes in heaven at Chingy's tenth birthday party? Man, I've been in love with that girl ever since." He shakes his head and then clamps his hand down on my shoulder. "Well, if I have to lose her to somebody, I'd rather it be to you." It's funny to hear Nestor say this because he's more GiGi's type than I'll ever be. Truth is, I don't know why lately she's been showing me so much love. As fine as she is, not knowing her motives makes it hard to enjoy her attention.

"Come back to AC, and she's all yours," I say.

Nestor laughs. "I have to make that paper, so you'll have to be my wingman. So, what's up with her?"

I tell him how GiGi got me in trouble in physics class and

offered to do my homework. "Says if I drop by her crib tonight around eight, I can pick up the assignment."

We reach the front of my building. I sit down on the stoop while Nestor cackles and does what Chingy calls his laugh dance. "Oh, snap, Efrain. You might be pickin' up somethin' besides homework." He flounces in place like a little kid who needs to pee.

"Shut up, man." The idea of getting it on with GiGi doesn't constitute an original thought, but I'm not keen on discussing it with Nestor. Maybe it has to do with a conversation we once had with Chingy's brother Baraka. We were bombarding him with questions about sex, and he was cool answering them until Nestor got ugly. He kept saying things like *I wanna beat this chick* or *I can't wait to hit that* and *Man, I would just gut her.* Finally, BK yelled, *Yo, we're trying to parlay about sex here, but what the hell you screaming about, kid? Rape? If that's how you want to talk about sisters, take that grimy conversation elsewhere.*

I finally say, "Nah, man, GiGi wants a dude who'll take her to all those celebrity hot spots or whatever, and I'm just not the one, kid."

Nestor sits down next to me. "But you can be."

That's my cue to bounce. I stand up and say, "Let me get upstairs."

Nestor stands up, too, grabbing my arm and blocking my path. "Look, E., I know you. In certain ways, you and I aren't all that different. Chingy, he's—"

I shake his hand off my arm. "Nah, man, don't talk about Chingy."

"Wait, let me finish." Nestor lays his hand on my arm. "I'm not trying to talk sideways about Chingy, because, despite every-thing, I still got mad love for that brother. But let's be real, E. Homeboy likes his bling, and you know his parents be spoiling him. And I ain't mad at nobody for that, and I'm sure you ain't either. But we both know our parents don't got it like that to give it to us. And who knows? Maybe that's why we have . . . How do they call it? Loftier ambitions!" I start to laugh. Nestor seems confused. He sees me eyeing his gear and gets it. "Okay, hold up. Efrain, look at me." I take in Nestor's Akademiks jeans with the swirl pockets, his Notorious B.I.G. T-shirt, and the denim days Air Force 1s. His kicks alone cost almost two hundred bucks. "This is just a uniform," says Nestor. "I rock gear like this to work, but study me good, E." He holds out his hands in front of me, palm side down so I can see the scar on the back of his left hand from the time when we were horsing around on some rocks on a class trip to Central Park. Then Nestor pulls the collar of his T-shirt away from his neck to reveal the simple gold necklace with the crucifix pendant his grandmother gave him when he made his first communion. "I don't rock any ice, and I'm not pushing a phat ride, but you know I get paid, so why is that?" Nestor doesn't wait for me to answer. "Because, just like you, E., I have better things to do with my money. I got plans beyond this place."

Suddenly a loud rattle comes from across the street. Awilda and her seven-year-old daughter Serenity come out of the Laundromat up the block. Serenity struggles to push a shopping cart overloaded with bloated canvas bags while Awilda juggles Rubio's baby on her hip even as she drags a stroller behind her. Serenity hits a crack in the pavement, and the laundry cart pops, then spills. The loud clang it makes when it hits the concrete scares Rubio's baby, and he shrieks. Awilda has her hands full because now the baby won't go in the stroller so she can give her daughter a hand. Nestor calls Awilda's name and motions for her to wait. He bounds down the steps and onto the sidewalk. "Ain't you comin'?"

"Nah, man, I have to go check on Mandy." My sister probably

sneaks over there after school while I work and then rushes home when she knows I should be on my way. Besides, the last thing I need is for Awilda to see me with Nestor and go flap to Rubio, who'll bother my moms again.

Nestor shakes his head as if to say *That's messed up*, so I shrug back to tell him *It's like that*. If he wants to be chivalrous, I ain't mad at him, but don't hate on me because I have my own family to attend to.

In fact, it's all I think about as I walk the three flights up to my apartment. My parents aren't officially divorced, and my mother has too much pride to sic the courts on Rubio for child support. From time to time, he swings by the crib to give us money or hands Mandy some cash when he sees her playing outside, but that's just it. From time to time, when it crosses Rubio's mind, if Awilda's not around to give him grief . . . In two words: never enough. And forget about hitting the man up for any money for something beyond the basics. What kind of man lets a woman tell him which of his kids he can and cannot father? Unless Awilda "tells" Rubio to do what he wants to do anyway.

Worst of all, my mother has to deal with this every day. Bad enough he played Moms dirty left and right; this time he had to go knock up some breezy around the way. Rubio wasn't even man enough to tell her about the pregnancy himself. Sleazy Awilda waited until she was four months along, rolled into Yannis's store, and lifted her T-shirt to show off her belly. "This," she said, "is Rubio's." My mother had heard the gossip before then—we all did—but she refused to believe it until the proof was literally in her face.

So now Moms makes Mandy and me lug our dirty clothes to the Laundromat three blocks away. She claims that the dryers across the street cheat you out of two minutes of the ten your quarter is supposed to buy. Mandy believes her, but I know she doesn't want to bump into Awilda or any of her people. It's one reason why I can't wait to leave for college. I can't stand to see the look on my mother's face whenever that *mujeriego*'s in her line of sight or she overhears some humiliating *chisme* about his latest exploits. But when all you make is seven twenty-five an hour, running an errand a quarter mile out of your way is the only escape you can afford.

Oscillate ♦ (*v.*) to sway from one side to the other

After I get upstairs and check in on Mandy, I jump on my college applications. When I started this process, I put myself on a schedule and stick to it. Homework can wait. Then I make the mistake of trying to tackle the financial aid forms on my own. Harvard costs thirty-two G's. So does Princeton. Yale is thirty-five. If I did want to go to Columbia and decided to commute into Manhattan every day instead of moving into a dorm to save eight thousand dollars each year in room and board, tuition alone would still set me back thirty-seven grand. I lose my way in the stack of paper and figures, and I try so hard to re-focus, I give myself a headache and have to lie down. Then the phone rings.

"You promised to call me, son," yells Chingy.

"Man, I forgot."

"Don't make me go over there and chop you in the neck. You didn't see GiGi yet, did you?"

"That's what I forgot."

"You must be on crack to forget that you had a date with Jessica Alba Junior."

I laugh hard. Chingy just kills me with his lines. "I swear, kid, I forgot. A brother has a lot on the mind."

"Even more reason to go over there."

"Chingy, after struggling for the past two months in physics,

50

how am I going to roll up in Mr. Harris's class with not one but two perfect assignments?"

"Yeah, that might make him suspicious."

"You think?"

"Shut up, cuz. I'm trying to help you. Okay, when you get the assignment from GiGi, jack up enough of the answers to maintain your lousy average."

"Ha, ha, ha." I hear the call-waiting beep. When things are not hectic at the store, my mother calls to check in on us. "Yo, Chingy, my moms is on the line. Let me holla back at you in a few."

"A'ight. One, cuz."

The beep sounds again. "Peace." I hit the Talk button on the cordless. "Hello?"

"Efrain!"

Who's this strange girl screaming on me? Then it hits me. "GiGi?"

"Don't get it twisted, Efrain," she yells. "I have better things to do than finish your stupid physics homework and wait for you to come and get it."

"GiGi, I'm really sorry," I say, and I actually find myself meaning it. "It's just that my mother works late, and I really can't leave my little sister here by herself." Not a total lie. Mandy's not so young that I can't leave her alone for a while sometimes. After all, she's alone for two hours every school day while I tutor. But when it gets dark earlier, my mother's not too keen on my leaving Mandy alone for too long. Truth is, I'm not too crazy about doing it either. I might hang out on the stoop, run to the bodega, or even catch a game of hoops with Chingy and some guys at People's Park. But if Mandy really needs me, all she has to do is throw open a window and holler, because my family is the only one in the free world without cell phones.

"Oh." GiGi almost sounds sorry, but in true girl fashion, she doesn't apologize, and Candace flashes through my mind. She says, "So, when are you coming over?"

"Man, GiGi, I appreciate you lookin' out for me, I really do." Again, I find myself meaning it. "But I just don't think I'm going to make it over there tonight."

GiGi sighs. "Well, how about I give you the answers over the telephone?"

"Yeah, that's peace." I reach for my worksheet and pen. "Ready when you are."

As she gives me the answers, GiGi is mad sweet, sometimes even explaining the right answer to me. I think it actually makes her feel good to help, but I have mixed feelings about her attentiveness.

After giving me the final answer, GiGi yells, "Now you owe me, Efrain."

All I say is, "All right, GiGi." I knock on my desk. "But I gotta go now."

"You owe me big-time!" GiGi finally hangs up on me.

I don't know what she wants from me, but I'm pretty sure I don't have it. I don't have what *I* want, and I don't even want it all. Being Brown and broke has been a seventeen-year-test in just how badly I want an average life. A life where doing the right thing is punished with the luxury of having to choose between the things I need and those that I want. Why does the valedictorian have to choose between his class ring and an SAT prep class? Why does a clean-cut teenager have to decide between showing up to his minimum-wage job and going to the movies with the most popular girl in school? Why do I have to fight so hard just for the mere chance to have it all?

A real knock on my door interrupts my funky train of thoughts. "Efrain, are you there?"

"C'mon in, Mami."

My mother pokes her head through my door. "You okay, honey?"

"Just studying."

"Did you eat?"

"No, I got caught up in homework. I was thinking of just running down to the pizzeria for a slice."

"That's a good idea." My mother reaches into her pocket and pulls out a twenty. "Why don't you pick up a pie for all of us?"

"Save that," I say as I slip on my kicks. "My treat."

My moms smiles at me in that sad way of hers and leaves the room. Did she always look like that when she smiled, and I'm only noticing it now because she has reason to be sad? Or has all the drama with Rubio broken her smile? Can I do anything to fix it even though I'm just a son? Can Moms stand strong for Mandy until I can reach back to them?

Mandy sits in the living room watching a stupid reality show where a bunch of D-listers move in together and work each other's nerves, hoping to convince the network to give them their *own* stupid reality show. "Turn off that garbage," I tease as I head for the apartment door.

She jumps to her feet and catches up to me. "Efrain, can I go with you to the pizzeria?" Before I can answer, she reaches for her jacket. Oh, so now she has love for her big brother.

"Nah, stay here." I didn't mean to snap at her. It's just that I really wasn't hungry, never mind craving pizza. I just needed an excuse to go outside without raising my mother's suspicions, and I can't risk Mandy overhearing my conversation. To make up for my nastiness, I ask, "So what you want, Beyoncé? Pepperoni or sausage? How 'bout both?"

She cuts me a look. "I don't care." Then Mandy spins around and marches back into the living room. Poor thing's been cooped up in the apartment all afternoon.

"Okay, I'll get half and half." I can't be mad at her. And she'll get over it.

When I hit the sidewalk, I cross the street toward the bodega where Nestor plies his trade. "What's up, E.?" He's with two other guys that are usually out there with him. The corner boys wish me peace, and I return the favor. In a neighborhood like mine, you don't turn your nose up at the thugs just because you don't roll with them. You holler but keep it moving to avoid static. My moms taught me that so I wouldn't be book smart but street dumb. That's the kind of thing a son should learn from his father, but Rubio was too busy looking for younger women to turn into single mothers.

Without breaking my stride, I say to Nestor, "Yo, roll with me to the pizzeria, kid. I need to holler at you about something."

"No doubt," says Nestor as he falls into step behind me. "What's up?"

"Can you hook me up with a job?"

Obstinate ♦ (*adj.*) not yielding easily, stubborn

Although I've been to Hunts Point to shop for clothes on Southern Boulevard, I've never walked through the neighborhood on the other side of the Bruckner. At first, it doesn't seem much different than mine in Port Morris. There are tenement buildings and walkups, bodegas and *lechoneras*, liquor stores and nightclubs. As Nestor leads me farther away from the highway, it becomes less residential—huge loft buildings, with no lights through the broken, dusty windows. On one side of the street is a McDonald's with an indoor playground, but on the other side is a strip club. A group of young girls strut down the avenue, trying to act grown.

Nestor juts his chin toward them. "Little hos."

"Malo." I jab him in the arm. "You wrong for that."

Nestor jabs me back. "For real, those little girls are on the stroll."

"You're kidding me?" I stare at one wearing a jacket that looks just like one Mandy owns. The thick eyeliner and heavy lipstick can't hide that she is not a day over thirteen. She turns and catches me. When she flutters her lashes, I look away.

Within minutes Nestor leads me to the most industrial part of the neighborhood, practically at the Bronx River. There are large factories with garages wide enough for trucks. I ask, "Just where are you taking me, kid?"

"Right here." Nestor leads me to this small door a few yards down from a closed garage. He pulls out a cell phone and dials a number. He says, "Yeah, it's Nes with my boy E. We're outside. Okay."

We wait for a minute, and the door opens. The Black guy behind it seems a bit older than we are. From the Pelle Pelle leather jacket on his back to the Air Tour Spectators on his feet, he's official. "What's up, son?" Nestor grips his hand, and they pull toward each other for what my sister calls an "ug." She says that boys don't get close enough to each other, so they should never call it a hug. The guy catches me smiling at the thought, so I switch up my grille so he won't think I'm an herb.

Nestor says, "Trace, this is my boy Efrain. E., Trace."

I offer Trace a pound. "Peace."

Ignoring my hand, he says, "Assume the position, yo."

Nestor gives a nervous laugh and flattens his palms against the wall as if he were just arrested. "Business precaution, man."

"Yeah, Snipes don't know you," says Trace as he pats down Nestor for God knows what. "You could be a snitch for Hinckley."

I don't even know who that is, but I mimic Nestor. Trace moves over to frisk me, patting me so hard on the crotch, I have to catch my breath and suck down the pain.

Finally, Trace backs off of us and says to Nestor, "You know where he is." Then he steps aside. Nestor leads me inside and into an office where a bald Latino guy in his late twenties pours himself a glass of rum and watches *SportsCenter*. Nestor says, "Snipes, this is my boy Efrain. The one I was telling you about."

Man, I feel like a fool. I had the entire stereotype in my mind, expecting Wesley Snipes in that movie *Sugar Hill* or *New Jack City*. I hold out my hand to him and say, "Pleased to meet you, sir. My name is Efrain Rodriguez," like Mrs. Colfax taught me in her professional development course.

Snipes takes one look at me, then says to Nestor, "Take off."

Nestor hesitates, then tells me he'll wait for me outside. As soon as the door closes, Snipes motions for me to take a seat and turns off the television. He rises from his chair and takes a sip of his rum, never pulling his gaze from me. Finally, he scoffs, "Get the fuck out of here. This ain't for you."

"Excuse me?"

"You heard me, Scout. I told you to get the fuck on up out of here! You ain't trying to work for me."

I know this is a test. I ace tests. I have to. "Yes, I am."

"What for?"

"Because I need the money."

"Who the hell doesn't?"

"But I'm the one who's here."

Snipes squints as if he wants to like my answer. "You in some kind of trouble?"

"No, sir."

"You owe anybody any money?"

"No." Then I come clean. "Not yet. Not if I can help it."

"Oh, I get it. You got some nasty habits. Gambling, drugs, or some shit."

"Not at all." Chingy pops into my mind. "I stay shy."

Snipes laughs. "You stay shy? Okay, Scout. Here you go." He reaches into his back pocket and pulls out a wad of bills. He peels off one hundred-dollar bill after the other, tossing them into a stack on the table. One, two, three, four, five, six, seven, eight, nine, ten. "Is that enough for you?"

I should take the money, say peace out, and never show my face around these parts again, but there's more at stake now than money. "Hardly." This man doesn't know me to rate my needs so damned cheaply.

Snipes bends down and hollers in my face, "How much is enough, then?"

"Thirty!" I yell back.

"For what?"

"College!"

"College?" He laughs like my name is Ernie and I want to buy a truckload of rubber ducks. "College?"

"I didn't stutter." I'm not two feet from Cerebus, and I unleash this pent-up bravado. Who is this guy, and why is he trying to get me killed?

"What freakin' college costs thirty grand?"

"The best."

"Oh, is that right?" Snipes laughs again. "What do they teach for thirty G's that you can't learn at the College of Mount Okey-doke?"

"How to run the world." It may sound like a slick response, but that's real talk. "And that's thirty G's *per year* and *not* including room and board."

Snipes finally straightens up. He finishes off his rum and sits back down beside me. "You really out there slinging so you can afford to go to some rich White boys' college? Da Man's University." He laughs at his own joke. I neither laugh nor answer. "You think a nickel bag here, a white top there is enough to take you where you trying to go?"

"With all due respect, why does it matter why I want to do this?" I ask. "So long as my incentives fuel my hustle and move your product, we're both good."

He leans over and scoops the money off the table. "You want Da Man's U that bad?"

"Yes, sir."

"I see you there," he says. "Not on no sellout shit either. I see you keeping it real. Representing. You gonna become one of my good friends in high places, aren't you, E.?"

I swallow. "Damn straight."

58

Conciliatory ♦ (*adj.*) friendly, agreeable

On Monday, when I rush out of physics to speak to Mr. Sweren before everyone else arrives, who's there with him but Mrs. Colfax. On another day, I would have held back and waited for her to bounce, but today I'm on a mission. "Excuse me, Mr. Sweren, but I need to speak to you about something important."

Mrs. Colfax puts her hand on my arm. "So, how are your college applications going, Efrain?" she asks.

Like you really care. I step out of her reach. "Fine."

She says to Mr. Sweren, "Efrain's intent on going Ivy League."

"Good for you," he says, not sounding the least concerned about my being overwhelmed.

Mrs. Colfax fidgets. "But don't you think Efrain should apply to a range of schools?" Her tone makes it obvious that Mr. Sweren should back her up.

He says, "That's right, Efrain, you want to apply to three types of schools. One, apply to a few dream schools. You know, the ones that seem like long shots for whatever reason. Then you want to apply to a few safe schools. Those are ones that you can afford and know you can get into with no problem. And then you want to have a few schools in between those two extremes. This way you're neither shooting too high nor aiming too low."

"Thanks, Mr. Sweren. I'll do that." I appreciate Mr. Sweren schooling me. I haven't applied yet to any schools in the middle, only concentrating on my dream and safe schools. He did more for me in one conversation than Mrs. Colfax ever did.

If Mrs. Colfax is hating, she keeps it to herself. She tells Mr. Sweren that she will speak to him later and touches me on the arm again. "Remember, Efrain, it's better to be a big fish in a little bowl rather than a little fish in a big bowl." I'm mad tempted to tell Mrs. Colfax what she can do with her fishbowls, but I don't want to shake Mr. Sweren's image of me as a respectable student.

Once she leaves, he asks me, "What was that all about?" When I explain that Mrs. Colfax thinks it's a waste of my time to apply to the Ivy League, Mr. Sweren's bushy eyebrows become one long caterpillar across his forehead. "Look, Efrain, I agree that you shouldn't put all your eggs in one basket, but Colfax is an idiot." After the initial shock, I belt out a whooping laugh. I never had a teacher dis another one in front of me like that. "Seriously, she's been feeding seniors like you that fishbowl crap for years. Yes, it's difficult for even the best student at Albizu Campos to get into an Ivy League college, but it has been known to happen."

"You mean since 1913?" I ask. That's when Pedro Albizu himself enrolled at Harvard. Eleven years later they opened our high school, although I bet anything it wasn't named after a Puerto Rican back then.

"Yes, a few times since," Mr. Sweren laughs. "There are always exceptions, and you won't ever know if you can be one if you don't at least aim for it."

"No doubt," I say. "Albizu Campos himself was a Harvard man, right?"

"That's right, Efrain." Mr. Sweren seems impressed that I know that. Then he says, "Let me guess . . . Señorita Polanco."

"All day, every day." Go to a school named "Washington," "Roosevelt," or "Kennedy," trust you'll learn all about who the school is named after, but no one taught us who Albizu Campos

60

was until Señorita Polanco returned to teach after graduating in the eighties.

Students start to come into the library, and even though I want to talk more with Mr. Sweren, better to get this over with before Chingy arrives. "Look, I don't want to do this, but I'm going to have to quit tutoring."

Mr. Sweren's caterpillar brow arcs its back. "Why?"

"I didn't do well on the SATs, so I'm going to retake them in January. But I need more time to study for them. That means giving up my tutoring job."

Mr. Sweren nods. "I understand. Sounds like you have your priorities in order, Efrain." He swats me on the back of my shoulder. "You'll be hard to replace, though. Good luck to you." Then he opens his folder, and takes out my time sheet. "Sign this before you go so we make sure you get your last check." He leaves the sheet on the desk and then starts to mark his attendance book as people roll through the door. Man, that was much easier than I thought it would be. I expected Mr. Sweren to try to convince me to stay or grill me or something. Somehow I don't feel relieved that he didn't.

As soon as I sign the time sheet and slip it into Mr. Sweren's folder, I turn around and bump into Chingy. "What's up, cuz?" he says as he offers me a pound. "Man, you flew out of physics. Kinematics got you shook?"

"Yeah, man, I had to quit my job."

"What?"

"Check it." I motion for him to follow me outside the library. Once we are in the hallway, I say, "Look, Chingy, I told Sweren that I need more time to study for the January SAT. The truth is, though, I took another job that pays better so I can enroll in a prep course at Fordham."

"Word? That's what's up. Where's your new grind?"

"I was on Southern Boulevard this weekend, and I saw a sign in the window of Jimmy Jazz." Damn, I shouldn't have said that. What if Chingy decides to drop by, wanting to say hi or apply for a better-paying job himself? Luckily, I chose a store with locations throughout the city. "But chances are they're going to assign me to a store downtown."

"The one on Delancey?"

"Yeah. Maybe. I don't know yet." I guess this is good practice for what I'll tell my moms. I haven't lied to her since Rubio made me. "Look, I have to bounce. I only dropped by to tell Mr. Sweren. . . ."

"No doubt. Do your thing. How 'bout I drop by afterward so we can chill? Maybe go play some hoops."

"That would be peace." Chingy may come over with a thousand and one questions about my new gig, but I really want to hang out with him. I'll deal with it as it comes like I did just now. Maybe I should pat myself on the back for being able to play this off so lovely, but instead, I really want out of here.

"Watch, I'm going to get stuck tutoring one of your herbs," says Chingy. "You need to compensate a brother by putting me down with your employee discount."

"Efrain."

Candace comes out of the library. Trying to keep my story straight while parlaying with Chingy, I hadn't even noticed when she arrived. "Hey, Candace."

Chingy grins, then backs up toward the door. "One, cuz."

"Peace out."

Candace waits for Chingy to go into the library and close the door behind him. She looks at me and says, "Mr. Sweren says you quit so you can focus on studying for the SAT."

"Yeah, something had to give." She nods but doesn't say anything. "So . . ."

"So . . ."

"So."

Candace smiles and rolls her eyes at me. "So!"

Now it's a game. "So!"

"Soooo . . ." Candace gives a slight shove to my shoulder. Then she smiles and casts her eyes away. "How am I going to return the book I borrowed?"

My heart starts to pound. I say, "Maybe we can hang out sometime." Studying, slinging . . . When am I supposed to do this? "You know, like, on the weekend."

"Like maybe Saturday afternoon."

I want to suggest Saturday night so it seems more like a date, but I have to grind on that corner so Snipes knows I'm about it. "Yeah, we can meet for lunch and then go to a matinee." I don't want Candace to think I'm cheap, so I add, "You know, go early so we can avoid all the 'hood rats who like to talk back at the screen and all that."

"I hate that!" says Candace. "Why do people pay to get into the movies only to do what they can do at home for free?"

"That's what I'm always saying."

We laugh for a moment, and then Candace gets serious. "Yeah, the afternoon is better for me. Ever since we moved to New York, my mother's been a bit overprotective. She really doesn't want me out too late at night."

"Cool." Right now an overprotective moms is an amateur slinger's best friend. "Give me your number, and I'll call you." I hand her my pen and notebook so she can write down her digits. "What time do you think you'll be home tonight?"

"On the way home, I pick up my little sister at the community center. . . ."

"St. Mary's?" When it gets too cold for People's Park, Chingy and I play hoops there.

"Yeah, so call me after six just to be on the safe side."

"Okay, I will."

"Okay." Candace nods a few times and then tiptoes to peck me on my cheek. "Bye, Efrain." Then she rushes into the library.

"Bye, Candace." I stay until the door clicks behind her. Then I practically skip out of the school like a little kid.

Novice ♦ (*n.*) beginner, someone without training or experience

"This is how we do this here, kid," he says as we hover between the Chinese takeout and the Dominican bakery. We're practically under the Bruckner Expressway, so we have to yell to hear one another. Sometimes I glance up and watch the truck exhaust gray the air. I pin my chin to my chest and pull my collar over my nose. "First of all, E., don't just run up on anybody who rolls through with wide eyes and slow feet, you feel me?" says Nestor. "Hunts Point's hard-core, man." He points to places as he mentions them. "You got the terminal market down that way, the hookers back here, the jail barge over there. . . ."

"Jail barge?"

"Eight hundred beds just floating on the water, bro. Remember when we were little how they were building that juvie right across the street from IS 162?"

"Yeah, Horizon." One day after Rubio got Mandy and me kicked out of St. Gabe's, he picked me up from 162. No matter how much I begged her not to, Moms told him I was having trouble with some of the other kids. On that walk home, Rubio pointed to my junior high school and said, "You go here," then he motioned across the street to Horizon, "or you go there." Like I needed to hear that. Rubio should've saved his bad attempt at cleverness for the ruffnecks that were wailing on me.

Nestor says, "While they were building Horizon, they put

some kids on that barge." Nestor's good for that kind of information. He's into all kinds of history and even mythology. I bet he watched *The Bronx Is Burning* and caught inaccuracies. Sometimes he veers into superstitious nonsense, but for the most part, the kid be on point. "With all that's going on down around here," he says, "the po patrol this area like you wouldn't believe."

Including us, I think. Then I ask, "So, how we go about stacking that paper?"

Nestor grins at me like I'm the Luke Skywalker to his Obi-Wan Kenobi. "Okay, check it. Someone rolls up on you wanting to cop. You see that cat over there leaning up against the lamppost?" Nestor points to this guy ogling a chick who wants nothing to do with him. He wears a golden yellow Yankees cap and matching jersey.

"You mean Frazzle over there?" Why would any major league franchise churn out merchandise that looks manufactured by Garanimals? "Stick to the navy and white, son."

"For real, kid!" Nestor cackles, laugh dancing and giving me a low five. "Not only is that, like, sacrilege, dude looks like an egg yolk with legs." We crack up good over that one. Nestor, Chingy, and I, we used to stay laughing. One time we were rolling so much, Moms swore we were sniffing markers or glue or something like that. I'm usually not the funny guy on the set, but hanging out with Nestor and Chingy would bring the jokes out of me. Man, I miss that.

Nestor returns to his businesslike tone. "Okay, first let me say this. Never speak plain 'cause you never know who's listening besides who you talking to. Don't worry, though, 'cause I'ma teach you all the codes and signals. So the customer tells you how much he wants, you quote the price, he pays you in full. And I don't care how well you think you know somebody, E. No pay, no product. If a customer stiffs you, Snipes dips into your pocket, so don't be getting charitable, you feel me?"

"No problem," I say. "I'm not here to *darle fia'o a nadie*." I have no time, money, or interest in extending credit and collecting debts.

"Then you signal to my man LeRon over there, and your customer swings by LeRon to pick up his package. Got it?"

"Why I can't I service him directly?" I ask. From what I remember from economics class, middle men cost money.

Nestor smirks at me. "C'mon, valedictorian. . . . Think about it."

I get it. "If the customer's five-oh . . ." My stomach flips so much, it rattles my rib cage. I remind myself that the guys clocking in front of the bodega across the street from my building are there day and night, week after week, and I've never seen the police arrest anyone. Then again, I don't live in Hunts Point.

Nestor motions for me to follow him. "Let me introduce you to the other guys." I should know where to steer the dope fiends and crack heads since I'm not trying to sell that mess, but, honestly, I don't need new friends. I just want to make my ends selling weed and go home to study.

As we make our way to the other end of the block, I see a few brothers hanging out across the street. Nestor stares straight ahead as we walk toward the corner. "And those are Hinckley's soldiers."

"Hinckley." Trace mentioned him the day I met with Snipes. "The competition?"

"That's another thing, E. We have our turf, and they have theirs. No trespassing." But there seems to be more to keeping the peace than sticking to our side of the street. My stomach gives another flip. An SUV pulls up to the curb, and LeRon lifts himself off the lamppost and approaches it. Nestor stops walking and signals me to hang back. As we wait for him to finish his transaction, I say, "Yo, Nes, do you ever think about quitting?" Without looking at me, he just shrugs. "C'mon, have you ever met an old corner boy?"

Nestor chuckles. "You right about that." He kicks at a tuft of grass poking out of two slabs of concrete. "Even a dude that lives for this can have a rough night and get to wondering where else he could be instead."

"So what crosses your mind on a rough night?"

"That at least I'm not dead. Or in jail."

I shove him. "You got jokes."

Nestor laughs and shoves me back. We shove each other all the way to the bodega, where he introduces me to Snipes's soldiers. But the entire time, I'm chasing a nagging thought around my head. I just let Nestor pull me into the game instead of pushing him out of it.

Chide ♦ (*v.*) to voice disapproval

I creep by the living room, where my mother and sister have fallen asleep in front of the television. Moms must've dozed off first because it is way past Mandy's bedtime. And rather than put herself to bed, Mandy just curled up into my mother's lap and fell asleep.

Even though I'm dead on my own feet, I remember to lock the door to my room before emptying my pockets on my bed. What do I have to show for my first night on the street? Forty dollars. I check my pockets for another ten- or twenty-dollar bill I might have missed, but there isn't anything in there but some pennies and the wrapper of a Halls cough drop.

Forty dollars.

Exhausted or not, I quickly do the math and get Nestor on the phone. He sounds all spry, which just annoys me even more. "Yo, Nes!"

"E.? Hey, bro, I think this is the first time you've called me in years. What's up?"

"I just counted my take. . . ."

"Yeah, count that paper."

"That's all it is, kid! Paper!" I check myself and lower my voice before I wake up my moms and sister. "Forty dollars ain't squat. I might as well go back to tutoring." I swear if I had Mr. Sweren's home number, I'd call him next.

"But Snipes doesn't take out taxes," Nestor laughs.

"Forget this," I say. "This ain't worth it." I don't need to be standing out on Hunts Point Avenue all hours of the night hoping I don't get sick. Or worse . . . busted.

"Wait, E., hold up!" Nestor finally gets serious. "Okay, I'ma be real with you. If you want to make more money, you have to do three things. One, you have to hustle. You're in sales, bro, and it's just not enough to wait until a customer approaches you. See how when a car pulls up the way other guys are on it? You want to make serious cash, you better start throwing elbows."

I don't like the sound of that. "Two?"

"You need to go harder. All that high and mighty about only selling weed?" Nestor's tone brims with annoyance so this is how he genuinely feels about my position even though he had pretended to be cool with it. "It might keep your conscience clean, but it's also going to keep your wallet light." When I don't say anything, he continues to lecture me. "Real talk, E. This is business. Supply and demand. If no one wanted coke, dope, crank, whatever, we wouldn't sell it. Plain and simple. And that's where the real money's at, so if you don't want to make it like that, E., fine. But don't judge another man who does or whine about being broke. Go punch a clock at Old Navy or Dr. Jay's or wherever your mother thinks you be at."

I'm too angry and embarrassed to speak, so Nestor barrels on. "And the third way to make money, E., is to move up. This ain't no different than corporate America. You start in the rank and file, pay your dues, prove your worth to the firm. You get promoted and make more money. The higher up the rank you climb, the more money you make."

Nestor finally hears something in my silence and softens his tone. "Look, E., I know you're on some other trip, and I ain't mad at you for that. Why should you be trying to come up under

Snipes with what you got going for you in the legitimate world? But you came to me, remember? You asked for an invitation to my neck of the urban jungle. Dudes push up on me all day, every day, son, asking me to hook 'em up, and I tell them to keep it movin'. Not only did I let you in, E., I'm trying to show you around and watch your back. So imagine how it's going to reflect on me to Snipes and all the other fellas if you quit after one day, especially behind some BS like this."

We both stay quiet for a minute. Then I finally say, "Let me go. I still have some homework to finish before I turn in, and I have to be up by seven."

"A'ight." Nestor hangs up the phone.

I sit on the edge of my bed and pull off my shoes. As I scrape the money off the bedspread, I count it again, still hoping to find another twenty stuck to one of the bills. No dice. I put the money away in a shoebox in my closet and crawl into bed with my clothes on.

The night has a way of raising the volume on the truth. Nestor's words echo in my head, crowding out my dreams and keeping me awake. In the dark, I take inventory of all that I have going for me in the legitimate world.

A mother who is long on love but short on cash.

A younger sister who used to look up to me but is now chasing her father.

A best friend who has some of the same goals but little of the same drive.

The highest GPA at a high school where the most crowded table at the annual college fair belongs to the U.S. Army.

A college advisor who's rolling the dice against me.

A few teachers who have my back but can't give me a leg up.

And a father who counts for so little, he's the last to come to mind, and only because the dark forces me to reach.

Since I can't sleep, I decide to get up and study for the SAT. I grab my vocabulary list and cross off the words that I'm confident I know. There are actually quite a few, which gives me a boost, so I work on the rest until the dark gives up on me and crawls away from my window.

Discern ◆ (v.) to perceive, detect

When I tell her I start my new job at Jimmy Jazz this Saturday, my moms sighs and says, "I guess your sister is old enough to stay by herself now." We both want to keep her young, but what choice do we have?

Obviously, I don't go to Jimmy Jazz. Instead, I take my first week's earnings and head downtown to the SAT prep center and put down a deposit for my course. Suddenly, the money seems like enough, and it feels mad good to take that step toward securing my future.

When I get back to the apartment, I try to study for the SAT before I have to pick up Candace, but I can't concentrate. This is my first date. I mean, I've hung out with girls, gone places with them, messed around with them a bit. . . . You know, we bump into each other at People's Park, grab some Mickey D's, and then sneak off to a parentless apartment somewhere. Or maybe we sort of agree to be at the same place at the same time. That's the closest thing to a date I've ever had. Despite the fact that I've just met her, I already understand that Candace is not just some breezy in the park. No wonder I'm nervous.

So I just bounce around my room until it's time to leave, changing outfits, re-counting my money, switching the hiding place of my shoebox, reorganizing my always tidy desk. . . . About fifteen minutes before I planned to leave, the telephone rings. "Hello?"

"What's poppin', cuz?"

"Chingy! How's it going, kid?"

"I'm here grindin'."

"Grindin'?"

"Yeah, man, I got your last check and something I want to show you. Is it okay if I roll through?"

"Nah, kid, you caught me just as I was about to walk out the door."

"So maybe I can catch up with you."

"Nah, I gotta pick up Candace to go see this movie."

"Ooooh—"

"Shut up, yo."

"It's like that, huh? That's cool, though. Just don't know why you can't inform a brother. Keepin' secrets and shit." But Chingy's just pretending to sweat it.

"What secret, kid? I just told you, didn't I?"

"Whatever," he laughs. "What y'all going to go see?"

"I don't know. Whatever the lady wants, I guess."

"Daaamn, look at you. All chivalrous and whatnot. I need to try your approach."

"What approach?" I tease. "That's called sincerity, son." The call-waiting signal sounds. "Yo, Chingy, someone's trying to call, so let me holler at you later."

"Maybe I can swing by tomorrow with the check and this thing I want to show you. Get all the juicy details while I'm at it."

Chingy kills me, gossiping like Leti. "Most def." The line bleeps again. "All right, man, I'll talk to you tomorrow." I switch. "Hello?"

"Efrain?"

I can barely hear her. "Candace?" She sniffles. "What's wrong, ma?"

"My mother won't let me go."

"But why?" I hear a woman in the background hurrying Candace to say her piece and hang up.

"She just won't." Her voice breaks. "I'm sorry. I said yes because I really wanted to go, but she won't let me because she doesn't know you." The woman in the background says more that I can't understand. Suddenly Candace says, "I'll see you at school."

"Candace, wait—" But she hangs up.

I toss the phone on my bed. No, nope, sorry, I'm not feeling this at all. Where does her mother come off making judgments about me? She don't know me! Shit, I'm the dude every woman should want for her daughter. I live clean, excel in school. . . . Didn't Candace tell her moms all this?

I leap on the telephone and call back Chingy. The second he answers, I just rip. I don't know how long I go on before it hits me that we might have been cut off. "Yo, Chingy, can you hear me?"

"Yeah, man, I'm just listening."

"So what you think, bro? Am I right or what?"

"You right, you right . . ."

"Why you say it like that, kid? Like her moms has reason to not let Candace go out with me."

"Well, it ain't like the woman has a reason to say *yes*. I mean, Candace is right. She doesn't know you." Chingy sighs, then says, "Look, E., if this was any ol' chick from around the way, I'd tell you to forget about it. Find you another, plenty of fish in the sea, and all that. But that girl and her family have been through things we can't even imagine. Maybe Ma Dukes got a right to be a little overprotective."

As much as I don't want to admit it, that's real talk right there. "Well, I'm glad I didn't, like, go off on her for standing me up."

"Nah, man, that ain't you," Chingy laughs. "You really feeling this girl?"

"I'm feeling her."

"I mean, you trying to get to know her, or you trying to get to *know her,* know her?"

"Know her, know her."

" 'Cause if you ain't really feeling Candace, if you ain't trying to get to know her like *that,* then leave that girl alone, E. But if you're really feeling her, if you think she's worth it, then figure out a way to let Ma Dukes *know* you."

That makes sense. And I do think Candace is worth it. I just have no clue how to win over her moms.

My silence must speak volumes because, without my asking, Chingy says, "You know what I'd do?"

Exorable ◆ (*adj.*) susceptible to being persuaded or moved by entreaty

I wait in front of Candace's building with my bags for about fif-teen minutes until someone leaves. Before the front door locks shut, I slip inside and walk up to her floor. Chingy had advised me to ring the bell and wait for someone in Candace's apartment to let me in, but I feel this is the better way to go. Yeah, I risk com-ing off brazen, and Candace's moms might think I'm being shifty or disrespectful. But my gut tells me that Mrs. Lamb has to *see* me, and that may never happen if I wait for her to be willing to meet me. And it beats standing on the street under her daugh-ter's window hollering her name like some ghetto knight.

Instead, I come to her door and gently knock. Before I came over, I followed Chingy's advice and changed out of my Crooked Ink hoodie and LRG jeans and into an Avirex button-down and pleated khakis. On general principle, I shouldn't have had to switch my gear, but if I'm taking this risk, better to not play into negative assumptions, as unfair as they might be. Behind the door, a woman says, "Child, how many times do I have to tell you to stay away from that door?"

Aw, man, her moms is going to open the door! I hear her slide the cover to the peephole. "Who is it?"

"My name is Efrain Rodriguez, ma'am, and I just wanted to drop off some things for your daughter."

The door clicks, then opens slightly. An ebony eye with wrinkled edges peeks under the security chain. "Come again?"

"My name is Efrain, and I'm a classmate of your daughter Candace, ma'am. She told me that you wouldn't let her go out with me for lunch and a movie since you don't know me. . . ." I hold up the two bags so she can see them. "So I thought I'd bring lunch and the movie to her so you could meet me."

The eye blinks at me a few times and then disappears behind the closing door. I wait, then hear the security chain slide across its axis. The door opens, and a middle-aged woman looks me up and down. She seems too old to be her mother and yet too young to be her grandmother. She squints at me. "Did you say your name was Rodriguez?"

"Yes, ma'am."

"Where are your people from?"

"I was born and raised here in the Bronx. So was my mother. She's Puerto Rican. And Ru— My father is from the Dominican Republic, but he's been living here for years. He finally became a citizen a few years ago."

"And do they know that you're here right now?"

"Well, my mother knew I had plans to go out with your daughter, but she doesn't know I'm here now. She's at work thinking we're at the movies."

"And your father?"

"Yes," I lie. "He works at the auto shop on Jackson and 139th Street."

"You see what I mean, Mama? I told you he was a nice boy." I look past Mrs. Lamb and see Candace in the hallway. Her eyes are red, and there are tearstains down her cheeks. "May I please go?"

Mrs. Lamb whips her head to yell, "No, you cannot, Candace." Then she turns back to me and steps aside. "But Efrain can spend time with you here."

Prescient ♦ (*adj.*) having foreknowledge of events

On Sunday afternoon, I sweat through my physics homework when Mandy yells, "Efrain, Chingy's here!"

Thank God, because I need the brother's help. Sometimes I spend the same amount of time on this mess as it takes to finish all my other homework combined. I jump up and toss open my bedroom door. "S'up, kid?" I say.

"It's an everyday struggle, yo," Chingy says. He always cracks me up with that line. When does Chingy struggle with anything? He hands me my last paycheck, bounds over to my desk, and switches on my computer. "Damn, E., Barney Rubble had a faster computer than this thing." It's true what Nes said about Chingy being spoiled. For his last birthday, his parents bought him a new laptop. For my birthday, my mother gave me a card with twenty bucks that immediately went to pay my library fines for overdue SAT prep books. At almost nine o'clock that night, Rubio finally cornered me in the bodega and asked me what I wanted. I answered him by walking out, leaving the candles I was buying for the cake Yannis's wife baked me on the counter.

"Tell me something I don't know," I say, putting the check into my backpack so I can take it to the check-cashing place tomorrow. "You done your physics homework yet?" Chingy nods as he hits the button on the disk drive to my computer. "Then give a brother a clue 'cause it's kicking my ass."

Chingy snickers. "All you gotta do is choose the right formula, plug in the numbers, and, bam, you got the answer." He slides a CD into the tray and closes the drive. BK's roommate at Morehouse is a deejay, so he's always sending him CDs of underground hip-hop mixes. They're usually fire, and I'm down to listen but after I'm free from physics.

"Nah, son, I have *no* answer, never mind *the* answer."

"You think too much, cuz." Chingy turns on my monitor. "But a brother's gonna hook you up with this here birthday present I made for ya. Sit down."

I grab my extra chair and pull it up next to him. "My birthday was over three months ago, kid."

"And what'd I give you?"

"What you give me every year. Nothing but a hard time."

Chingy laughs as he clicks the mouse. "Well, happy belated birthday, E."

The hourglass on the screen bursts into a giant spreadsheet with a dozen columns, each headed by the name of a school I'm applying to. For each school, there is a list: *GPA, SAT, Class Ranking, Interview,* and other things colleges consider when weighing someone's application. "What's this?"

"This here is the Rashaan Perry College Admission Probability Calculation System," he announces. "You enter the data, right? Your grade point average, your SAT score, or whatever, and the system calculates your odds of getting admitted."

"That's dope! Slide over." Chingy moves aside, and I drag my chair in front of the monitor. Under *Harvard,* I enter *4.0* for *GPA* and *2400* under *SAT.* Pure fantasy, I know, but I'm curious. The last cell in the *Harvard* column flashes a number: *95 percent.* "You could make mad paper selling this."

"I proposed this as my final project for my advanced programming class thinking it'd be easy, but man . . ." Chingy whistles.

"My teacher says if I can get it to work, I should enter it into a few competitions. Get my scholarship on. I figured you'd be my perfect beta tester."

"No doubt."

"In order to be as accurate as possible, I couldn't just develop one code. I had to create a unique algorithm for each and every college."

It takes me a second to grasp his point. "Because Hunter College may place more emphasis on your class ranking than your SAT score than, say, Harvard might?"

"Exactly! And there's no way to really assess that unless you talk to someone at every admissions office or, better yet, compile statistics on incoming freshmen." I get a kick out of seeing Chingy so serious about something. "Plus, let's say an interview is optional. Whether it should increase your odds depends on how well it goes, right? That's mad subjective, yo, so how much weight should the system place on it?"

"Still," I say, "this program's fire, son."

But my boy's in another world, trying to figure out how to perfect his invention. "I think I'm onto something by accounting for the averages. For example, in the algorithm for Harvard, I included the average SAT score for an incoming student, which is 2100—"

"Don't remind me." But being a glutton for punishment, I enter *1650* into the *SAT* cell and watch my odds of admission plummet. I'm surprised my computer didn't just crash.

"—Did that for each of the schools. Same with percentage of applicants who are admitted at each college, too. Factors like that." Chingy leans back and sighs. "It's a work in progress, and I've got a long way to go, so treat it like a game, E., a'ight? Don't OD and take it too seriously."

I play around with the numbers and say, "So when I take the

SAT again in January, which score should I use?" Please say the better one.

Chingy throws up his hands. "Damn, I forgot about that!" He jumps to his feet and hunches over my keyboard. "Slide, yo."

I plant myself in his way, laughing. "C'mon, man—"

"Nah, man, I got to account for that." He clacks away at the keys. "I guess I should just average them."

"No!" I yell. I may suck at physics and may not be as good at math as Chingy or Candace, but I know damn well that averaging my scores will kill me. "Wouldn't it be more accurate to weight the second one more than the first one?"

Chingy considers it. "You might be right." He tinkers with the spreadsheet, changing *SAT* to *SAT1* and adding a row named *SAT2*. "But let me tell you something, bro. You better rip that sucker 'cause if you don't do as well or better the second time around, it'll hurt your odds more than if you never retook it, ya feel me?"

As if physics weren't enough to worry about. At least I'm feeling better about my chances now that I've registered for that SAT prep course. Not that I bring that up with Chingy in case he asks me how much it costs and other questions I don't want to answer.

Corroborate ♦ (v.) to support with evidence

"Man, E., what you keep smiling about?" asks Nestor. "All ear to ear and whatnot." Then his mouth pops into a big *O*. "You finally got some!"

"Shut up, yo." But my face hurts from grinning so much. I can't control it.

Nestor laughs. "You be all secretive, Efrain, but I knew it all along. I figure in time you'd spill the beans. GiGi González?"

"No, nope, sorry."

"Yeah, she ain't trying to mess with you."

As stupid as it is, I get upset. "What's wrong with me?"

"Same thing that's wrong with me. You ain't Snipes." Nestor gives me a slight shove. "Why you getting bent out of shape? Two seconds ago when I asked if you were going out with GiGi, you were all *Hell no!* Now you offended."

"Whatever."

"Come with me to Fratelli's. I'll treat you to a pizza or a hero or something." Nestor starts to walk east on Hunts Point Avenue. "So what's her name?"

"Candace."

"No wonder you're whipped! Candace is, like, the title of a female ruler in ancient Africa," says Nestor, a huge grin busting across his face. "Sisters who be running shit like the queen of Sheba."

While I like the idea of having a girlfriend with a name of distinction, I'm not too crazy about being called whipped. "Shut up."

Nestor, of course, keeps on. "For real. *Candace* is the Latin version of *Kandake* or something like that. Is she Boricua? *¿Dominicana?*"

"Black."

"Ah!" And the clown breaks out into his jig. "I should've known."

"Yeah, yeah, yeah." I should play cool and keep it at that, but I can't help myself. "I got me a nice Southern girl."

"You're going out with some chick from Brooklyn?" Nestor laughs as he dodges my chop to his neck. "Yo, I'm only messing with you. I may be a high school dropout, but I know where the South is. So is she, like, from Texas, Alabama, Georgia, or what?"

"Louisiana." I hesitate for a second, wondering if I should say more. Candace might not like me putting her on blast even to one of my closest friends. But I want to tell someone about her, and I don't plan on introducing Nestor to Candace anytime soon. "New Orleans."

Nestor's eyes open. "K-Ville? Yo, was she living there when Katrina hit?" I nod. "Damn . . ." He gets an extra bop in his walk. "How did she get out?"

"I don't know. We haven't talked about it yet." I increase my stride to keep up with him. "We're still getting to know each other, so I don't know where she is with all that. I'm afraid to ask her and stir up any painful memories, you know?"

"I feel you." Suddenly Nestor punches his hand into his fist. "You know that jail barge I was telling you about? It was built in NOLA."

"Get out."

"For real, kid. Cost, like, 160 million." We walk a few paces in silence. Then Nes gets angry. "You see that, E.? All that money for a jail in the 'hood, but folks in K-Ville still living in trailers."

"If that," I say. Candace's family is hardly the only one spread throughout the country. I wish she would talk more about it. Or at least give me some kind of permission to ask.

"What Kanye said on TV during that fund-raiser?" says Nestor. "That was truth right there."

"Real talk."

Nestor and I get to Fratelli's and order a couple of sausage heros. After grabbing some sodas from the refrigerator, we decide to wait outside while they prepare our order. Nestor asks, "And what about Chingy? Who's that player messing with these days?"

I don't like dodging him, but I like the idea of betraying Chingy's confidence even less. "Never mind Chingy. What about you, kid? Who're you seeing?"

Nestor shrugs. "I hit this one here, smash that one there. Nobody worth naming, you know. As nice as it would be to have someone official like that, a brother in this game can't keep a decent female. If a girl knows you're slinging and still wants to be with you, you have to wonder. . . ." Nestor walks over to a parked car and leans against it. "Does she like me for who I am or what she thinks I can do for her?"

"But if the girl doesn't know how you make your paper," I say, "no need to worry about that."

Nestor takes a deep swig of his soda. "But then what do you really have if you can't be real with her? A man is what a man does, you know?"

"That's not true." I pace the sidewalk in front of Fratelli's. "A man is more than what he does to make ends meet."

"I didn't say that was all he was, but . . ." Nestor gets off the car. "Okay, what does Rubio do?"

I give him a dirty look. "Don't talk about him, yo."

He throws his hands up. "What I say? Did I say anything bad about your pops? No. I just asked you what he does for a living."

Nestor knows the man's a mechanic. Before his father bounced, he used to take his car to Rubio's shop all the time. Those two probably used to swap boasts about their jump-offs. "I heard what you asked, and I'm saying leave Rubio out of this conversation."

Nestor sighs, then says, "Okay, what does Chingy's father do?"

"He works for the Department of Labor in some office at the Hub. Something to do with veterans." It comes back to me. "Yeah, he helps other veterans get jobs."

"Right. Okay. When he's not at work, what kind of things does he like to do?"

I have no idea where Nestor is taking this, but I have to admit he has my attention. "He and Mrs. Perry like to go to Atlantic City every once in a while. And he's part of that bowling league. In fact, he's the captain of his team." All those trips to Harlem Lanes come back to me. It'd be just us guys, and, man, would we have fun! Nestor's father even came along from time to time. Mr. Perry always invited Rubio, but he could never be bothered. I remember wondering out loud to my moms if it was because he was prejudiced. She had a fit. *How could you say something like that about your father? Do you think he would let you be friends with Rashaan if he were a racist? Do you think he would've married me?* And on and on and on. She lit into me, but then later I eavesdropped behind their bedroom door as she went after Rubio. Telling him things like the Perrys were *buena gente,* that he was offending them by never going bowling with us, and how did he think it made me feel to be the only boy whose father never went. . . . Rubio said that he was a grown man who could choose his own friends and had the right to spend his free time in whatever way he pleased without anybody's assumptions and judgments. What Moms and I didn't know then was that all those friends were females, and all that running around on her didn't leave Rubio any time or energy to go bowling with me.

Nestor starts to count off on his fingers. "Okay, Mr. Perry's a husband, a father, a veteran, a . . . What do you call it when you work for the government?"

"A civil servant."

"Yeah, that's it. He's a husband, father, veteran, civil servant, bowler, gambler. . . ." I shoot him a look. "What? I didn't say it like *that*. Like he's Pete Rose or some shit. I meant it like the bowling. A hobby."

"A'ight."

"So Mr. Perry is all those things, but let me ask you this, E. Where does he spend most of his time?"

"At his job, I guess."

"So the man spends most of his waking hours at the Department of Labor helping veterans find jobs. That's his primary role in life. No, the man's not only his job, but the job is the main part of who he is." Nestor pauses as if to give the point time to sink. "And if you think about it, E., it makes perfect sense. A man's job says a lot about him. It tells you what he's good at, what kind of people are around him most times, who relies on him for what. . . . Man, just the fact that he has a job—no matter what it is—says something about the kind of man he is. So, no, how a man makes his ends may not be the end-all, be-all of who he is, but it's a big part of it, E. A real big part. So when I say a girl gets with you knowing that you're slinging, you gotta hold her suspect—"

"And what if your girl doesn't know?" I ask.

Nestor thinks about it for a second. Then he just shrugs. "Then I guess the one who's suspect is you." Then he lifts himself off the car and heads back to Fratelli's. "Hope them heros is done, 'cause I'm starving."

Buttress ◆ (*v.*) to support, hold up

From the first meeting of my SAT prep course, I feel a thousand times slicker. These instructors got tricks, yo. Like I can increase my score just by *skipping* entire sections of the test. I mean, I still have to boost my vocabulary and memorize mathematical formulas and whatnot, but this so-called aptitude test is as much about how to take the exam as it is about what material is on it. If I bust a score of 2200 in January, I basically paid two bucks per point. That's a steal, if you ask me.

I feel so good when I leave Fordham that when I jump off the Bx19 bus, I head straight to Candace's place. After a few more chaperoned visits with rentals and takeout, Ma Dukes finally agreed to let me take the girl off the block. Candace is mad excited. Even though her moms forbids us to leave the Bronx, she insists I take her someplace downtown. At first, I was having none of that, but Candace pleaded and schemed, and I finally agreed to take her to this restaurant called the Delta Grill so she can have a taste of Louisiana. I kind of like that my "nice Southern girl" has an edge, and I want her to feel the same way about her valedictorian. Could never have been able to afford that restaurant tutoring, that's for sure.

When I arrive, her aunt lets me into the apartment. "Child, you're a half hour early," says Miss Lamb. "Candace hasn't returned from her doctor's appointment yet."

She never mentioned any appointment. "Is Candace sick?" I ask.

Miss Lamb's eyes open with the realization that she spoke out of turn. She nudges me back toward the door. "It's probably best that you wait at home and come back in thirty minutes," she says. "A lady doesn't like to be caught off guard by her suitor, Efrain."

What else can I do but step? When I get home, I reach out to Chingy, but his mother says he's playing hoops at St. Mary's. So I trip for the next half hour. Why would Candace keep something like that from me? Does she have an illness or disability that I can't see? Is this why Candace said that sometimes she gets sick of people being nice to her?

I freshen up and arrive at her building on the hour. Instead of buzzing me in so I can head upstairs, Candace comes down to meet me. On sight we both know what's up. She knows I know about her aunt's slip of the tongue, I know she knows, she knows I know she knows. Just one nerve-racking metaphysical mess of a moment, man.

I say, "Ready to go?"

Pretending to fuss with her jacket to break eye contact, she just mumbles, "Yeah."

"Still wanna go downtown?"

"Uh-huh." Usually when Candace and I hang out, I take her hand or she links her arm through mine. It happens naturally. But today when we walk toward the subway, a yard of tension hangs between us. "Hey, how was your class?"

I tell her, trying to muster the same enthusiasm I had when I left the campus. I fake it long enough for the 6 train to come. Once we find seats on the subway, I finally ask, "How's your day been so far?"

Candace takes a deep breath. Then she smiles. "Your ears must've been ringing, because I was talking about you."

Her answer surprises me. "To who?"

"My group."

Here it comes. "I didn't know you were part of a group."

"It's not something I tell just anyone. The few people outside my family who know either had to know or . . ." Candace finally looks me in the eye. ". . . I decided to trust them." Like I told Chingy, I'm trying to know this girl. I mean, *know her,* know her. So I take her hand, and Candace squeezes it as if to transfer the truth without words. PE to KE. "It's a support group for kids like me, you know, teenagers who survived Katrina. And Rita, too. Anyway, the doctor my bigmouth aunt told you about?" I laugh as she rolls her eyes, and the tension between us bends. "She runs the group. I meet with her one-on-one every Wednesday after school, and on Saturday mornings, we have group . . ." She hesitates to finish her sentence, and I squeeze her hand. ". . . therapy."

Candace waits for me to say something. My girlfriend is in therapy. She sees a psychologist, psychiatrist, or whatever. Her problems are serious enough that the doctor needs to meet with her alone in private. I remember the rumor about why Candace transferred from Mott Haven to AC. I just shrug and say, "It's all good." What a stupid thing to say, E.! "I mean, not the reason why you have to go, obviously! Just the fact that you *do* go." Man, I'm making a lot of assumptions. I ask, "Do you feel like it helps you?"

Candace nods. "My doctor says that she wishes I would talk more during group, but it helps me a lot to just listen. To know that I'm not alone. But today I talked a little." And the way she looks at me says that even though I'm not a part of the group, I'm part of the therapy.

"Can I ask you something?"

Candace sighs with relief. "Please!"

"You promise you won't get mad?"

"No, but ask me anyway."

"It's something I heard, and I just want to know what's true." I throw my hands up ready to block blows. "It's not like I already believe it or anything like that."

"Will you ask me already? And will you please put your hands down, Efrain? Everyone's staring at us like a bad reality show couple."

"My bad." I drop my guard. "Okay . . . Is it true that . . ." I can't keep it that real. How do I repeat the hurtful gossip about her now that I know she trusts me? ". . . you got expelled from Mott Haven for stabbing some girl and burying her under the football field?"

Candace hits me in the arm. "Shut up!" We laugh a bit, and then she says, "I was taking an elective in environmental justice, and I did my final presentation on New Orleans since Katrina. I knew things were bad at home, but, man . . ." She looks away from me, and I follow her eyes to the MTA's Train of Thought ad across the car. In silence, we both read it.

> *There are roughly three New Yorks. There is, first, the New York of the man or woman who was born here, who takes the city for granted and accepts its size and its turbulence as natural and inevitable. Second, there is the New York of the commuter—the city that is devoured by locusts each day and spat out each night. Third, there is the New York of the person who was born somewhere else and came to New York in quest of something. . . . Commuters give the*

91

city its tidal restlessness; natives give it
solidity and continuity; but the settlers
give it passion.

Candace smiles at the ad, then turns back to me. "The school system in New Orleans was always bad, but now it's worse. The crime rate's off the meter. . . . Anyway, I finish my presentation, and the teacher asks if anyone has any questions. I'm one of the last people to go, and nobody's been asking anybody questions all week. Then this girl Dacia yells, 'You one of them refugees?' And everybody starts laughing at me. Well, maybe some people were just laughing 'cause Dacia was supposed to present next if there was time left in the period."

"Yeah, she was just asking questions to waste time."

Candace shrugs. "Anyway, I say, no, I'm not a refugee, but the girl is like, 'You kept saying how New Orleans is the City That Care Forgot and how the Black folks there were treated in an un-American way or whatever and that things are so bad that you had to leave and you can't go back. That means you a refugee!'"

"And the teacher didn't shut her down?"

"She tried. She explained that a refugee is a person who flees a foreign country to escape danger or persecution. Then the teacher asks me if there's anything I want to add. I say, 'Yes,' and I look straight at Dacia and say, 'Don't call me a refugee.' Then the teacher says it's her turn, and I can go back to my seat. Then she starts clapping, and everybody else claps, too, but as I pass Dacia's desk, she says, 'Nice job, refugee.' So I threw my notebook at her." I start laughing. "That's not funny, Efrain!"

"Did you break her jaw so the doctor had to wire it shut?"

"No!" But her eyes flash with horror.

"You hit her, though." I can't stop laughing. "You connected, didn't you?"

"I would've missed her except she kind of walked into it so the edge of my book caught her in the nose." A lot of girls I know would be bragging about that, but Candace sounds embarrassed. "Her nose bled a little, but I didn't break anything, I swear."

I stay laughing. "I believe you, *mami*."

"What do they say about me at school?"

"That you hung some dude from the bleachers." Before she can answer, I add, "And there's another one that goes *Candace snuck an AK-47 into the school and shot up her gym class.*"

She finally smiles. "Uh-huh, I did that." Candace no longer cares about the hurtful rumors, and that's all that matters to me. "And you fixin' to be next, so keep it up."

"There's one more story about you that they used for an episode of *Law & Order.*"

"Efrain, stop exaggerating!" Candace leans into me giggling.

Her touch pumps the idea into me like a transfusion. PE to KE. "I'm taking this year-long civil rights class and have to do a senior thesis," I say. "Would you mind if I did something related to Hurricane Katrina and, you know, used your presentation as part of my research? Don't worry, I won't plagiarize."

Candace glows. "You'd never do anything like that." Then she kisses my temple. "You're the best guy in the whole school."

Inimical ♦ (*adj.*) unfriendly, hostile, having the disposition of an enemy

The block's poppin' more than usual even for a Thursday night. "It's warm for November, the city workers got paid today . . . ," says Nestor. "I smell cheddar." We had to re-up an hour earlier than usual, and I make money hand over fist. It's dope to not grind for pennies. If every night were like this, I can see how dudes get caught up.

I only break for dinner, treating myself to *un biftec empaniza'o* with yellow rice and black beans at Floridita's, a Puerto Rican restaurant across the street. When I walk out of Floridita's, a disheveled guy wearing a week's funk bops up to me.

"You got?"

"What you need?"

"I heard those white tops be whispering sweet nothings in a nigga's ear," he says.

It still bothers me to sell crack. The money is usually too good to resist, but I don't need the extra sale tonight. "I'm out," I lie, "but let me introduce you to my man over here."

The throwback shakes his head. "Nah, man, never mind. My cash has to go long this weekend. You got any weed?"

"No doubt."

"Hit me up with a nickel, then." He gives me a ten-dollar bill, and I pocket it. I start to signal LeRon when I feel a hard yank on the hood of my jacket. I fly backward until I crash against the brick wall of the restaurant. A forearm slams across my throat, and my Adam's apple reaches for my eyebrows.

Then milky dark eyes breathe the tang of stale endo into my face. "What the fuck you think you doing?"

With both hands, I grab at the arm and try to pry it off my neck. "Get the fuck off me, yo!"

"You run with Snipes!" The stench of old reefer invades my nostrils again, followed by another thrust of the forearm to my throat. "You one of Snipes's boys, right?"

I close my eyes and brace myself for the blow. But then the forearm whips off my neck as if someone was rewinding a video. Then all I hear is a bunch of guys cursing, feet pounding, jackets chafing. I finally open my eyes to catch boys from my crew pulling back Nestor while some guys from Hinckley's posse restrain one of their own. I run into the middle of the drama. "What the hell's going on, man?"

"How you gonna try to hustle on this corner?" says this Latino kid I've never seen before. "All in our face like we ain't shit."

"You got it twisted," says Nestor. "That's all I was trying to explain, man. It's just a misunderstanding 'cause my boy's new, that's all."

"New, my ass!" shouts Reefer Breath. He's a skinny, yellow-skinned dude with a knotty Afro and pointed jaw. "He's been out here slinging long enough to not even be thinking about plying no trade on this side of the street." He jabs his finger toward my face. "You finna get smoked?"

Nestor reaches into his pocket and moves toward Reefer. His boys crowd around him so our crew closes ranks around Nestor. Nestor takes a few steps back and raises his hands in the air, waving a fifty-dollar bill. "Look, let's squash this before someone calls the po and we all get knocked, okay?" Soldiers on both sides mutter *Word* and *For real*. "Just consider this compensation for any inconvenience."

Reefer Breath paces in a small circle like a mutt about to settle on a rug. He starts toward Nestor, but the Latino kid in his crew clamps a hand on his shoulder. "C'mon, Julian, squash it."

Julian knocks off his friend's hand. Eventually, he faces off with Nestor, but homeboy doesn't blink. He just raises the bill and dangles it in front of Julian. They stare each other down for a few seconds with both posses set to jump. Finally, Julian snatches the fifty out of Nestor's hand and walks around him to me. He points in my face and says, "This time it was a mistake. Next time . . ." His boys follow him, mean-mugging as they bop past me.

My crew makes its way across the street while Nestor hangs back. "What were you thinking, bro?" he asks.

"I wasn't, man. I came out of the restaurant, this guy steps to me, and without thinking twice about it—"

"Damn, E.—"

"I know. I'm sorry. Trust me, it'll never happen again."

"No worries." Nestor slaps me on the shoulder. "Just to be on the safe side, don't even cross the street." And with that, he motions us to head back to our side. "For real. This is Hunts Point, kid. You can get your *empaniza'o* on anywhere you look."

I snicker as I dodge through the oncoming traffic. "No, nope, sorry. I'm not giving up Floridita's *empaniza'o* for nobody."

I'm just joking, but Nestor looks mad serious. "I'm not trying to son you, E., but these streets are on some other shit, okay?" When we reach the other side, and I try to bounce, he grabs my arm to pull me back. "It's not like you, Chingy, and me scrapping with those kids from Cypress Avenue on the court after a hard foul, ya feel me?"

"Yeah, yeah, yeah." I shrug him off me. Like I don't feel enough like an herb.

He takes a deep breath. "Look, bro, I saw how that punk Julian just yoked you from behind. That you didn't even see him coming."

My cheeks grow hot. "Let it go already."

But Nestor gets in my face. "You better listen to me but good, E. Compared to cats who've been hustling since they were yea high, you *are* a Boy Scout. Just because I have your back out here doesn't mean you can skip down Hunts Point Avenue like it's the Yellow Brick Road, got it?"

I get it. Still, I say, "Whatever."

Nestor shakes his head at me. His cell phone rings, and he fishes it out of his pocket. He reads the screen, taps out a text message, then puts his cell away. "Snipes wants to see you."

"What?"

Nestor shrugs. "Hey, when you don't make friends and influence people, trust that some kiss-ass is going to run tell when you have drama. Heads be griping that you punch in and clock out without ever stopping to chitchat by the water cooler, you feel me? Saying *That new kid Scout, he's just a schoolboy playing gangster until Mommy calls him home for supper.* When Julian rushed you tonight, the brothers fell in for me. For Snipes. Not you, and you better take that shit personally."

I know he's right, but I can't do a thing about it except hope that Snipes dismisses it as just another day on the grind. Worse things have happened, haven't they? Thinking about that makes me shudder.

"Don't get shook, E.," says Nestor. "I'm responsible for you. I'll go talk to Snipes."

"Look, man, thanks for having my back. As always." My shame just isn't deep enough to man up and face Snipes myself.

"No doubt, bro."

"And before I forget." I reach into my pocket, peel off fifty dollars, and hand it to Nestor. Ouch. But it's the least I can do.

He backs away from the money. "C'mon, it ain't like that. Not between us."

"Take it anyway." Nestor pockets the cash, and we get back to work. Although the tide is still strong, I have no swagger. Customers approach me, but because I'm slow on the take, other cats in my crew muscle in on the sale. Now every time somebody beats me to a customer, LeRon yells out something like, "Uh-oh, Scout, he's gunning for your badge." I consider quitting, but pride won't let me. Instead, I stay longer than I ordinarily do. I even borrow Nestor's cell phone, take a walk over to Jimmy Jazz, and give my mother a story about overtime as if standing by a display of sweaters makes it less of a lie.

Gregarious ♦ (*adj.*) drawn to the company of others, sociable

My routine is insane. From Monday to Friday, I walk to school with Chingy and go to class. After eighth period, I jet home to check in on my sister (if she's not over at Rubio's) and do my homework. When dusk falls, I put away my schoolbooks and grab the train to the Point. I sling till midnight, maybe one in the morning. Sometimes during my "meal break," I get on Nestor's cell phone and check in with my mother and sister. Then I go home and crash unless I'm too wired to sleep. On those nights I study for the SAT, sometimes until two, three in the morning. Sleep or no sleep, I wake up at six on Saturday mornings to finish my SAT prep homework before taking the bus to my class at Fordham. After class I go the library and study some more (or take a nap) until Candace comes home from her doctor's appointment. On Saturday afternoons, we have a standing date. Mrs. Lamb doesn't let us venture far from the neighborhood, but that's fine by me because when the sun goes down, I have to grind on that corner, all the while having everyone think I'm working a register at Jimmy Jazz.

With school closed this Monday because of Veterans Day, I pretend to take a day off from the store just to sleep in, especially since I have a practice test in my SAT prep course this Saturday. The extra sleep feels awesome, and I even had some cool dreams. My moms smiling proudly as I give my valedictory speech at graduation. Me giving Chingy a tour of the Harvard campus. Candace and me . . . Whenever I wake up, the nice feelings cling to me like the sheets still wrapped around my body, so I just roll over for more.

That is, until my mother barges into my room wearing a housecoat that adds fifteen years to her age. I leap up in bed and say, "Mami, what's wrong?" She usually works on Veterans Day.

"Nestor is at the door," she says. Her voice is cold and thin like the films of ice that now cover our front steps.

I start to climb out of bed, but my mother doesn't budge from the doorway. "Mami, I gotta get dressed." She huffs and then slams the door behind her. If this is not major, I may have to smite that kid.

I throw on a raggedy sweat suit, slip on my *chancl'as,* and bolt out of my room. In the living room, my sister sits in front of the television watching music videos. "Where's Nes?"

"Huh?"

"Nestor. Mami said he was here. Did he leave?"

Mandy shrugs. "He didn't come in here."

As I cross the hallway to the apartment door, I see my mother's shadow across the floor before me. I open the door to find Nestor bobbing his head to the *reggaetón* on his iPod. "Nes!" I yell, waving my hand in his face to get this attention.

He notices me and pulls the earbuds out of his ears. "What's poppin'? With school out today, I thought we'd go shopping for some new gear. No disrespect, 'cause I don't think anything's wrong with your look, bro, but Snipes kinda ordered me to take you to get a flashier collar to pop, you know what I'm sayin'? Fit in better with the crew."

"Shhh." I crack the door in case Moms is eavesdropping from the kitchen. "Lower your voice, kid."

"My bad," Nestor whispers. Then dude leans over the threshold and yells, "¡Hola, Doña 'Lores!"

My moms steps back from the kitchen counter and comes into view. "Hello, Nestor," she says, barely making eye contact. The three of us have a moment of silence for the conversation that used to follow Nestor's greeting. *Come in, come in. We have Oreos. Do you want chocolate in your milk? How's Carmelo? He's going to be such a heartbreaker when he grows up, that one. ¿Y Marlene? I'm worried about that girl, Nestor, I have to tell you. Isn't your mother worried about your little sister?* Then my mother disappears from our sight.

"Look, we're Snipes's representatives on the street. With Hinckley and his boys trying to steal our customers, we always have to look like we're the ones with the hotness. It attracts customers, impresses the hungry, makes Hinckley's boys think about switching teams, and all that."

It sounds like bull to me, but after the Julian incident, how can I dis Nestor? "Fine, but don't expect me to wild out. Meet me at the pizzeria, like, around two."

Nestor glances down at his cell phone from where it hangs off the belt loop of his jeans. "Damn, E. That's, like, two hours from now."

"Look, kid, I can't run out of the apartment five minutes after you show up at my door. It'll make my moms suspicious. I gotta play it off like you just dropped by to say hi and head out much later so she'll think I'm with Chingy or my girl."

Nestor stares at me for a few seconds. He finally backs away from the door. "A'ight." He shuffles toward the staircase like a sad puppy, muttering under his breath how I need to get a cell phone.

I close the door and hustle toward my room, praying that my moms didn't hear him. But just as I reach my door, Moms comes out of the kitchen. "What did Nestor want, Efrain?"

"He wanted to me to go to the Hub with him, but I said no." Moms has known Nestor since we were nipping at her knees. She never liked his family but still allowed me to play with him all those years. Okay, usually she insisted that Nestor come over here or that we play outside where she could see us, but Moms never tried to stop us from being friends. So what he sells drugs? He's still the same Nes. Would it have killed her to invite him inside and offer him some *chocolate*? Dude's not going to sell herb to Mandy in our living room.

I don't say a word, though, too relieved that she seems content that I got rid of Nestor quickly. I try to get more sleep, but the whole situation weighs on my mind.

Chaos ♦ (*n.*) absolute disorder

I catch a break when my mother goes into her bedroom with the telephone and closes the door. Must be Rubio and it can't be good. Still, I take this opportunity to creep, grabbing my jacket and telling Mandy that I went to St. Mary's to play hoops with Chingy.

But when I get to the pizzeria, Nestor's nowhere to be found. The counter guy says he hasn't even seen him. I have a slice while I wait, but Nestor never shows. I'm halfway back home when something makes me head over to Nestor's building. It's been so long since I've been to his apartment, it takes two wrong guesses to remember which buzzer is his. Finally, I hit 3E, and one of his sisters comes over the intercom. "Who?"

"Efrain."

"Who?"

"Efrain!"

"Efrain?"

"Yeah, damn!"

She finally buzzes me into the building, and I bound up the steps two at a time to the third floor. As I near the apartment, I hear several voices chatter over the bass line of the hip-hop blasting on the stereo. Some things never change, I guess. I bang on the door, knowing that no one's opening it until I almost kick it in. That's just the way Nestor's family gets down.

Nestor's older sister Claudia opens the door. She's twenty-two, twenty-three now with two kids. When Claudia has a boyfriend, she and her kids move in with him. When the relationship goes sour, she moves back here. By the way she's dressed—stained baby tee, faded pajama pants, and torn *chancletas*—she must be between baby daddies. And to think Chingy and I used to fight over who was going to get with her when we grew up. It's not that having kids has made Claudia less pretty. Some of the baby fat she got while pregnant lingers in all the right places. But after having two kids with two different cats, neither who's worth a damn, Claudia's bitterness hangs off her like an ugly suit.

"Oh my God!" Claudia peers at me. "Is that Efrain?" She squeals and hugs me as if I were Nestor's older brother Leo come home from his second tour in Iraq. No one believed he had enlisted until he sent us a picture from basic training wearing his desert camouflage gear. Then it really sank in when they shipped him out to the Middle East for the first time. Can you believe that crazy dude volunteered to go again? "Come in. Marly, turn down that freakin' music already!"

With only two bedrooms for seven heads, Nestor's apartment has always been mad cramped, but now it's just a mess—half-broken toys everywhere, old store circulars piled on tables and the floor, clothes on the backs of the chairs. I take three steps into the corridor when I stub my toe against a stroller blocking my path. "Is Nestor here?"

"Yeah, he's in his room." Claudia makes no move to get him for me, so I ease by the stroller only to bump into a walker. "So, how're you doing, Efrain?"

"I'm good." I don't want to be rude, but the moment I crossed the threshold, the chaos sucked up my patience like a vortex. Claudia's baby cries from the master bedroom. She mumbles that his nap was way too short and that he'd better sleep through the night. I almost joke that it's too quiet for him and Marlene should blast the radio again, but maybe Claudia won't find that funny.

I run an obstacle course, including hurdling over a playpen, to make it to Nestor's room. The stainless steel lock on it looks out of place in this old tenement apartment, probably the only lock inside the place. I knock on the door. "Nes, open up. It's E."

After some shuffling from the bed to the door, the lock turns. Nestor throws open the door and pulls out his earbuds. "E.!" He gives me a pound and an 'ug and motions for me to enter. The place looks like it belongs in another apartment altogether, with all the technology and tidiness. "Man, you have this place all pimped out, son. Why bother going through all this trouble with Claudia and the kids going back and forth all the time?"

"Enough was enough," Nestor hisses. "I permanently relegated their behinds to the living room."

I drop myself onto the leather lounge chair, which gives heat *and* massage. I reel in the remote by the cord and turn on both. The rollers start to wave up and down either side of my spine. "Your moms back you up on that?"

Nestor sits on the edge of his bed and winds his earbuds around his iPod. "C'mon, man, what choice did she have? I pay the bills up in this piece. How's the man of the house going to sleep on some lumpy-ass sofa bed with an eight-year-old?"

On the one hand, I feel what Nestor's saying. If he's the only one maintaining the apartment, it's unfair to make him camp out in the living room like some overnight guest. But, on the other hand, it seems kind of foul to force Claudia and her two babies to sleep on some hideaway. "So where does Melo sleep?"

"In here with me, but he ain't allowed in here when I'm not around. I don't want him jacking up my stuff." He doesn't want Melo to find any "business-related items" either, I'm sure. That's the true reason for the lock on the door.

It makes no sense to me, though, since the kid should be sleeping while Nestor's hustling, but where do I go overanalyzing another man's business? I say, "Yo, I thought I told you to meet me at the pizzeria."

"The way you was frontin' back at your crib, I didn't think you would show up." He stands up, ready to roll. "So, you down to go to Brooklyn? The Fulton Street Mall?"

"I don't know, man," I say, leaning back into that leather slice of heaven. "I'm feeling this chair, kid. I may have to go *mimir* right here." I shove my thumb in my mouth and pretend to sleep.

"It's hot, right?" Nestor laughs. "Word is bond."

"It's *born,* not *bond.*" We fight about this all the time. "How many times do I have to tell you that it's a biblical thing? God created everything just by naming them. He said, *Let there be light,* and *boom!* There was light. Then He said, *Let there be land,* and *bam!* There was land. On the power of His word, everything in nature came into existence or was born. That's why sometimes heads will say *Word to life* 'cause word is *born.*"

"Uh-uh." That's all the dude has in response to a brother's lengthy reasoning. "It's *bond.* Short for *My word is my bond.*"

"*Born.*"

"*Bond!*"

"I'm telling you, kid, it's *born!*"

Our age-old debate is interrupted by a timid knock on the door. "Who?" yells Nestor. Who, who, who . . . Them Irizarrys are a bunch of Puerto Rican Whos like out of Dr. Seuss. And they all short, too. I laugh at my thoughts. Nestor gives me the *What's so funny?* look.

"It's me," says his little brother Carmelo.

Nestor goes to unlock and open the door. There stands Little

Mellow Man. He looks exactly like Nestor did when he was that age, I swear. "What's up, Little Man?" Nestor asks.

Melo speaks in a voice so low I can barely hear him. "Can I play Strike Force?"

"What's that?" I ask.

Nestor replies, "Bowling game on the Xbox." Then he says, "Maybe later. E. and I are about to go out now, and you know I don't want anyone in my room when I'm not around. Okay?"

Melo's eyes fall to his feet. "Okay." He's so sad as he shuffles away from the door. Nestor closes and locks it again.

"Malo." I say.

Nestor gets defensive. "What?" He walks to his closet and pulls out a pair of Skechers boots.

"He didn't just want to play with the Xbox." So unlike Nestor to miss the obvious. "Melo wants to play with *you.*"

"Nah, it's all about the Xbox, bro." Nestor shrugs as he sits on his bed and pulls on his boots. "I really got it for him anyway. I'm usually too busy to play."

"So put it in the living room so he can play with it whenever he wants."

"Forget it. Nobody here knows how to take care of anything. Claudia lets her kids get into everything, and Melo gets carried away, breaking stuff because nobody's minding him. . . . That's another reason why I don't let nobody in here when I ain't around. I'd have nothing if I did." Nestor knots his boots. "And neither would Melo." He stands up. "Ready to bounce?"

"Yeah." I grab the remote and turn off the massage chair.

Once we walk out of his room and down the hallway, Nestor stops at the living room. Poor Melo. Boredom has him on the brink of death as *Blue's Clues* plays on the television. Claudia's baby lies facedown on a comforter while her toddler bounces around in a swing. "Little Man, when I come back from Brooklyn, you want to go with me to Harlem Lanes? I'll show you how to bowl for real like a big boy." Melo's eyes flare, but he doesn't smile, as if he's afraid to say yes for nothing. "Yeah, Mellow?"

"Okay."

I say, "I'll hold him to it, Mellow Man."

"Come over here and show me some love." Melo scrambles off the couch, runs over to Nestor, and throws his arms around his legs. "That's what's up. My Little Man."

We finally leave the apartment and head down the stairs. "Yeah, he's a good kid," says Nestor. "I gotta spend more time with him."

Abjure ♦ (*v.*) to reject, renounce

"Efrain, get up." Scrawny fingers grab and shake my shoulder, and I get a whiff of flaky chocolate. I open my eyes to see Mandy's dusty brown fingertips with butterfly stickers over chipped purple nail polish. "Efrain . . ."

Man, the last thing I want to do is get up. I hit the block after taking Candace home and didn't get into bed until almost two this morning. My mother even woke up when she heard me come in and asked me what took me so long. I muttered some nonsense about staying late because we were short and the manager needed help with inventory. Moms mumbled something about calling next time so she won't worry but quickly fell back asleep. She believed it because she has been in that situation plenty of times. I crawled into bed just to stare at the ceiling for another half hour before I finally crashed, so I don't want to know about a damn thing before noon.

"Efrain!"

I smack Mandy's hand off my shoulder. "Amanda, if you don't stop bothering me, I'm going to tell Moms you be using her nail polish."

"Jerk!" The brat goes and chops me in the neck.

"Just for that, I'm going to tell her you've been eating the Cocoa Pebbles out of the box, too."

Now she looks scared. As hard as Moms works, she keeps this apartment immaculate and hates it when we do unhygienic things like eat dry cereal out of the box and drink juice from the carton. Mandy yells, "Chingy's here, stupid."

Just like I'm not allowed to hit her, she's not supposed to call me names. "Why couldn't you just say that, then, instead of shaking me and whining in my ear?" I know I shouldn't stoop to her childish level, but Mandy's being such a brat, and it's first thing in the morning. First thing in *my* morning anyway. "You need to stop spending so much time around little kids and babies 'cause you starting to act like one."

"Shut up, Efrain." She whips around like a top and storms toward my door.

"Yeah, that's really mature." I throw back the covers and climb out of the bed. "Get out of my room." She slams the door behind her. Hopefully, Chingy won't mind if I just meet him on the basketball court at St. Mary's in a couple of hours.

When I open the door, Chingy flies into my bedroom. In a flash, he spots the Joe's I wore last night draped over the chair by my desk. Chingy snatches the jeans and clenches them in his fist. "New gear, huh?"

"Yeah, I got those on sale," I say. Yeah, I OD'd a bit when I went shopping with Nestor. Don't I deserve some new clothes that aren't already a year behind the style when I get them? I bought Christmas presents for Moms and Mandy, too. And nothing I bought could I take home anyway, hiding everything at Nestor's except for this one pair of jeans.

"The five-finger discount?"

This is so unbelievable, I laugh for a second. "How're you going to roll up into my crib and accuse me of boosting some jeans?"

" 'Cause that's how you get down now, right?" says Chingy. Then he throws the jeans at me. If I had not been quick on the catch, the button would have caught me in the eye. "That's how you living, right?"

I fling the jeans onto my bed. "Yo, why you tripping?"

Chingy saunters over to me. "At least when Nes went foul, he was man enough to be open about his shit. I give him that much. He didn't front like some altar boy."

"Ain't nobody fronting, man." The words don't come out as angry as I feel them. I can barely hear myself say them.

"Then how come I have to find out that you're slinging rock at Hunts Point from Leti, GiGi, and them?"

I can't believe those *bochincheras*! None of them have actually seen me do anything to be running at the mouth, never mind exaggerating like that. "You're supposed to be my boy, but you jump to believe the first person to talk sideways about me?"

"Don't even try to turn this on me!" Chingy interrupts. Now he's in my face. "How long, son?"

Although I don't back away, I can't look him in the eye. "Since around Halloween."

"And all the times we've hung out since then, were you dirty?" So ever since GiGi and her friends yapped, Chingy's been running scenarios through his head. He's been imagining us hanging out—playing ball, eating pizza, heading to the movies, or whatever—and the cops suddenly rolling up on us, finding crack vials on me, and then hauling us both to jail. He done worked himself into a tailspin like the Tasmanian devil.

"No, man, I swear. I don't bring my work home. And I certainly don't mess with that shit myself."

Chingy smirks at me. "That's what I'm talking about. Fronting like you're some kind of saint. Living dirty and calling it work. Keeping secrets."

I say, "Maybe if you weren't so damn righteous, I would have told you." That hits Chingy because he falls back some and doesn't say anything for a few seconds. "Who can confide in you when you're so freakin' judgmental?"

Chingy backs up toward my door. After opening it, he pauses to look me in the eye. "You're right, E. I am righteous. I am judgmental. I'm lots of things, some of which ain't too cool. But at least with me, what you see is what you get. I'm out."

"C'mon, Rashaan—"

Chingy slams the door behind him. I stand there for a few seconds contemplating whether or not to go after him. I decide against it since my sister is home, and God knows how much of our argument she already heard. Snatching a fistful of Cocoa Pebbles out of the box is nothing compared to what Mandy may have on me now.

Disdain ♦ (v.) to scorn, hold in low esteem

As I walk Mandy to school the next day, she chatters on about some stupid dating "reality" show. At first, I just laugh with relief that my argument with Chingy is out of her mind and off of Moms' radar. Then again, I thank God Moms can't hear all this mess about stripper poles and booty claps and whatnot. Just yesterday my little sister was all about Hannah Montana and the Cheetah Girls. I give it to my mother for preserving Mandy's innocence for as long as she has, but I'm scared to death that any day now she might morph into Marlene! And it'd be nobody's fault but Rubio's. Had he been on point, Moms wouldn't have to work such long days, and my sister wouldn't have television for a babysitter. Hell, she's probably watching that garbage at *his* place, since we can't afford BET and VH1!

I drop off Mandy at her school and head to the corner of 141st Street and St. Ann's Avenue as always. Today I wait for Chingy to come running up his block yelling *Son, did you see the way Strahan sacked Hasselbeck?* But he never shows.

I jump into my seat in Spanish class just as the bell rings. I feel lucky to arrive on time yet avoid *las chismosas* when Señorita Polanco starts to pass out a test on the future tense. I had planned to study for it, but it completely slipped my mind with everything else crowded in there. Luckily, after I take a moment to gather my wits, most of last week's lessons come back to me.

I have social studies second period, my first class of the day with Chingy. He stands by the window with Marco and Stevie yammering about last night's Giants game. Instead of heading over there, I go to my seat and dump my books on the desk.

Leticia clacks down the aisle in high-heeled boots as if she were still in the running to become America's next top model. "Hi, Efrain!"

I don't even look up. "Hey."

"Did Chingy tell you?" she says. "GiGi and me think we saw Nestor and you at the Fulton Street Mall the other day. We weren't sure, though, 'cause we were on the other side of the train platform and haven't seen Nes in a looong time. I mean, GiGi swore up and down it was you, but I was, like, *If that's Efrain, where's Chingy?*" The bell rings, and Chingy takes his seat next to me. "Chingy, why weren't you with Efrain and Nestor on Fulton Street?"

Chingy squints at her. "Where was I supposed to be?"

"Nothing, I'm just saying y'all used to be like the Three Musketeers, but I never be seeing the three of y'all together no more, so I'm, like, what's up, you know?"

"Chingy was doing like Chingy do. Keepin' it real." After a sneer in my direction, Chingy adds, "And keepin' it right."

I say, "Whatever." The bell rings, and I open my textbook just to have something else to look at.

Leticia's eyes volley back and forth between us. "What's with you two?" she asks. "Y'all fighting?"

Both Chingy and I say, "Mind your business."

Leti hisses at us, "Later, then, for you two *pendejos.*" And she whirls around in her seat, her hair whipping in the air.

Ordinarily, that would have been enough to set things right between Chingy and me. We would have laughed at the way we both dissed Leticia and made an unspoken agreement to forget our argument ever happened. But that was before yesterday.

The tension between Chingy and me becomes more obvious with every passing class, even in gym, when Chingy doesn't choose me for his team. "Get over it, fellas," Coach Moretti cracks. "She's not the first; she won't be the last." Now all the herbs who were oblivious to the static are tuned in, talking about *er, huh, what?*

So I spend my lunch period in the library. I don't want to listen to Chingy and the rest of the guys who sit at our table jawing for forty-five minutes about the Giants' game anyway. Until we get right, sixth period will sound like *SportsCenter* all day, every day, and I have more important things to do, like study. Never again will I get caught out there unprepared for a test. Never! But five minutes into my vocabulary list of the one thousand most common words on the SAT, I conk out until the seventh-period bell rings.

Caustic ♦ (*adj.*) bitter, biting, acidic

After sleepwalking through my civil rights class, I walk into physics to find GiGi sitting on my desk. "Hi, Efrain."

"Hey." She looks good in her Southpole jeans. Too good. "Excuse me, please," I say as I motion her to move her butt off my desk. That apple bottom is a quadruple threat now. I'm involved with Candace, my boy Nestor wants to get with her, Chingy and I are on the outs, I'm dead on my feet. . . . The girl has to go.

But GiGi plants herself at Chingy's desk. "So what'd you get the other day in Brooklyn?" Chingy walks into the classroom. I need him to reclaim his desk, but, instead, he just scorns me, taking GiGi's seat in the front of the room. "I bet you got something really nice for your girlfriend."

I don't need all this attention right now. I wouldn't appreciate the interrogation if GiGi were ugly, but she's the business. And she smells good, too. The bell finally rings, thank God. A brother has never been so eager for physics class to start.

Mr. Harris hands back our latest homework assignments. GiGi leans over to crack her gum at my grade. "Bummer," she says to my big, fat sixty-five. I shove the work sheet into my binder, even though Harris is reviewing the answers.

GiGi pretends to drop a pencil to toss a note on my desk.

> Listen Efrain if you want help, you can
> come to my house after school so I can
> tutor you.

I guess GiGi's forgiven me for standing her up a few weeks ago. Honestly? I want to go to her crib. Not only do I seriously need the help before my physics grade wrecks my average, I'm craving the company. I could go to the tutoring program after school, but how's that going to look? Besides, I'd much rather get tutored by a dime like GiGi than some dude like Chingy who's not trying to have my back these days anyway. GiGi winks at me, then tosses her hair, sending a hint of coconut my way so strong, I almost feel her hair brush across my face. Damn.

I catch Leticia at the front of the room sitting sideways at her desk so she can stare at GiGi and me, all giggling and whatnot. Does that *chismosa* ever quit? I flip GiGi's note and scribble an answer across the back.

> Thanks, but I'm straight. Besides, I have
> to work.

When Mr. Harris turns around, I drop the note on GiGi's open notebook. She grabs and opens it. Two seconds later, a crumpled piece of torn loose-leaf sails into my face and lands on my binder. I glance at GiGi. Her nose flares as she pretends to concentrate on Harris's review. I take the crumpled note apart and read it.

> You call a 65 straight??? Whatever Efrain!!!

She's trippin', yo. Would GiGi be checking for me if Leticia and she hadn't seen Nestor and me shopping for gear? GiGi's hot and smart and sometimes even sweet, but she's also the female equivalent of an *asqueroso* who hollers at women on the street. Like I taught Mandy, the only right answer is no answer. He doesn't care what you say to him—dis his mama if you want to—but the second you acknowledge him, he's won. This is what I have to do with GiGi, even though just the idea of being alone with her is so exciting, it scares me.

GiGi waits for my response, but, instead, I pay attention to Mr. Harris. Then she flings another note on my desk.

> Just don't come looking for this Butta
> Rican when you're done with your MORENA
> PHASE!!!!!

Okay, I have to put an end to this. I couldn't care less if a girl is Black, Puerto Rican, Dominican, or whatever so long as she's down for me no matter how I make my paper or how I spend it. I start to write *I'm into* mujeres decentes. *Chickens need not apply* but check myself. Mr. Harris will catch her, then punish *me,* and no way can I give that foul *morena* comment any traction. Instead, I just correct the spelling and grammar on her note and grade it. Then I fold it into an airplane and fly it over to her desk. I mean, Chingy's desk.

> You call a 65 straight??? Whatever Efrain!!!
> Just don't come looking for this Butt~~a~~er
> Rican when you're done with your <u>MORENA</u>
> PHASE!!!!!

> **75=C=Average**

GiGi reads the note and crumples it into her fist. Then she turns and throws it in my face. *"¡Pendejo!"* She's lucky I'm not some beast who hits girls.

Harris turns from the board and yells, "What's going on, Miss González, Mr. Rodriguez?"

I say, "Nothing." Then I can't help myself and start to laugh. "Believe that, Mr. Harris." GiGi's doing her best to not turn in her seat right now, but I know my laughing upsets her.

Harris looks to where GiGi usually sits and finds Chingy at her desk. "Miss González, why are you sitting there?" Even with his back to me, I know Chingy is grinning like a hyena.

Without missing a beat, GiGi says, "I've just been diagnosed with hyperopia, Mr. Harris."

"Excuse me?"

"You know, I'm farsighted. My old seat is too close to the board. I see it much better from back here." GiGi's slick. Got to give her that. She probably had that excuse planned all along when she decided to colonize Chingy's seat. On any other day, that'd be mad sexy, but she lost major cool points for acting like a gold digger and making that *indirecta* about Candace. Just goes to show that GiGi is smart only when she wants to be, which is why when she acts ignorant, it's far worse than helpless stupidity à la Lefty Saldaña.

"Get back to your seat, Miss González." Obviously, stupid Harris ain't. "Bring in a note from your eye doctor, and then I'll reassign you. Mr. Perry . . ." Chingy reluctantly gathers his things and heads back to his seat.

GiGi jumps out of Chingy's desk and grabs her books and jacket. I mumble, "See ya, hate to be ya."

"Don't speak to me."

I wave her away like a housefly. "Done."

GiGi huffs past Chingy, almost knocking him into the kid seated in the next row. "Damn, what'd I do?" he says. The class laughs. When Chingy reaches his desk, he has this bewildered flicker in his eyes. He's dying to know what this is all about. I'd volunteer the 411, but since he's too good for a brother . . . *pues, sufre.* He could've gotten the real deal straight from the horse's mouth, but now let him consult the rumor mill like everyone else.

Enamor ♦ (*v.*) to fill with love

The rumor mill grinds at lightning speed, because when eighth period ends, Candace is waiting for me in the hallway.

"What a nice surprise!" I kiss her on the forehead without checking to see if anyone is watching. That was for Candace only. "Everything okay? Aren't you tutoring today?" If she feels like playing hooky from work, I'd be down for that.

But Candace looks mad worried. "Yeah, but . . ." She pulls me into the stairwell and waits for the crowd rushing home to die down. "Listen, I need to ask you something, and I want you to tell me the truth."

Oh shit. She knows. I say, "All right." Then I hold my breath.

"There are rumors going around that you and Chingy are on the outs over a girl." By the look in her eyes, not only does Candace find the gossip plausible, she suspects that the girl is not her.

I exhale without miraculously blowing the poor thing down the stairs. "No, ma, that's not what's up between Chingy and me." I reach out and caress her cheek.

She sighs with relief. "I wasn't accusing you of anything, Efrain. I figure that if Chingy and you had fought over some girl, it'd have been before we got together." It's mad cute the way Candace says *some girl*. Obviously, the rumor mill supplied a specific name. "And I know that just because we're together now doesn't mean that you guys are going to squash your beef just like that. I know how that goes."

"First things first. This girl who likes me—"

Candace spits, "GiGi."

One useful thing I learned from watching Rubio in action: your girlfriend doesn't want her suspicions about a potential rival confirmed, and just saying her name is confirmation enough. No matter if she's some 'hood rat you'd never mess with: speak her name, ask for drama. And if she's a banger like GiGi? *Olvídalo*, kid. You might as well say *Yeah, I'm hitting that all day, every day*, even if she thinks you're a troglodyte. It's still a wrap for you with your girl.

"This girl wants to stir up trouble because she's jealous that I'm with you and ain't checking for her." Let me segue to the beef between Chingy and me and convince her that it's not female-related. "But Chingy and I are on the outs over this dude we used to hang with. He dropped out of school, got into some stuff, and, well, Chingy doesn't want to hang out with him anymore, and he's mad at me because I stay friends with him."

Candace chuckles and shakes her head. "I thought only girls did things like that."

I tell Candace as much of the truth as I can without giving myself away. "This guy, the one that Chingy and I used to run with, he started . . . selling drugs." Then I rush to clarify. "I mean, he's not living like Scarface or pushing crack on kids or anything like that. He's just chillin' on the corner selling to whoever rolls through." The weight of my own truth forces me down on the step.

"You don't think there's anything wrong with that?" Candace asks, taking a seat on my lap. She doesn't ask with that tone of voice somebody uses when their mind is already made up and they just want you to sink yourself in deeper. Candace truly wants to get me.

But I'm not ready to be gotten like *that* just yet, so I avoid one truth by offering another. "You just don't throw away a good relationship because your friend makes a choice that you wouldn't." Now my leg feels like it's overrun with ants, more from the weight on my conscience than on my lap.

Candace fidgets. "You okay?" Before I tell her my leg's falling asleep, she lowers herself two steps and leans her head against my knee. "So you were saying . . ."

Man, she makes it so easy that it's hard. I want to tell her everything—about Nestor as well as me—and yet that's precisely why I can't. "Candace, have you ever done the wrong thing for the right reason?"

She takes a second and says in this unwavering voice, "Yes, I have."

"Really?" Even though I asked, I wasn't expecting her to say that.

She nods, rubbing her cheek against the denim across my knee. "After the hurricane." I want to hear more, but something tells me not to push right now. The fact that she reveals this much is enough for me.

"My friend's the man of the house. He can't do right by his family asking people *Do you want fries with that?*" I stroke Candace's hair as I speak. "His father isn't worth a shit, so the fate of his family relies on his success. It is what it is, and I don't think you cut a guy off because he's doing what he feels necessary to improve his chances in life. Especially when he intends to reach back and pull up those he loves. Doing one bad thing doesn't make him a bad person."

"You talk about him like a brother," says Candace, smiling.

"He's the closest thing I've ever had to one. Chingy, too, so it's like one brother asking me to choose him over the other, and I don't think it has to be that way." At this moment, my anger with Chingy for insisting on it surprises even me.

Candace pops up her head and turns around to face me. "Maybe I can talk to him for you."

"Who? Chingy?"

"Yeah. Maybe I can speak to him when I see him at work." And when Candace says that, we both remember that she has a job to go to. I'm supposedly late for ringing up designer jeans myself. Man, sometimes it slips my mind how many lies I have to tell to maintain my cover.

"No, ma, you shouldn't do that," I say as I stand up. Especially since Chingy actually knows the truth. What if he resents that Candace is with me and blows up my spot? I hate thinking this way about my oldest friend. Even though he's never done anything like that to me before, I can't chase the possibility out of my mind. "This is one of those in-between-men things, you know. But I appreciate the offer, though."

"You know what?" Candace shakes her head and smiles to herself. "Never mind." She tries to reach for the door, but I grab her by the waist.

"Nah, nah, nah," I say, pulling her back toward me. "Spill it."

"I'll tell you some other time."

"No, tell me now." I lean on the wall, and Candace presses herself against me, burying her face in my chest. Despite all the drama around me, at this moment, my life couldn't be more perfect. Nestor, Chingy, Rubio, GiGi—nobody exists but Candace. I wish I could freeze us in time.

She looks up at me and gives me a smile that would melt ice. "So, you're still having trouble in physics, right?"

Freakin' *bochincheros,* man! "Who told you that?"

Candace looks at me as if I'm kidding. "You! The same day we became friends. You said you were worried about how it would affect your GPA." I totally forgot about that. I said all that to Candace on Day One? Damn. No wonder Nestor teases me. She nuzzles her face into my collar. "That's another thing I like about you, Efrain. You won't settle. A lot of boys go all out when playing sports or video games, but for the things that really matter, they're content to just coast. Not you."

We lean against the wall, holding each other and feeling each other. I mean, really feeling one another. Does Rubio feel like this with every woman he has been with? Is this why he sticks and moves? Is he hunting for this feeling? Candace and I haven't done anything except kiss, and I'm feeling her in a way I've never felt anyone. Imagine what it will be like when we take it to that level. No, Rubio couldn't possibly feel this way. If he did, he would never be able to leave.

All I can say is, "Thanks, boo."

"You can come over to my apartment, and I can help you with physics." Candace pulls her head from my chest and looks up at me. "I promise, I won't tell anyone." Her deep brown eyes remind me of the staurolite I learned about in elementary school geology. The girl has got me all poetic.

I kiss Candace on the temple, lift her chin with my finger, and then kiss her again on the lips. If I should be embarrassed that my girlfriend can tutor me in science, I'm not. And I can't lie. A part of me hopes that Candace is borrowing a page from GiGi's playbook. Except with Candace, I don't feel stupid or manipulated. Just mad lucky.

Dissent ◆ (*n.*) disagreement

I fiddle with the timer as Candace grades my practice exam for the physics Regents. Without looking up from her calculations, she mumbles, "Efrain, please." She jabs the eraser of her pencil into the keypad and starts over again.

"Sorry." I put down the timer and drum my fingers on the table. Candace reaches out and slaps her hand over mine. I turn my hand to curl my fingers around hers. That keeps me until she finishes adding up my score. Candace puts down her pencil. "So?"

"Efrain, even though you won't learn some of this stuff until next semester, I'm surprised that you just skipped the questions. Why didn't you at least guess?"

"Because I'm not supposed to," I say. "The SAT penalizes you for guessing. It's better to leave the answer blank and get no points than to guess wrong and lose a quarter of a point."

"But this is not the SAT, babe, it's the Regents."

"I know, but that's what I'm learning in my SAT prep class. It took me forever to squash the impulse to guess. I'm afraid if I fall back into my old habit of guessing, I won't be able to switch gears when I have to retake the SAT at the end of January."

Candace shakes her head. "It's a stupid test."

"Word!" I throw up my hands. "Who ever heard of punishing someone for trying to solve a problem?"

"Especially when they always say you should at least try."

126

"Like that stupid poster in Mrs. Colfax's office."

"The one that says 'You'll always miss one hundred percent of the shots you don't take'?"

"Yeah, man. It doesn't say anything about losing a quarter of a point if you miss." Candace laughs. Man, I must sound like such a baby. "I don't mean to be whatever. I just got to suck it up and train myself to guess the answer when I can and to skip the question when I shouldn't." I barely catch the sweetest expression on Candace's face. As soon as I notice it, she goes sad, and I don't know what to make of the sudden change. "Hey."

"Hey." She turns back to her French textbook.

"What's the matter, boo?"

She shakes her head. "A year from now, you'll be sitting at a table somewhere at Harvard or Princeton . . . probably with another girl." Candace's eyes glisten even in the fluorescent light of the kitchen.

I reach across the table and take her hand in mine. "Maybe we could go to the same college." This is the first time the thought enters my mind, and it fills me in this indescribable way. Katrina cost her a semester, so I would have to wait for Candace, but I'd do it gladly. When I'm grinding to keep up with my classmates from Andover and Exeter, knowing someone I care about is coming to be with me will get me through that first year.

"You probably have a better chance of getting into Harvard than I do," I laugh.

"Or you could go to Dillard."

"But, ma, if you had a chance to go to a school like Dartmouth or Brown, why would you pass on that?"

"Because just as much as you want to go to an Ivy League school, Efrain, it's important to me to go to an HBCU. You know, a historically Black—"

"I don't need you to explain *HBCU* to me," I interrupt.

127

"Don't interrupt me," says Candace. "I hate when boys do that!"

Oh, so like that I'm just another boy? "I'm only saying that I know what a historically Black college is. Howard, Morehouse—"

Now Candace interrupts me. "You obviously don't know enough. Even though only three percent of the colleges and universities in this country are HBCUs, most Black professionals—doctors, lawyers, entrepreneurs, whoever—graduated from them. In fact, one out of four African Americans with college degrees went to an HBCU. Ever had a Black dentist or teacher, Efrain? Chances are that person went to an HBCU and not one of your precious Ivy League schools."

I close my schoolbooks and stack them on the table. Nothing I can say to that. Look, I understand being proud of your culture and history and all that, but even if there were HPRCUs or HDCUs or even HLCUs, I wouldn't go to one. There, I said it, okay? To be the Pedro Albizu exception instead of the Nestor Irizarry rule, I need more than my culture and history can provide. Real talk. I want to be a credit to my culture, a highlight in our history, not just another statistical stereotype. What's so bad about that?

Candace watches as I slide my books into my bag, leaving behind the paper she had written for that class that eventually led to her being expelled from Mott Haven High School. "Efrain, I'm only trying to make you understand that just as it's important to you to go to Harvard or Yale, it means a lot to me to go to an HBCU down south. If I can respect your reasons for wanting to leave home, why can't you respect mine for going back?"

I can't answer that either. It feels too much like one of those no-right-answer questions girls ask, like *Does this make me look fat?* or *My best friend is so pretty, right?* And this question is much worse because the answer actually matters. College means so much to both of us, which just makes this argument that much more ironic and even dangerous.

I stand up, grabbing my bag and pulling my jacket off the back of the chair. Candace just watches me without saying a word. I know she doesn't want me to leave but won't ask me to stay. Candace follows me to the door, then watches me as I walk out of the apartment and down the hallway to the elevator. Only when it arrives does she finally say, "I can't believe we're arguing over something good that we both want." Then she closes and locks the apartment door.

Funny, I was thinking the same thing. But there is more to this than getting a college education. This is about wanting to be with each other. I thought we both wanted to make this last, to stay together as long as possible. This is what I get for thinking that.

Consolation ♦ (n.) an act of comforting

I walk into my apartment and find my mother in the living room watching a rerun of a Jennifer Lopez romantic comedy on television. She usually watches TV in her room when my sister is home and is surprised to see me home so early. "Efrain!"

"Hi." I stand in the doorway of the living room. "Mandy's still at Rubio's?" My moms laughs. "What's so funny?"

"That you call your father 'Rubio.' "

"That's what everybody else calls him."

"Efrain . . ." She shakes her head at me, then asks, "What are you doing home so early? I thought you were going out with Candace."

I walk into the living room and sit down on the sofa. "We got into a fight."

"First one?" I just nod. "About?"

"College."

"Doesn't she want to go?"

"Yeah. In New Orleans." I was going to leave it at that, but my mother points the remote at the television to turn down the volume. "I thought she might want to go to the same school together, or at least close to one another, but she's dead set on going back to Louisiana even if it means breaking up."

"That's understandable, Efrain. After all, that's her home."

"I'm willing to leave home."

"Yes, but no one is forcing you to go." A sad look comes over

130

my mother's face. She knows that I'm mostly applying to colleges outside of New York City, but I guess I never spoke this plainly about wanting to leave. "If Candace had her way, she never would've left New Orleans."

"I know I'm young and new at all this romantic stuff or whatever, but I thought if you found something good, you were supposed to do whatever you can to keep it going," I say. "That you're supposed to compromise."

"And what compromise did you offer?" Moms waits for me to answer, folding her arms across her chest. "So, compromise means what Efrain thinks is best for Efrain even if it may not be what Candace thinks is best for Candace?"

"No, nope, sorry!" I didn't think of it like that at all. That's some Rubio-type selfishness. "How can going to an Ivy League college not be best for Candace? I mean, New Orleans . . ." I almost say *New Orleans will always be there,* and a heavy blanket of shame envelops me. Damn, my moms just caught me out there!

But instead of shaming me, my mother strokes my hair. "Sometimes what it takes to keep a relationship going is too much to ask of one person," she says. "Would it be too much of Candace to ask you to sacrifice your Ivy League dreams to go to a college down south?"

I kick off my sneakers, put my feet up on the couch, and lay my head against my mother's lap. I don't want to think about that. "If there's such a thing as too much to ask, then maybe it wasn't meant to be."

"Honey, relationships are not so cut-and-dried, least of all romantic ones," she says. "That's why even the best ones are hard work with no guarantee that they're going to last because of your efforts."

I expected her to say something like *There'll be other girls, Efrain,* or *Your education has to be your priority.* Good moms say those kinds of things even when they know it's the last thing you want to hear. Great moms keep it real.

Sometime later my mother shakes me awake. "Efrain, telephone."

"What?" I fell asleep on her lap.

"The telephone's ringing." I sit up, and she motions for me to go to the kitchen. "Since you're up . . ." Moms got jokes. I push myself off the couch, groaning like an old man. "You're much too young to be so tired, Efrain, and it's probably for you anyway."

I shuffle into the kitchen and take the phone off its base. "Hello?"

"Hi."

Candace.

"Hey."

"Listen . . . I know you probably have plans with your family, but you want to come over on Thanksgiving? Maybe after dinner with your family, you can come here to have dessert with mine."

"Yeah," I say, grinning from ear to ear. "I'd like that a lot."

Cleave ♦ 1. (*v.*) to stick together firmly 2. (*v.*) to divide into parts

On Thanksgiving I spring for a cab to City Island, and Mandy, Moms, and I go to Sammy's Fish Box. This is my moms' favorite restaurant and where we celebrate special family occasions. Back when he was good for something, Rubio started the tradition. He brought Moms here for dinner, took her for a boat trip around the island—supposedly a major heart racer for my mother because she loves the water, while homeboy is the only Dominican on the planet who can't swim—and proposed to her on the Long Island Sound. Since that time we have come here after Mandy's baptism, my and Mandy's First Communion, my confirmation, you name it. When I graduate from AC in June, Sammy's Fish Box is where you'll find us. There are a lot of positive memories in this place, and I'm happy that Rubio's absence doesn't change that.

Instead of eating turkey with stuffing or even *pernil* and *ceviche*, the three of us share the Italian Feast for Two: lobster, shrimp, clams, mussels, snow crab legs, king crab legs, *and* hard-shell crab with fresh pasta and garlic sauce. And Moms kills us with one story after the other. My favorite is the one where she destroyed the first *lechón* she ever tried to roast for Thanksgiving in a disastrous attempt to impress her boyfriend's mother, an uptight *blanquita* who was always correcting her Spanish, referring to her as *la Americana* as if that made her a lowlife, and otherwise talking sideways about my moms to anyone who would listen. I almost choke on a crab leg when my moms goes off on the matriarch in front of all her guests, tells Dude not to call her until he "grows a set," and runs out with the half-frozen pig under her arm like Eli Manning breaking out of a pack of Patriots. I never thought about my mother's life before us, but somehow hearing about her past makes me hopeful about all of our futures.

She's in such a good mood, Moms even lets Mandy order a virgin piña colada and pours me a little of her sangria. When the check comes, we fight for it. "Efrain, you shouldn't spend your money on things like this," Moms says. "Save your money for your senior ring and graduation pictures."

But I won't give up the tab. "You cover the cab ride back."

The Dominican cabbie's a trip, too, playing this corny *bachata* song and fishing for my moms' marital status. *"Ella está casá,"* my sister snaps at the poor guy.

I say, "No, she's not." Of course, this clown isn't for my moms, but I just want to give her the heads-up that if she wants to look for someone who will keep her happy, cool with me. Still, I have mad respect that Moms doesn't hook up with every guy who tosses a smile her way in an effort to prove something to Rubio.

As we pass Nestor's block, I imagine the huge *pariseo* going down at his crib and wonder how long before someone sets off drama over something ridiculous. One Thanksgiving Nestor's father and his older brother Leo came to blows over the Turkey Bowl. When my family came back from my grandmother's place, we found Nestor pitching a handball in our lobby. His people didn't even realize he was missing until my moms called his apartment. Moms invited Nestor to stay at our place for the rest of the weekend. At first, Rubio was pissed about this, but eventually he took us all to the movies and Mickey D's. That goes to prove that dude can be decent when he wants to be and not because he has no other choice.

And as if I conjured him, Moms tells the cabbie to turn onto Awilda's block. I feel ambushed. "Why are we going there?"

"I'm just dropping your sister off so she can spend some time with your father and brother today."

"Oh." So long as she doesn't expect me to stick around.

Mandy says, "Mami, come upstairs with me."

"No, sweetie, I'm tired and stuffed."

"But Awilda said to invite you."

My mother can barely hide her contempt. "Tell her I said thank you."

"Mami!"

I snap, "Mandy, stop whining."

The cab pulls up in front of Awilda's building, and not for nothing I'm glad I'm not paying for this ride. Mandy bounces out of the cab and runs to the gate. Meanwhile, when the driver thinks I'm not looking, he slips his card in my mother's hand along with her change. I'd laugh if I weren't upset about being here.

My mother and I wait by the curb as Mandy leans on the buzzer. "Enough, Amanda, that's obnoxious."

Finally, the gate buzzes, and my sister shoves it open. She stops to turn around and look at me. "Efrain, come on."

"Nah, I have to go to Candace's house."

Moms says, "Just call me when you want me to come pick you up, honey."

Mandy pouts, then disappears into the building. Without a word, Moms and I start to walk toward St. Ann's Avenue. After a few paces, she says, "We really do have much to be grateful for, Efrain."

"Yeah." Even though my head knows this is true, my heart doesn't feel the same way it did a half hour ago.

Moms and I reach the corner. She beckons for a hug. *"Te quiero mucho, m'ijo."*

"I love you, too, Mami."

As she holds me, she says, "No matter what happens, I'm always thankful for my family, especially you kids." Then Moms pulls away, brushing her fingertips across my cheek. "Tell Candace and her family I said happy Thanksgiving, and that I hope to meet them very soon."

"I will."

Then my mother takes a left, and after wondering for a second if she truly wants to be alone today, I head to Candace's.

Pathos ♦ (*n.*) an emotion of sympathy

After two heaping servings of vanilla ice cream and homemade pecan pie, Candace asks if I want to go for a walk. And true to the secret manual that must have been written for kid sisters worldwide, Nia insists on going with us. As we reach People's Park, her sister races toward the swings while Candace and I sit on a bench and hold hands. She says, "You know, it's not so cold out here today."

"I hate to break this to you," I laugh, "but you're talking like a New Yorker."

"For real?" Candace smiles at the thought. "Don't think I don't like New York, Efrain. Sometimes it's tough, but this city's been good to me."

"It's just not home." I try to say it without resentment, but I don't know if I succeed.

"For now it is, and it will be for a while." Candace reaches inside her coat and pulls out the Katrina presentation I had asked to borrow only to leave it behind after our fight about college. I take the paper from her and tuck it into my inside pocket. Then Candace leans her head against my shoulder. "I wish we could spend more time together."

"Me too." We watch Nia make friends with some other kids and turn the playground into an obstacle course. "So, is everything okay with you? You know, with school, work . . . group."

Candace flashes a grin at me. "Did you hear about your friend Dominic?"

I'm actually relieved to hear some gossip. As curious as I am about her therapy sessions, I'm not always sure I can handle it. "What did that fool Lefty do now?"

"I caught him selling weed to one of Chingy's tutees in the stacks, and Mr. Sweren kicked him out of the tutoring program."

"Word?" It makes me a hypocrite, but I say it. "They need to expel that moron."

"Mr. Sweren said he would've called the police if he had caught him in the act, but that's okay." Candace raises her fist. "Free at last, free at last, thank God almighty, Candace Lamb is free at last!" I laugh, even though my intestines feel braided. I kiss Candace to make myself feel better, and it works. For the most part.

She suddenly pulls away, her eyes fixed on something past my shoulder. "Nia, get down from there. It's not ladylike to climb the monkey bars in a dress. That girl, I swear—"

Then Candace gasps. "Oh my God, I didn't invite your sister over for dessert, did I? She was totally welcome to come. Your mother, too. Efrain, I'm so sorry."

"Don't feel bad," I say, squeezing her hand. "Moms could use some time to herself, and Mandy's over at her father's place."

"Oh, I just assumed you two had the same dad."

"We do, but . . ." Besides Chingy I have never spoken to anyone about Rubio. Even that was on some little-boy-lost feebleness that embarrasses me to this day. But I can only dodge Candace about this for so long. "Rubio and I don't get along."

"As in rube?"

"Yeah, exactly," I laugh. But the truth is Rubio is far from naive or unsophisticated. Dude could stand to be a bit less slick.

"Nah, I'm just playing with you. His real name is César. *Rubio* means 'blond' in Spanish."

"So why don't you get along?"

"He did some funky things to my moms and put me in the middle of it." Candace waits me out. "My father's a first-class womanizer, and around the time I turned ten, he started taking me along on his little escapades. He'd tell my mother we were going to play ball but end up at his so-called girlfriend's place. Just drop me off in front of her television while they did their thing."

"And one day you told your mom," says Candace. The fact that she assumes I did the right thing makes me want to kiss her. The knowledge that I did no such thing makes me want to push her away. "Of course you didn't. You were just a child, and no child wants to hurt his mother or have his father angry with him."

On the drive from Yankee Stadium that particular night, I had been bouncing off the walls of the Civic, juiced on lemon ice and an Alfonso Soriano home run. Then Rubio made the detour where it finally clicks. As we drove home from his mistress's apartment, Rubio tried to chat me up while I sat there, doing a calculus I was too young to understand and praying for my stillness to betray me. But he never asked why I was suddenly so quiet. Eventually, I blurted out, "What were you doing in Christina's bedroom?"

"Tenía que arreglar algo."

"You never have to fix anything in the kitchen or bathroom," I said, recalling the previous detours. "It's always the bedroom."

Rubio finally confessed. *"Janguiando con mi novia."*

"But Mami's your girlfriend."

"No, Mami's my wife. That mean she my best girlfriend. My favorite one of all."

"But you're not supposed to have *any* girlfriends once you

get a wife." Said it just like that, closing myself to any more of his creative interpretations and insults to my intelligence. "That's what God says."

No wonder when Moms finally put him out, Rubio stopped paying my tuition at St. Gabe's. At the time, though, he laughed. "And when God say that to you?" Then Rubio said, "As long as he take care of his wife and his children, it's okay for a man to have a girlfriend, too. I take good care of you and your sister and Mami, ¿verdad?" I didn't understand this then, but now I would say, *You put me in a good school but don't come to my spelling bees. You buy me toys, but you don't play with me. You can't take me to Yankee Stadium or the Bronx Zoo without stopping at a girlfriend's house on the way home.* "But a good man keep his girlfriends a secret from his wife so he no hurt her feelings. There are many good women but very few good men, so all the good women have to share. The women don't like the truth, *pero así son las cosas.*" I broke his code, though. If I told my mother about Rubio's girl-friends and stomp her heart over something she could do nothing to change, then I would be just as bad as he.

"I tried to call it out, Candace." Child or not, I need her to understand that. These days my hands are so dirty that as deeply as they're buried in my pockets is the overwhelming urge for her to know how pristine they once were. "I might've been a kid, but I knew he was doing something wrong, and I tried to check him from jump. Rubio spun it as if he told me the truth on some father-son bonding shit," I say. "He thought he was going to play me like he did my mother, using me as his alibi, but I wouldn't let him. Eventually, when he'd say, *Frankie, you want to go see the Yankees?* I'd be like, *No. I want to go to Chingy's house.* Rubio finally got the hint and left me out of his charades. Long before they split, he made me choose between her and him. I chose her." This is the most I've said to anyone about this in years, and I feel raw. Only quid pro quo can right the scales. "What about your father? You never talk about him either."

Candace traces her fingertips along my sideburn. "He's dead," she says.

"My bad."

"That's okay. I didn't really know him all that well. He left for Texas to work when I was really young, came back for a little while . . ." Candace laughs. "Long enough to plant my sister, I guess. Then he left again for another spell. A few years before Katrina hit, he came back with heart disease. My mom cared for him until he passed. I hate to admit it, but when he first came back from Texas, I avoided him."

"Were you afraid to be around him, you know . . . because he was dying?"

"At first, I didn't feel anything, Efrain, because he was a stranger to me. Then I felt so guilty, but I couldn't stand that. It became much easier to be angry. I thought, *All this time away from us and now you only come home to make us watch you die.*"

I imagine how I might feel if Rubio was dying. My mother breaking the news to Mandy and me. Awilda trying to upstage my mother during his final days at Lincoln Hospital. Another woman and her child turning the funeral into a *telenovela*. The reading of the will and Rubio leaving my mother nothing but the six-figure hospital bill since they're still legally married. Yeah, anger is mad easy.

"My mother snapped me out of it, though," Candace laughs. "As hard as I tried to hide it, she sensed what was going on with me."

"Moms just be like that."

"I remember once yelling at her *I don't know that man*. And my mother yelled back *You don't know 'that man' because he worked himself to death to buy this roof over your head and those clothes on your back. You don't know 'that man' because he loves you. That's all you need to know about 'that man.'* " Candace pretends to scout the playground for Nia, but I know that now she feels as raw as I did a few minutes ago. "That's when I started bargaining with God for miracles, but he wasn't interested in any of my offers. Still, he gave me one small consolation."

"What was that?"

"Before he died, I got to tell my dad that I loved him, thank him for all he'd done for us, and say goodbye. I think he could've lived a hundred years, and I still never would've known him all that well. But we told each other all we needed to know."

"Come here," I say. Candace and I wrap ourselves around each other. We still feel raw, but at least we are raw together.

Veneer ♦ (*n.*) a superficial or deceptively attractive appearance, facade

There is so much business tonight, Nestor and I race back and forth between the building and the curb as if in an endless relay. In between sprints, he chats up nonsense. Nestor insists that all the scuttle about gang initiation rites—you know, flashing headlights and slashing ankles—is just propaganda to make people think that gang members prey on random White suburbanites, but to this day he still believes Tommy Hilfiger dissed minorities who wear his clothes on *Oprah*. I humor him, though, because stacking paper builds a man's patience.

"Yo, Nes, don't you think if that were true, it'd be all over YouTube?" I ask as I pocket the cash handed to me by my latest customer and then whistle for LeRon. "Yo, RonRon, introduce my man there to Judas."

LeRon nods. "Done."

"Claudia says she saw that episode herself," says Nestor. "You know she be into all those talk shows. Says Oprah owned him, too, bro. Kicked his racist ass off her set and told everyone to boycott his brand. That's why you'll never catch me wearing that nigga's shit. Never, son!"

Claudia's a liar, but what do I care? "Yeah, okay." I check my watch. "I'ma bounce."

Nestor peeks at his cell phone. "You kidding me? The set is jumping, and it ain't even ten yet!"

"More money for you, then," I say. I made more tonight in three hours than I have made all week, and I'm ready to go. "I've got homework to finish and a test first thing in the morning, so I'm not trying to be up all night." Plus, I want to get home so I can call Candace at a decent hour.

Nestor says, "Yo, E., when you go to college, you think you might join one of them fraternities?"

"I don't know." It crosses my mind sometimes. Apparently, the real benefits of joining a fraternity kick in once you graduate. For example, a fraternity brother might get me into a choice law school or give me a dope job. But then I remind myself that I'm not headed to a Morehouse or Howard. "I'm going to a college where I'ma be a minority, and to be real with you, kid, I don't think I can let some rich White boy haze me, ordering me around and smacking me up and all that." I had enough of that mess at IS 162 before Nestor told the bullies to fall back. I'm not the one anymore.

"Yeah, that couldn't be me either, bro," says Nestor. "But if you go to the Library of Congress down there in D.C., they got a whole file on that stuff." I suck my teeth at him. "For real, E.! Back in the fifties when that cat McCafferty was running around accusing everybody of being a communist—"

"McCarthy, kid, McCarthy."

"Whatever, yo, listen to me! Back then the government made all the frats and sororities give up their secrets to prove that they weren't commies, and it's all documented in the Library of Congress. But check it . . . there's still mad info missing."

I sneer and say, "I bet."

"You think somebody like J. Edgar Hoover or the head of the CIA or even the president himself is gonna expose their boys? No way, man! You know they're gonna use their influence to keep their most secret rituals out of that file."

I start to ask with all those exceptions, how Nestor can be so sure that such a catalog even exists when I see Lefty Saldaña across the street. I pull my hood over my head and inch closer to Nestor, letting him ramble on to the next topic on his list of favorite urban legends while stealing glances across Hunts Point Avenue. Is Lefty looking for me? No, can't be. Least of all around these parts. Chingy may know I'm slinging now, he may be angry with me about it, and he may like to parlay with Leti and the other *chismosas,* but no way would he put my secret out on front street.

Still, I keep my eye on Lefty while pretending to listen to Nestor yammer about some talk show psychic who predicted one of the campus massacres. With a huge grin on his face, Lefty approaches that Latino guy in Hinckley's crew who convinced Julian to accept Nestor's money and back off me. They hug like long-lost relatives and kick it for a minute in front of La Floridita. A few minutes later, Julian turns the corner, and his boy calls him over. The way Julian and Lefty nod as he speaks, and then exchange pounds, I gather that he just introduced them. But then they burst out laughing and slapping five as if they've known each other forever.

"Damn, I hate when you do that, E.!" yells Nestor. "I be talking to you, and you be zoning me out. What you staring at, man?" He rides my gaze across the street and cackles at the sight of Lefty. "Oh, that's the AC Super Senior!" Then Nestor spits on the ground. "He used to be down with us, but then he got too hungry, so Snipes told him to kick rocks."

I don't confirm or deny out of fear of drawing attention to ourselves. It makes no difference because suddenly Julian looks across the street and busts Nestor and me eyeballing him. I quickly look away, and Nestor put his hand on my shoulder. "Don't do that, bro. Don't look away." And yet Nestor sidesteps in front of me, blocking Julian and me from one another's sight. He whispers, "It's okay to get shook out here sometimes, but you can never show it, you feel me?"

I shrug his hand off my shoulder. "I'm not shook." And to prove it, I jam my quivering hands into my pockets, bop over to a parked car, and lean against it with my back to Julian. Hopefully, this move lets me have my cake and it eat it, too. It avoids the staring contest I can't win and yet signals to Julian *I'm not afraid to turn my back on you.*

Nestor doesn't buy it, though. Still, he perks up and asks, "Yo, but did you hear about the time Method Man scared this White lady in a hotel elevator?" See how he lets me be? That's why we're boys.

But when I first heard that urban legend a few years back, it was Kobe Bryant. And then it was Reggie Bush. The last time I heard it—from Nestor himself, in fact, only a year ago—it was Jay-Z. But I leap off the car and say, "Yeah, dude steps on with his boys, and she starts clutching her purse and whatnot because she doesn't realize he's rich and famous. Then later he picks up her dinner tab at the hotel restaurant, and the woman's, like, *Duh.*" I feel my back burn, and I take a glance over my shoulder. Now Julian and Lefty are alone, both eyeing me from across the street and talking out of the sides of their mouths. I turn back to Nestor and say, " 'Cept when I heard the story, the Black dude was 50 Cent."

"No! Whoever told you that done lied, bro. How is that story going to work with a cat like 50 Cent?" Nestor laughs. "If Fiddy stepped on my elevator, I'd grab my shit, too."

"What about Fiddy?" LeRon yells from his post. "You want to talk sideways about my boy, you need to kick rocks 'cause I love that nigga. No homo, though."

Nestor says, "You see, this White woman is staying at this

146

fancy five-star hotel and gets on the elevator to go to the restaurant for dinner, right? . . ." As he recounts the legend, he walks toward LeRon, and I follow. The other guys in our posse crowd around Nestor, reacting enthusiastically to his story. As much as I want to go home and crawl into my warm bed with Candace's voice in my ear, now is the time to close ranks. When Nestor gets to the part where the woman realizes that the Black "thug" she encountered on the elevator is a celebrity who just paid for her dinner, I laugh louder than anyone else. That's the best way to show 'em you're not shook.

Sanguine ♦ 1. (*adj.*) consisting of or relating to blood   2. (*adj.*) optimistic

Candace has family visiting New York City during the holiday, so we decide to exchange gifts on Christmas Eve Day. We sit on the floor in the living room by her tree while her sister Nia watches television a few feet away. Meanwhile, Candace's mother, aunt, and grandmother throw down in the kitchen for all the guests they expect tomorrow. I hand Candace a large gift bag and say, "Ladies first."

She kisses me on the cheek. "Thank you, E." Then Candace tries to tuck it under the Christmas tree.

I reach out and clamp on to her wrist. "C'mon, open it now!"

"No," she says while making no effort to pull away from me. "We have to wait until midnight at least."

"But I won't be here then to see the expression on your face." This girl can be so stubborn! Katrina never stood a chance against her. I lower my voice and say, "Unless at midnight you're planning, you know, to climb down a brother's chimney. . . ."

Candace gently socks me in the knee. "Shhh!" She jerks her head toward Nia.

"She can't hear me."

"Yes, I can!"

"Nia, stop being so nosy!"

"You and Efrain stop being nasty!"

Now I'm the one who tells Nia to hush. Then I say to Candace, "That's your fault. You should've just done what I asked you."

Candace reaches inside the gift bag. She pulls out the large but thin gift box. When she opens it, peels away the tissue, and finds another wrapped box, I pretend to cough to cover up my laugh. Candace smirks playfully at me as she tears away the wrapping paper and opens the box. In the box is another gift bag. "Efrain!"

"Blame my sister," I say laughing. "It was her idea."

Candace opens the gift bag and pulls out yet another box. After unwrapping the gift box, pulling back the lid, and peeling away the tissue paper, she finally finds the envelope. "Oh, a gift card!" she says. "For where?"

"Someplace you really love," I say.

She runs her finger under the triangular flap, tearing it away from the envelope. Then she pulls out the ticket. It takes Candace a second to read it and understand. "You bought me an airplane ticket to New Orleans?"

"Round-trip. And it's an open ticket, too, so you can leave and return whenever you want so long as it's before then," I say, pointing to the expiration date. "You still have to make a reservation in advance, but, you know . . ."

"Oh, E. . . ." Candace's eyes fill with tears. Good tears. She leans forward and kisses me in a way she shouldn't with a little sister and all those matriarchs only feet away.

When we finally part, I say, "I have something else for you, but you have to wait until *los Tres Reyes*. I mean, Three Kings' Day." I know I should save every cent, but I can't resist the desire to spoil her a little.

"We celebrate the Epiphany in New Orleans, too," says Candace. "My grandmother makes the best king cakes. She'll be baking and mailing them from now till Mardi Gras, but I'll save you a piece."

A dirty thought pops into my mind, but at least I know better than to *say* it with Nia in earshot. Instead, I say, "Thank you."

"No, Efrain, thank *you*."

"You're welcome, sweetie." We sit there for a few seconds, our foreheads pressed together and holding hands, wishing each other a Merry Christmas just by breathing in time. Then I yell, "My turn!"

Candace giggles and reaches under a tree for a small, flat package. "It's not much, but I think you'll like it."

The package feels hard in my hand. With no grace whatsoever, I rip away the wrapping paper. It's a book called *Letters to a Young Brother: MANifest Your Destiny*. The Black dude on the cover looks mad familiar, too. "Is this guy on TV?" I ask.

Candace nods. "Yeah, that's Hill Harper. He's an actor on *CSI: NY,* but . . ." She opens the book and points to the short biography under his photograph. "Not only did he go to Brown, he also has a law degree *and* a master's in government from Harvard."

"Word?" As much as I like to read, I haven't read anything unrelated to school and the SAT in a minute, so Candace's gift is perfect. "I'll probably read it in one night."

"Well, the gift receipt's in there if you'd rather exchange it for a CD or something."

"You're crazy!" I tease her. "Of course I'm going to like it. This brother's been exactly where I'm trying to go." Saying that makes me think of Chingy's brother BK, the only person I know in college. I wonder if he will ask for me now that he's home from the ATL. What will Chingy say? As lucky as I am to have Candace, I still feel a bit sad to not be hanging with my boy this Christmas, but it is what it is.

"Efrain, what's wrong?" asks Candace.

"Nothing, boo," I say. I don't want her fretting over me, least of all on Christmas. "Thank you." Then, just as I lean for another scandalous kiss, I hear my name.

"Efrain?" Mrs. Lamb stands in the doorway of the living room, beckoning me to her. Candace shrinks as if trying to disappear herself by sheer will.

"Told y'all stop being nasty," says Nia.

I jump to my feet but take a decade to cross the living room. When I come within reach, Mrs. Lamb takes my arm and leads me into the kitchen, which is now full of stovetop aromas and devoid of other people. The lady wants to hurt me for pushing up on her daughter, and made sure to clear the room of witnesses.

"I have something for you, Efrain." Mrs. Lamb hands me a small gift bag. "Promise me that you won't tell Miss Candace."

"Wow, Mrs. Lamb, that's so generous of you." I try to hand it back to her. "I can't accept this."

She pushes my hand away. "Yes, you can. You must." Mrs. Lamb motions for me to sit down at the kitchen table. She leans forward to whisper, "Has Candace ever told you about the things we went through because of the hurricane? The things we still go through?"

Not as much as I would like, but I answer, "A little, yes."

"And she probably talks about it more to you than to any of us." Mrs. Lamb points to the gift bag and says, "Even though we survived the hurricane, Katrina still killed my family. A family is a living thing where every person plays a role. Candace was our heart. She was our spirit, our hope, our jazz, and Katrina took her from us. We were broken, shattered, torn apart, in the same way the winds destroyed our house. For a long time, we were just the shell of family. A group of evacuees with the same last name. Then Candace met you, and you pumped life back into her. And by giving her back to us, you made us a family again." Mrs. Lamb

151

gestures toward the gift bag that I'm now clutching in my fist as if it were gold. "It isn't much, but my mother, my sister, and I wanted you to have it. Open it."

I remove the tissue paper and find a jewelry box. Inside the box is a gold necklace with a pendant of St. Expedite. *Expedite* (*v.*) *to execute promptly, accelerate the progress or process of, speed up.* "The saint who never existed," I say. They call him that because so little is known about him that the Roman Catholic Church refuses to officially recognize him. "People pray to St. Expedite when they need quick solutions to their problems. Especially financial ones."

"And he's quite revered in New Orleans," adds Mrs. Lamb. "He's our unofficial patron saint."

To say that I'm moved doesn't cut it. "I don't know what to say except thank you, *señora*." It hardly seems enough. "And please thank your mother and sister for me, too."

"Just keep being good to my Candace."

I want to make that vow, but I can't find my voice right now. So I just nod and think, *No doubt, Mrs. Lamb. No doubt.*

Relish ♦ (v.) to enjoy

It takes only a few rips for my sister to see the Baby Phat logo. "Oh my God!" She tears away the rest of the wrapping paper and hugs the suede handbag to her chest.

"No more Boo Boo Kitty for you," I say as I wink at my mother. It's not the iPod that I wanted to get her, but that would've drawn too much attention. Moms is busy, not stupid. That's why, despite Nestor's harassment, I refuse to get a cell phone. My mother bought Mandy an off-brand MP3 player from Yannis's anyway.

"I love it!" Mandy jumps to her feet and rushes to hug me. "Thank you, thank you, thank you. I love you, I love you, I love you!"

I laugh. The telephone rings. "I'll get that. Mami, open your gift already."

"No, I want you to be here when I open it."

"Nah, I don't need all that mush." It started when I was five and gave her a lumpy ashtray I made out of clay, even though Moms hasn't smoked a day in her life, and it hasn't ended. When I get to the kitchen, I recognize my grandmother's number and jump on the phone. *"¡Feliz Navidad, abuela!"* Then I remember what I was taught to say as a little boy when I would visit her before she moved from the Bronx back to Guavate. *"La bendición."*

"Que Dios te bendiga, m'ijo. ¿Y cuándo vienes a Puerto Rico pa' verme?"

Without giving it a second thought, I say, *"En el verano."* Why not? In fact, I'll take Moms and Mandy, too. Summer vacation in Puerto Rico is something that we all need and deserve. I'll pretend I won a radio contest or something. *Abuela* proceeds to list all the things she's going to cook for me when I visit her. *Pasteles, arroz con gandules, lechón* . . . She intends to fix a Christmas dinner in June to make up for our not being together now. The more I talk to my grandmother, the better my Spanish flows, and the more I miss her.

She finally asks to speak to Mandy. When I get back into the living room, my sister is already taking a pair of scissors to an old St. Gabe's T-shirt while following a pattern in *99 Ways to Cut, Sew, Trim, and Tie Your T-Shirt into Something Special* (Moms' alternative to all the designer clothes she wanted). Meanwhile, my mother still hasn't opened her present, and I'm glad she waited.

"Candace helped me pick it out," I say.

"I would've been happy just to have met her for Christmas," says Moms as she peels away the wrapping paper.

"Soon."

It takes only a peek at the burgundy leather to make my mother's eyes water. "Efrain!" She pulls the jacket out of the box and slips it on as if it were made of delicate lace. "I had one just like it that I absolutely adored."

"I know," I say. "I've seen the pictures."

Suddenly, my mother drops the jacket on her lap. "How did you pay for this?" My heart starts to pound. "You bought this off the street, didn't you? Mandy's bag, too!"

I roll with that. "Mami, it was the only way I could get you something really nice." This heat I can take. I don't know which offers more relief—the fact that my mother isn't slipping or that I've become so adept at lying. "The guy was parked in front of the school with a trunkful of them for almost nothing."

154

"What if you had been caught?" she scolds without yelling. "*¿Y que 'taba pensando, chico?* You haven't been working so hard to get arrested for buying stolen property in front of your school, have you?"

"No, *señora.*" How can I splurge on my girlfriend and not spend a little on my mother and sister? It's the least I can do since I haven't figured out a way to pay a bill here and there. Once I almost sneaked into the check-cashing place to pay the telephone bill and just pretend that Verizon made a billing error in our favor. But Moms is too honest. She'll call them up and tell them they made a mistake, and then she'll realize that somebody paid the bill. God help us all if she thinks it was Rubio! "But it's not like I can return it."

As much as she tries to hide it, Moms is happy about that. "Promise me you'll never do anything like that again, Efrain."

"I promise. Merry Christmas, Mami."

She motions for a hug. "Merry Christmas, Efrain." As I smell the soap on her neck, I realize I miss her, too.

Fidelity ◆ (*n.*) loyalty, devotion

"Efrain, do you mind if I come in?"

"Sure, Mami." My mother peeks inside my room, and the smell of *pasteles* boiling in the kitchen wafts in over her head. I point my new digital camera at her. "Smile!"

I wait for her to hide behind the door and fuss with her hair, but, instead, my mother curtsies and smiles for my camera. "So you really like everything?" she asks, pointing to the scruffy portable player (furnished three Christmases ago from Yannis's Discount) as it plays one of the CDs she gave me this year. Moms closes the door and walks toward me with a lockbox under her arm.

"Yeah, I'm going to take this on my college visits." My mother always reminds me that, no matter how busy she is, she's paying attention. Right now Chingy's pretending to love some wack hip-hop albums that his mother chose for him simply because there's no parental advisory sticker on them. I show Moms her photo, wishing she looked like this all the time. She had just turned twenty when she had me, but you'd never know with the streaks of gray in her hair and the frown lines around her mouth. But when Moms is happy like she is today, the gray and lines disappear. I point at the box. "What's that?"

"Another Christmas present for you." She sets down the box on my dresser and turns the key in the lock. "I was saving this for your eighteenth birthday, but I figure you could use it now." Inside is an array of forms, folders, and envelopes. She reaches for a business envelope, hands it to me, and fishes around for something else.

The return address is from Banco Popular. I tear it open and pull out the letter. Attached to the bottom of it is a bank card with my name on it. "A gift card?" I ask.

"No, sweetie, that's the bank card to your savings account. Your father and I opened it when you were born, and whenever anyone gave you money—you know, for your baptism, your birthdays, your Holy Communion—we just deposited it. We never touched it, letting it grow and build interest. Anyway, you're old enough now to use it as you see fit. Maybe buy your class ring or take Candace to the prom. Whatever you want. You're a such good kid, honey, always working so hard at everything. You deserve to have some fun." She hands me more papers. "That should be the PIN, and this is the latest statement. I have the bank addressing them to you now."

I look at the balance on the statement, and I remember the years of spiced ham and cheese on Monday, peanut butter and jelly on Wednesday, and tuna fish on Friday. I remember the Medicaid days when Rubio's auto shop was struggling and we lost our health insurance, so Moms took a day off we couldn't afford to take Mandy and me to the enrollment office in the basement of Lincoln Hospital. Just like that, I'm fifty-five hundred dollars richer.

But it's never just like that, is it? Difficult as it may have been, Moms managed to save for my future no matter how bleak the present seemed. Meanwhile, Nestor has had bad credit since he was born because his trifling parents got a charge card with his Social Security number. And no matter how tough things were, Moms insisted my money stayed mine. How many single mothers in the 'hood can say they have a college fund for their kids? Not too many, believe that. Moms saved almost six thousand dollars

157

over seventeen years while I have nearly as much sitting in my shoebox that I made in almost eight weeks. But she's proud of her savings, and I'm not.

"Please don't tell Mandy about this," Moms says. "When I tell her she can't have those designer jeans or expensive shoes, I don't want Miss Runway throwing in my face *Well, what about my savings?* Her money is not for things like that."

I laugh. "She wouldn't do that." Immature or not, she's still my mother's daughter.

"Well, keep your mouth shut, and we'll never know, okay?"

"Okay." I'm breaking in my new debit card by registering for the January SAT. "Thanks, Mami." We stay quiet for a while. We seem to have so much more to say, but neither of us knows where to begin.

Finally, my mother lays her hand upon my shoulder. "Look, Efrain, I also came to ask you a favor." Moms sits down at the end of my bed. "Go with Mandy to see your father today."

"Why?" Bringing over my mother's *pasteles* to Awilda's place and watching Rubio play Santa for his new "wife and kids" ain't my idea of a merry Christmas. "He put you up to this?"

"Every time I ask him about that financial aid form he needs to fill out for you, he says *Why didn't Efrain bring it to me himself?*" Your father wants to spend time with you, honey. . . ." My mother hesitates. "And he thinks that I'm getting in your way."

"That's bull." Never has my moms kept me from Rubio, and I don't appreciate him guilt-tripping her about it. He blew father-son time all by his lonesome.

"You know that as well as I do, *m'ijo*." My moms stands up. "I feel I've done my best to shield you and your sister from our problems, but you're a young man now and can make your own decisions."

"So why are you asking me to go over there when I don't want to?"

"Why don't you want to?"

" 'Cause I just don't!"

"Efrain, that's a child's answer."

"If I'm old enough to make my own decisions, I'm old enough to keep my reasons for them to myself."

My mother stares at me for a while, then throws up her hands. "What can I say? You're right. It was selfish for me to ask." She heads for the door.

I sit up in my bed. "Are you trying to get back with him?" The last thing I need in my life right now is for Rubio to come back after all this time trying to be king. "Why is asking me to see him selfish like you're going to get something out of it?"

"Maybe I shouldn't care what Rubio thinks, but I hate being accused of keeping you from him when I was never the one to play such games. Your father makes it extremely difficult to be the bigger person, yet I try for your sake and Mandy's. But I'm only human." She places a hand under my chin. "Having a relationship with your father, Efrain, does not mean betraying me."

"I don't care," I say. "Why would you want me around him the way he be?"

"Because I have faith in the way *I'm* around you." Then she says, "If you need something from your father, Efrain, don't hesitate to ask him. If there is anything that I can't give you— whatever it may be—go to Rubio. Not only will you not hurt me, I want you to."

"And what if I don't need him?" I ask. "What if I don't want anything to do with Rubio?"

"If this is truly how you feel, Efrain, so be it," says Moms, but her expression tells me she doesn't believe me. "But you look

Rubio in the eye—son to father, man to man—and you tell him that."

The telephone in the kitchen rings, and Moms leaves to answer it. She returns a few minutes later to find me standing dumbstruck where she left me. "It's Candace," says Moms as she hands me the telephone and softly closes my door.

"Hello."

"*Joyeux Noël, mon chéri!*"

"Merry Christmas."

"What's the matter, boo?"

"Me? I'm good."

"You'd tell me if you weren't, wouldn't you?"

"Sure."

"So . . ."

"Everything's cool." I'm so unconvincing. "My mother just asked me to go see my father today."

"You should, then," Candace says.

"She says that my father accuses her of coming between him and me," I say. "Dude's an egomaniac who can't imagine anyone not dying to be in his orbit."

"You can stand him for one day," Candace giggles. "After all, you put up with me."

I laugh, too. "All day, every day."

"And, besides, Efrain, maybe he'll surprise you. Maybe today your father will make you feel something besides angry. Wouldn't that be a cool thing to get for Christmas?"

I can't imagine it. And some surprises ain't so cool. Like Candace taught me on Thanksgiving, angry is easy.

Empathy ♦ (*n.*) sensitivity to another's feelings as if they were one's own

When we get to Awilda's floor, Mandy flies down the hallway to knock on the door. It opens, and Awilda stands there, looking Christmas corny in a red velour sweat suit with gold tinsel hanging around her neck. She shakes a baby bottle in her hand and throws a white cloth over her shoulder. "Rubio!" she yells, tossing back the door to let us into the apartment and heading into the kitchen. No "Hello," no "Merry Christmas," no nothing.

Mandy bounds in like she lives here. Feeling like an intruder, I follow her into the living room. Serenity's on the floor in front of a three-story dollhouse wearing a shirt that says "I came for the presents." "Mandy, come look at what Santa brought me!" Mandy never got a mansion from "Santa."

"Wow, you must've been really good this year!" says Mandy. Even though she's past playing with dolls, she kneels on the carpet next to Serenity and helps her arrange the furniture. And to think of all the times I thought Mandy only came over here foolishly trying to stake a claim on Rubio's heart through his wallet. I just stand in the doorway, watching them and feeling proud of my sister. Mandy talks to Serenity the way I talk to her—at least, when she's not being a pain. Either she's a natural at the older sister act or maybe I taught her something.

"*¡Efraín!*" The devil himself stands behind me now, grinning like the Cheshire cat and offering me his hand. *"Feliz Navidad."*

I hesitate but finally shake his hand. "Merry Christmas." Before I can pull away, homeboy yokes me into a hug. I can't remember the last time Rubio's been this close to me. The stubble on his cheek rubs against my own, and I smell the cheap cologne on his collar. The kind of cologne a kid saves pennies to buy his father at a discount store like Yannis's. Serenity probably gave it to him, and he splashed on a handful.

"Give me your coat y *siéntate.*"

"I'm not staying long," I say. "I just wanted to walk Mandy over, help her carry the *pasteles* and presents."

"You have to open your gifts," says Rubio, "and meet your brother." He motions for the coat. I start to insist on keeping it when I peep Awilda eyeballing us from the doorway of the kitchen while feeding the baby. She would love for me to set something off so she can tell her girlfriends that I'm a *malcria'o* as an insult to my mother, so I pull off my jacket and hand it to Rubio. "Serenity, play Santa *para Amanda y Efrain,*" he says before leaving to hang up my coat.

"Okay, *tío!*" says Serenity, dropping the miniature chair in her hand and scrambling over to the Christmas tree. They got her calling him *tío?* If I hadn't given up my jacket, I would have bounced right there just the way Awilda greeted us. No "Goodbye," no "Merry Christmas," no nothing.

Serenity runs over to me with a large, wide box. "Santa left this here for you, Efrain." She's actually a cute kid, so I just give her a little smile and say thank you. I pull off the lid and peel back the tissue paper. It's a pair of Eckō jeans with painted canvases for back pockets like Nestor and LeRon be rocking. So not my steel-o.

From the doorway of the living room, I hear a shriek. "Do they fit?" I look up, and Awilda's standing there burping the baby. "Stand up. Let's see."

Instead, I pretend to peek at the tag. "They fit."

Awilda grins like a jack-o'-lantern. She yells, "Rubio, they fit! I told you!" Damn, does she have to be that loud with the poor kid trapped under her big mouth? It's a miracle he's not crying, but maybe he's accustomed to the freakin' racket. Awilda gives me a smug look. "I picked them out. You like them?"

No, I don't care if they're all the rage. I'd never walk down the street looking like an art gallery exploded across my ass. But I nod and say, "Thanks."

"Serenity, give Efrain the rest of his stuff." Rubio comes back into the living room. When he leans against Awilda's shoulder to coo in the baby's face, I look away. In Spanish, Awilda instructs Rubio to take his son so she can give my sister her presents. Meanwhile, Serenity piles box after box beside me.

Rubio scoops the baby off Awilda's shoulder and into the crook of his arm. The baby starts to fuss, and Rubio shushes him. The baby continues to whimper as if he's already resigned himself to some sad fact of life. Rubio seems embarrassed. "He wants his mother," he explains to me. He rocks the baby while walking toward me. "Junior, *mira quien 'ta 'qui. Tu hermano.* Don't cry. You big brother Efrain come to see you."

Just to have something to do besides watch this, I open the first box on top of the pile. Two Eckō hoodies, one an off-white pullover with a red lining, the other a white zip-up with argyle diamonds in different shades of gray. Chingy would like the pullover. Maybe I can give it to him as a peace offering. And now I can finally bring home my new gear from Nestor's and just tell my mother that Rubio gave the clothes to me.

I feel this nudge to my side. Next thing I know, Rubio tries to slide the baby into my arms. "Junior, this is your big brother Efrain."

When I was a kid, I used to love holding my little sister, but this is different. I don't want to hold the baby, but Rubio is all up on me with him. If I don't take him, he'll fall and might get hurt. Imagine the *bochinche* if I send Awilda's kid to the emergency room on Christmas.

So I take him. His Onesie says "Dear Santa, I can explain. . . ." Man, he does look like me, just much lighter. I may have dark brown hair, eyes, and skin like my moms, but like it or not, Rubio, Junior, and I have the same shape eyes, the same kind of nose, the same size lips. Those Rodriguez genes must be mad potent.

"Junior likes his big brother," says Rubio. *"Mira como se dejó de quejar."*

He *did* stop crying. Maybe Junior already knows not to get attached to the man. They say babies are mad intuitive, you know. *'Manito* probably gets an overpowering feeling whenever he lies in Rubio's arms that the man's not built for longevity.

And as if he can read my thoughts, the baby raises his fist toward me like a little homeboy. "Oh, you want a pound?" I laugh. I poke out a knuckle and tap it against his fist. "What's up, bro?" I give Junior another pound, and he actually smiles at me.

Awilda yells, "You wanna change him for me?"

"Uh, no." Then I say to Junior, "No offense, kid." And he laughs like he ain't mad at me!

"Fine." Awilda motions for me to hand him over to her. "Your brother just came to get his gifts." Yeah, I wanted nothing more for Christmas than to become a walking museum.

Rubio growls at Awilda, *"Te dije ya . . ."* The look on his face could shatter glass. *"Él no vino pa' 'cer lo que tú 'ta supuesta 'cer."*

When I hear him say that I didn't come here to do her job, I jump up and say, "Give him to me. I'll change him." I can't explain it, but something about that bothers me. "I was only playing."

Awilda eagerly forks over the kid. "The wipes and diapers are in the master bedroom." She waves us away as she heads back into the kitchen. As I carry Junior out of the living room, Rubio reprimands her in Spanish under his breath while Awilda sucks her teeth.

When I reach the bedroom, I close the door behind me. I carry Junior over to the changing table and lay him across it. "I'ma tell you right now, kid, don't get used to this." Junior's eyes follow me as I bend over to get the box of wipes and a fresh diaper from the shelf under the table. I grab two of them and hold them over the baby. "Teddy bears or fishies?" Junior gives a little kick toward the teddies, and I think of Mrs. Colfax. "That's right," I say laughing. "No fish." I hold my breath while I undo his diaper. Thank God, he's only wet.

I wrap my hand around Junior's plump little ankles and hoist him high enough off the table to slide the soiled diaper out from under him. He blasts a cackle like newborns do. "Oh, you like that, huh?" I lift him again, and he laughs some more, his eyes so shiny and mouth all gummy. I keep doing that while I clean him, using a second wipe for good measure. I sprinkle powder on him and fold the new diaper over his little belly.

After I tape him up, I lift Junior off the table and place him across my shoulder. I don't want to go back into the living room, so I stay in the master bedroom and pace across the carpet. Junior's a real good baby. He knows how to chill. Moms says I was the same way. If you bounced me around on your knee, cool. If you put me in the swing, gave me a good push, and went about your business, no problem. According to Moms, I only cried for the basics—a cup of Gerber's, a fresh diaper, or some Z's. I bet Junior's the same way, no easy feat with that megaphone for a mother.

My grandmother jokes that Rubio was restless from conception, kicking his way out of the womb two weeks before the doctor said he was due. Yeah, that's just like him. I don't know how Junior and I could be his sons, seeing that Rubio needs so much attention. Maybe it's one of those recessive genes that sometimes skips a generation.

As I pace with Junior in Awilda's bedroom, I imagine what it might be like to grow up in that apartment. How old will he be when his father takes up with the next chick? When will Rubio decide he's old enough to do it in his face and tell him to lie to Awilda about where they've been? Will there be any money to send Junior to college if Rubio knocks up the latest jump-off? And Awilda being the type of chick who doesn't think anything of lying down with a married father of two and getting pregnant, what kind of *tíos* are going to be around him when Rubio moves on?

Junior raises his fist to me again. I give him another pound with my knuckle. "Don't worry, Little Man," I say. "I got you."

Collusion ♦ (*n.*) a secret agreement, conspiracy

"No, nope, sorry," I say as I step off the curb.

"C'mon, E., why not?" pleads Nestor. "Oh, I get it." Nestor closes the gap I created between us. "For all your talk about *You more GiGi's speed,* you're hedging your bets."

"No! Why you pressing me for this double date, kid? You asked her out; she done said yes. *Se 'cabó.*" I have other reasons not to want to break bread with that breezy. Like Candace finding out just how close Nestor and I truly are. "Damn, as long as you've been pining for that chick, you ain't fiending to be alone with her?"

Nestor stares at his Jordans as he shuffles in place. "Okay, here's the deal. I may be more GiGi's speed, as you like to put it, but she ain't exactly some 'hood rat, you know what I mean?"

"No, not really." A car creeps up to the curb. I peek inside at two scruffy White boys barely a few years older than I am. "What's up?"

The driver asks, "Have you seen Hayden around?"

"Yeah, I know her."

The passenger grabs my arm. "And I'm looking for Ana." Nervous little amateur, isn't he? I would've figured him for a Clemenhead, too, from the bone-crushing grip he has on me. "Ana lives around here?"

"Yeah, I know both those girls. You can catch Hayden at ten."

In other words, ten bucks will buy the driver one aluminum packet of horse. "Ana gets off at one." That means the gym candy will cost his friend a dollar per capsule. Both driver and passenger reach into their pockets and hand me some cash.

As I start to step back from the car to signal LeRon, Clemenhead grabs me again. "Hey, what about Ruth?"

The driver nods like a bobblehead doll. "Yeah, Ruth!" He and Clemenhead cackle like hyenas and slap a five.

I draw the line at roofies. How can I sell that when I have a sister? Backing away from the car with a scowl, I say, "Nah, Ruth moved." I spit on the curb and signal LeRon so he can service these aspiring rapists with two packets of heroin and a bottle of anabolic steroids and get them out of my sight. As the car crawls further up the block, LeRon steps into the street. Meanwhile, one soldier runs off to get the product where it's tucked behind the icebox in front of the bodega while another runs down the street to the abandoned building where the steroids are stashed.

Nestor says, "Popeye must be desperate." Yeah, it's not typical for 'roid users to cop on the street. Especially no White boys. Not in this neighborhood. That's why the pills had to be fetched at the stash house like some kind of special order. "So like I was saying about GiGi, she may have that thug bug, but she a schoolgirl, too," he continues. "Don't you be having classes with her?"

I still don't see what he's getting at. "Yeah, she's in the honors program, too." I'm crazy about Candace, but sometimes I look at GiGi and the nasty thoughts flow. Don't get it twisted. I would never play my girl, but I'd be lying if I said if Candace and I hadn't met—

Nes says, "So that got me thinking that even though she got a thing for street cats, GiGi wants her man to be . . . you know . . . smart."

I shake my head at him. "Just 'cause you're not in school

doesn't mean you're not smart." Nestor rolls his eyes at me. "Look at that dude Lefty"—I lower my voice even though no one's in earshot—"who runs with Julian and them."

"And that cat's, like, twenty-three." Nestor laughs. "All that smack about social promotion. They should've socially promoted Lefty's ass out of AC in the nineties."

"See, you're informed, kid! How many cats grindin' out here know what social promotion is? If GiGi wants to politick, you can hold your own." Truth is, I can't see GiGi talking about much of substance. She may be a schoolgirl, but that doesn't mean she watches CNN.

Nestor's not buying it. "C'mon, man, do me this solid, E. If my conversation gets simple, I know you'll have my back and feed me a line or two."

I think Nestor just wants GiGi and me in the same room so he can be sure that we're not feeling each other. I want no part of it even if Candace is there. She might notice something between GiGi and me that's not supposed to be there.

"I'm just asking for one meal," says Nestor. "And let's flip it like a coincidence. Like I take GiGi to a movie, right? That's two hours where I don't gotta say squat 'cept *Would you like some Junior Mints?*" I don't know if he's trying to make me laugh, but I snicker anyway. "Afterward, we parlay about the movie in the cab on the way to the restaurant. Just when that conversation runs out of steam, we get there, and, oh, snap!" Nestor throws his hands in the air like a jack-in-the-box. "*¡Mira quien 'tá 'quí! Efrain with his dime. Yo, you mind if we sit with y'all?* Two plus two equals zero."

"What?"

"Two people plus two more people equals no awkward silences."

Until someone forgets that Candace thinks Efrain works

at Jimmy Jazz. "Nah, man. Can't do it." Sometimes silence *is* golden.

"Why, Efrain?" Nestor's mad now, and he doesn't rile up easily. "Just tell me why you can't do me this favor."

"Nestor?" This chick with fading blond streaks of stringy hair runs toward us. "Hook me up with sugar stick." I recognize her as one of the prostitutes that work the area. On the street, selling her body, hooked on heroin. Seventeen just like me. I can't stand to look at her, and I'm happy that she isn't trying to cop from me.

"No can do, ma," says Nestor as he eyes her empty hand. "You want to buy on credit, take your ass to Julian." The girl curses him and crosses the street. That's when Nestor notices my face and says, "Candace still doesn't know how you make your skrill, does she?" He scoffs, shaking his head. "You be out here day in and day out, E., grinding right beside me, keeping it from your moms and your girlfriend, but you're ashamed of me. Whatever, man." Nestor starts to walk away from me.

"C'mon, bro—"

"Save it," he yells over his shoulder. Then he crosses the boulevard to I-don't-know-where. I doubt Nestor knows where he's headed either.

Elucidate ♦ (*v.*) to clarify, explain

"Y'all just came from the movies?" I ask as if I don't already know. "What did y'all go see?"

"*Evacuation,*" says Nestor as he pulls out GiGi's seat. "You gotta see it. The effects were sick, bro!"

"That's the one where Will Smith plays the president, right?" I say. "We've been wanting to check out that joint."

GiGi shrugs. "The story wasn't realistic."

"What?" yells Nestor in disbelief. "See, these terrorists—not from the Middle East on some yee-had or whatever, but these White dudes, American citizens—"

"They're planning multiple attacks on major cities all across the country for the same exact time," GiGi continues. "So all these people are going to die 'cause these big cities don't have adequate evacuation plans or whatever for that kind of disaster."

In the softest voice ever, Candace says, "Sounds realistic to me." I reach over and place my hand on her knee.

Oblivious, GiGi rolls her eyes at Candace. "If you live in a big ol' city, just take your ass to the suburbs. Plenty of room up there." Nestor and I look at each other, both of us scrambling for the right way to intervene. Then she says, "And I don't think Hollywood should be making movies about terrorist attacks on New York City anyway."

Nestor says, "Ma, it's just a movie. Entertainment." He puts his hand over GiGi's, but she snatches it away.

"Nine-eleven wasn't all that long ago," she says, wagging her finger at him. "Three thousand people died. Making 'entertainment' out of that is mad disrespectful!"

We fall into that awkward silence Nestor was so desperate to avoid. Then Candace says, "I agree. It's too soon." Then GiGi finally remembers where Candace is from. As her face softens with embarrassment and sympathy, GiGi never looked prettier to me.

But now it's Nestor's turn to be oblivious. "Will Smith is the man, yo!" he shouts. "That's my nigga right there."

GiGi whirls in her seat and punches him in the arm. *"¡Estúpido!"*

"Ouch!" And in case he missed the point, GiGi hits him again. "Damn, girl, what's up with the sudden outbreak of violence?"

"¿Cómo tú vas a usar esa palabra enfrente de ella?"

"Thank you," I add. It's one thing to use that word while chopping it up with LeRon and them on the street, but how's he going to drop it in front of Candace?

Nestor finally gets it. He says, "I'm sorry, Candace. I didn't mean no offense."

Candace just smiles. "I used to say it as if I needed it like the air I breathe. You couldn't tell me I had no right. But then, after Katrina, it seemed so petty, even stupid, to defend it. That's no right worth fighting for." I put my arm around Candace.

Nestor asks, "If you don't mind my asking, how'd you get out?"

"Yeah, is your family okay?" asks GiGi.

"Yeah, we all got out. I mean, we were separated for a few weeks, but we're all together here."

GiGi makes the sign of the cross. *"Gracias a Dios."* The waitress comes over with the *pilón* of *mofongo* for Candace and me to share, and Nestor and GiGi order the breaded steak for him and a bowl of *sancocho* for her. We also order a round of Cokes and some water. "But how did you find each other with all that chaos?"

asks GiGi. "Is it true what they said about people refusing to evacuate?"

Nestor says, "On the news, they showed bodies floating in the water."

"That's disgusting!"

"But it's true!"

"Chill out!" I yell. All heads in the restaurant turn toward our table, but I don't give a shit. I understand Nestor and GiGi's curiosity because I have a thousand and one questions myself, but how're they going to come at my girl like that? "You don't have to talk about it if you don't want to, ma," I say. And as much as I want to know, I mean it.

Candace says, "It's okay. To this day, *I* have questions, and I went through it all. It helps me to talk about it." The waitress returns with a tray and sets the four Cokes and a pitcher of water in the middle of the table. When she leaves, Candace says, "I had snuck off to a friend's house when the levees broke. I know. *How are you going to be hanging out with a friend when a hurricane is about to hit?* You have to understand. We lived through these hurricanes year after year. We've survived so many of them. They pressured us to evacuate for Ivan in oh-four, and that turned out to be a false alarm."

"But isn't it better to be safe than sorry?" asks GiGi.

"Sure, if you have money or own a car. If nobody in your family is old or sick. If you have people elsewhere who can take you in. But most of us in the South couldn't evacuate if we wanted to. The only *if* we could afford is *What if the safest thing to do is stay?*

"So I decided to stay at my friend's house until the hurricane blew over. I was trying to call my mother so she would know I was okay, but I couldn't get through. Then I heard this banging in the street. When I ran to the window, I saw this garbage can bouncing down the block like a rock skipping across a lake. A pipe must've burst because the water in the street was bubbling and steaming like a witch's cauldron, and I could smell the salt in the rain that was pounding against the window. I even reached out to touch the water and taste it. That's when it hit me: the river was coming. This time we should've left.

"I ran to tell everyone that maybe we should seek higher ground at one of the hotels downtown. That's what we call vertical evacuation. They thought I was crazy. *Girl, it's too late.* Meanwhile, we had to yell to hear each other over the wind beating down the roof of the house. It was as if an army had surrounded the house and was trying to knock down the walls. But my friend's mother said, *Just go upstairs and try to sleep. It'll be over in a few hours.* She blew up an air mattress for me, then gave me a few pills to help me sleep through the noise."

The waitress returns with our orders. No one says a word as she sets our food down before us. Even when she leaves, no one moves.

"When I woke up the next morning, my blanket was soaked, and the mattress was floating," Candace continues. "I called the name of everyone in that house, but nobody answered me. I grabbed something floating in the water—I don't remember what—and used it to break the window so I could get out of the house."

"Do you know how to swim?" asks GiGi.

Candace nods. "Not that you wanted to be in that water."

Nestor bristles. "Why not?"

"The sewers flooded, so the water was contaminated. I could see the swirls from gas and oil in it. I even saw a few snakes the hour I was drifting out there."

GiGi asks, "You didn't see anybody else?"

"Yeah, they were stranded on roofs holding up sheets with *Help!* written on them. One guy on a balcony had a little girl on his shoulders waving a red towel. People would call across the street to one another. *Hold on! Please come and get me! I can't swim, but don't worry, they're coming.*"

"Who's 'they'?" says Nestor.

I mumble, "That's the million-dollar question."

"People were outside waving signs and flags, and meanwhile, there was no more wind," says Candace, shaking her head. "It was, like, almost a hundred degrees out. Humid, too. No wind to wave anything. Anyhow, even though my family decided to stay, we planned years ago that if a hurricane got really bad, we would head to the Superdome. That would be the place set up for people with special medical needs, and my grandmother has diabetes. I finally drifted toward some projects where people were actually walking through the water, which was almost chest-high. One woman and her two little kids were floating in a refrigerator with no doors, using pots to paddle through the water. Finally, I came across this building, and some of the people who lived there had boats."

"Say word?" laughs Nestor. "Nobody in no New York projects owns no boat!"

A little smile dances on Candace's lips, letting us know that it's okay to laugh along with him. I mean, it *is* kind of funny. Then Candace says, "The folks with boats were shuttling people back and forth to the bridge, so I got a ride with them."

I ask, "How did you find your family, though?"

Candace explains, "There were thousands of people at the bridge. Whole families even. But there were also a lot of folks walking around with pictures of their relatives, asking other people if they've seen them. And some people . . ." Candace stops, lowers her head, and closes her eyes. Seconds later tears seep through her lashes and down her cheeks.

I rub her back with my hand. "It's okay, ma." I dig my fork

into the *pilón* and scoop up some of the garlicky mashed plantains. "Eat some of this before it gets cold."

Candace opens her eyes. "I'm sorry."

Nestor and GiGi rush to dismiss her apologies and even dive into their own plates. We all seem especially grateful for the good food before us. Candace even loves the *mofongo* and asks how it's made. GiGi explains, and the four of us go on for a while about our favorite foods as we finish eating.

Eventually, GiGi pushes away her empty bowl. Candace stares at it, making GiGi self-conscious. "Oh my God, I'm so sorry! Did you want to try some of the *sancocho*? I must've been hungrier than I thought."

Candace says, "No, it's not that, . . . Every time I see a bowl that was just emptied, I think of home."

Nestor gives a nervous laugh. "Why?"

But Candace only stares at the bowl. She has shared so much already, and I'm so proud of her. She shouldn't have to say any more, but folks need to learn and understand.

Remembering what I had learned while reading Candace's paper, I reach for the pitcher of water and slide GiGi's empty bowl into the center of the table. "New Orleans was built seven feet below sea level." On one side of the bowl, I place Nestor's glass of water. "To the south is the Mississippi River." Now I grab GiGi's glass and place it on the other side of the bowl. "To the north is Lake Ponchartrain. When Katrina broke the levees—" I suddenly grab both glasses and gush the water into the bowl until it runs over every side and across the table. "That's how New Orleans drowned."

Overwhelmed by the mess, no one rushes to clean it up, the same way no one jumped to save or rebuild New Orleans, and now even I finally understand why it matters so much to Candace to go back home.

Apprehend ♦ (v.) to seize, arrest

The cold infiltrates my layers of clothing like a snitch. I shiver so hard, I know a headache is coming. Still, I stay on my hustle because thirty-seven degrees with a windchill factor of twenty-four doesn't keep cokeheads and dope fiends at home.

Nestor heads back to the curb after servicing some brothers in an Escalade. "Man, you would think with all the running back and forth, I'd be warm by now." He bounces up and down like a boxer in his corner.

"Kill that," I say. "You're making me dizzy. Bad enough I'm freezing." Nestor stops jumping and closes his eyes. A silly grin comes across his face. Suddenly he snaps out of it, flicking his eyes open and sucking his teeth. "For real, kid, the cold is eating away at what little sanity you have left," I say. "What was all that about?"

"I was imagining myself chilling on a beach in PR, but it didn't work. Guess it's because I've never been."

"You've never been to Puerto Rico?"

"Nah, man, and why you say it like that's a crime and shit?"

An Elantra inches up toward the curb. I notice it first, but I motion for another guy in our crew to make the sale. "My bad." The cold has Nestor and me bickering like two *viejos* all night. "Just surprised is all. Don't you have fam there?"

"I've probably got some distant cousins I've never met." Nestor starts to bounce again. "Sure wouldn't mind making their acquaintance right now." A Rio drives up to the curb, and he elbows past another dude to work it.

I rub my hands together and close my eyes. I imagine stepping off a plane in Ponce and the slight humidity making the hair on my neck curl. Cool air hits my face as I enter the terminal, and seconds later, I hear a woman call my name. I turn to the voice and see my *abuela* smiling and waving. When I hug her, I smell a mix of my mother and lavender. We climb into her beige hooptie, and she asks me if I want to get something to eat before we head to her *urbanización* in Guavate. I say, "No, *'uela,* take me straight to the beach, and I'll get us some *empanaditas* there." Now I feel the sand between my toes and smell—

"Yo, Scout!" Nestor waves at me to come over to the car.

I jam my hands into my pockets and jog over to the car. The driver is an African American woman about twenty-one, twenty-two. She has a big, pretty smile with short, deep dimples. Her friend looks Latina, a little younger, with bone-straight brown hair and blond highlights pulled back into a ponytail. They definitely fit Nestor's idea of preferred customers.

He says, "This is my boy Scout. Kayla and Martita wanted to meet you." He nudges me in the side, and when I glance at him, he's motioning toward Martita as if to say *Especially her.*

Girlfriend or not, I have to look out for my boy. Besides, it's just conversation, and I'm loving the hot air blasting through the vent on the dashboard. I take off my glove and offer Kayla then Martita my hand. "Nice to meet you."

Martita holds on to my hand and peers into my eyes. "Never seen you out here before." She presses a folded bill against my palm.

"Look at that baby face," says Kayla. "No wonder you call him Scout."

Martita asks, "How old are you?"

"I'm going to be eighteen in July." I take a quick glance at the bill in my hand—a twenty—before I stuff it in my pocket.

"Guess I'm going to have to come back then."

Kayla laughs. "So who's gonna hook us up?"

I point to LeRon. "Check out my man over there."

"You mean the one that looks like Frazzle?"

Nestor and I laugh hard at that, and this is the warmest I've felt all day. I say to her, "Thanks for that, love." Then I step away from the car.

Nestor adds, "Y'all have a good night and holla at us again soon."

"We will," says Kayla, and then they crawl up the block to get their order from Frazzle. I mean, LeRon.

Nestor says, "Yo, Martita was feeling you, bro."

I'm glad he noticed, but I play it cool. "She's just flirting, hoping to get hooked up."

"Nah, man, she was checking you out. Fine older woman, too." He squeezes his eyes shut and shakes his head as if he just swallowed hot sauce. "You frontin' like nothing."

"I don't mind being your wingman, but that's all I can do for you," I say.

Nestor keeps shaking his head. "You need to stop denying your true nature."

"Leave that alone, Nestor."

"Don't get me wrong, man. Candace is a sweetheart, but it's in a man's blood to have more than one female at a time, E. Especially yours, player. You know, Rubio must've—"

Suddenly a Nissan screeches up to the curb. Some guys jump out and run up on us, slamming us against the wall of the building. The dude on me pats me down and then yanks my wallet and loose cash out of my pockets. When I turn to look at his face, he grabs my head and presses it against the brick. "Easy, Efrain, easy." He must have read my school ID card. "Efrain Rodriguez, you're under arrest for criminal sale of a controlled substance." As he continues to read my rights, he grabs one wrist and twists it behind my back. Cold metal tightens around it, and he treats my other arm to the same. Then the plainclothes yanks me away from the wall and drags me toward a police van. He guides my head as I climb inside, joining some other guys, including Julian and other dudes in Hinckley's crew. Within seconds, Nestor follows, and I'm too relieved. He plops down next to me and says, "No matter what they say or do, keep your mouth shut."

I turn to peek out the window. Some of the other guys in our posse bop away like innocent bystanders who just happened upon the commotion and quickly grew bored with it. But a uniformed officer grabs LeRon, pins him to the ground, and yanks a bag of vials out of his pocket. Nestor hisses, "Freakin' Frazzle."

Egregious ♦ (*adj.*) extremely bad

I expect the paddy wagon to take us straight to the precinct, which is a short walk away from the block. Instead, it cruises the Bronx for another two hours, following one raid after another. One kid—he couldn't have been a day over thirteen—mumbles, "The breezies." No one says anything, but we catch eye. He asks me, "You sold to two females in a Rio, right?" The hulk beside him gives him a hard head-butt, then tells him to shut the hell up. The kid bites his lip while a single tear crawls down his face. After every stop, the police stuff in more guys like dirty laundry in a front-loading washer. Soon we have our knees in each other's backs, and it reeks of street grime and gym musk. When we finally arrive at the precinct and the cops open the back door, dudes tumble onto the asphalt, stretching and sighing with relief as if this is home.

Within minutes after we enter the precinct, a detective named Mendoza hauls me into a room and leaves me there alone. I aced a class on criminal law last year where the teacher repeatedly emphasized how things were not like the way they're depicted on television shows, yet I sit here for hours like a murder suspect on *Law & Order*. As much as I rack my brain, I don't remember learning anything that can answer the questions racing through my mind. Why would they separate me from the others? Are they all in rooms by themselves, too? If they're going to question me, why are they taking so long? This just isn't textbook.

Mendoza returns with his partner—a Black guy named Mays—who removes my cuffs. They spend the next twenty minutes firing questions at me. I answer the simple ones. Name, age, address—all the things they must already know since they confiscated my wallet. I dig for the courage to ask for a lawyer, but every time the words scale up my throat, I swallow them down. They start to ask questions about Nestor, LeRon, and other foot soldiers in Snipes's crew. Why do they call me Scout? They're my friends, aren't they? Do any of them go to Albizu Campos with me? As harmless as the questions seem, I exercise my Fifth Amendment right to keep my trap closed. Despite my silence, the questions come faster, sharper. Nothing fazes me until Mays asks, "So, I guess you don't know anything about this turf war between Snipes and Hinckley?"

He might as well have slapped me. Mendoza realizes Mays caught me off guard and says, "Frankie, Frankie, Frankie . . . You're five months away from graduating high school, you have no priors. . . . What are you doing out there, kid? Really. Did you get your girlfriend pregnant?" Something in his eyes makes me want to tell him, but I force that down, too. Finally, Mendoza says, "Okay, if that's the way you want to play it." He motions for me to stand, and Mays cuffs me again.

They toss me into a cell with some random guys, including that kid who guessed that Kayla and Martita were undercover officers. He acts grown, adding his two cents when the others crack jokes and make comments about every female officer who enters their line of sight. I just stay close to the bars, gripping them tightly while searching for someone I know. *Apprehend (v.) to seize, arrest.* The SAT vocabulary words ambush my conscience. *Grievous (adj.) injurious, hurtful, serious or grave in nature.* At first, I try to fight them. This is no time to be thinking about the damn SAT. *Fractious* (adj.) *troublesome or irritable.* Soon I welcome them because I have no other friends here.

"Rodriguez, Efrain." A female officer comes to the holding cell. She ignores the catcalls and leads me to an area where she fingerprints and photographs me. Finally, she allows me to make my telephone call. At this hour, she can still be at work, already home, or on her way from one to the other. I take my chances.

"Yannis Discount."

"Mami . . . It's Efrain." *Mendacious* (adj.) *having a lying, false character.*

"Hi, honey! I was just on my way home. Do you need something?"

"I'm . . . at the precinct." *Unctuous* (adj.) *smooth or greasy in texture, appearance, manner.*

"Oh my God! Did something happen at work?" I see the scenario running through my mother's imagination. I'm ringing up a sale when a masked gunman sticks a pistol in my face and orders me to empty the register. . . . "Efrain, are you still there?"

"No. I got arrested—"

"Arrested?"

"They're holding me at the Forty-first Precinct." *Incorrigible* (adj.) *incapable of correction, delinquent.*

"Efrain, what happened?"

"Time's up," says the officer.

"Just come down to the Forty-first Precinct on Longwood Avenue, and they'll explain everything."

"But, Efrain—" The cop takes the receiver out of my hand, hangs up the phone, and brings me back to the cage. *Egregious* (adj.) *extremely bad.*

Timorous ♦ (v.) timid, fearful

Before my mother can make it to the precinct, the police chain a group of us together and pile us back into the van. I don't know anyone else, and I suspect that this is no coincidence. The kid starts singing "Ninety-nine Bottles," and everyone laughs except me. To settle my nerves, I switch my recall from vocabulary words back to criminal law.

We arrive at the courthouse, and they bring us handcuffed into the building through a back entrance and down several flights of stairs to more holding cells. Before I can orient myself to the place, they remove the handcuffs, only to put us on a line that seems to have no end. It inches for hours until the guard finally ushers me into another cell where a man sits at a table. He makes final notes in the file before him, then adds it to the high stack beside him. Finally, the man stands and extends his hand. "Efrain Rodriguez?"

"Yes." He motions for me to sit in the seat across from him. While he reviews my file, I guess that he has only three or four years on me. Five tops. "Are you my attorney?"

"No, I'm with the Criminal Justice Agency," he deadpans as if he is asked that constantly. "I'm just going to ask you a few questions." Criminal law class floods back to me. This is the first step toward my arraignment. His job is to interview me, and based on his report, the judge will decide whether or not to set bail and, if so, how much. If I'm at this point in the process, my fingerprints are on the way to Albany. My belly softens. When they return, everyone will know that I'm a youthful offender who has never been arrested before, and the judge will likely release me on my own recognizance into my mother's custody.

Moms. The police have probably told her I'm here now, and she's on her way. My stomach tightens again.

Once I finish the CJA interview, they cram me back into another fifteen-by-twenty-foot cell with others waiting to meet their public defenders. After a few hours, I lose track of time and run up on despair. An officer and a thin man wearing wiry glasses and a wrinkled suit approach the cage. "Rodriguez, Francisco?" I and two other guys rush to the bars.

"Me! Here! I'm Francisco Rodriguez!"

"Yo, you meant Francisco Dominguez, right?"

The anguish in their voices makes me nauseous. I cringe at the thought of being as pathetic. Still, I shudder, hold my stomach, and ask the guard, "Can you be sure they got my name, please? Efrain Rodriguez. Not E-p-h-r-a-i-m. It's E F-r-a-i-N."

Once the attorney leaves with the chosen Rodriguez, Francisco the Unlucky spits on the floor of the cell. "Man, it's gotta be almost one already. Y'all know what that means." Some guys grunt while others suck their teeth in agreement. "Night court's done, man." Dominguez throws his back against the wall of the cell. "Ain't nothing happening 'round here at least for another eight hours," he says to the uninitiated hiding in plain sight. Then he slides down the walls as if to settle in for the night. "Damn, I wish I had a cigarette."

The weight of his announcement forces me, too, to lean against the wall and slide down to the floor. I sense eyes making the descent with me, and I fight to keep my head up and my gaze hard. When I feel the show of strength has served its purpose, I fold my arms across my knees, put down my head, and pray I don't cry in my sleep.

Forlorn ♦ (*adj.*) lonely, abandoned, hopeless

"Efrain Rodriguez!" I wake up lying on my side and facing the wall. Someone wedges his foot into the back of my thigh. "You Efrain Rodriguez, right?" I roll onto my back and squint up at Dominguez. "If you Efrain Rodriguez, they just called your name."

I want to leap, but it seems I've aged five decades overnight. "Right here!" I yell as I fight my aching bones to get to my feet. "I'm Efrain Rodriguez." As I stand up, I chide myself for rushing. Like they might think I got tired of waiting and went home.

I walk to the bars, where a woman with locks and a pantsuit waits for me beside the guard. He opens the cell, and I follow her to the opposite side of the room. "I'm LaTonya Avery from the Bronx Defenders," she says over her shoulder. On the way, we pass a single cell no larger than two by two feet. Locked inside is a woman, but just when I think how unusual it would be to mix the sexes in a place like this, she lifts her head, and I see the razor stubble peppered around her—his?—smeared lipstick. Before I can get over my shock, we pass the next single cell, where a man rocks in the corner and sings, "Peeeg, it will come back to you. Peeeg, it will come back to you." And in the next cell is that kid. With a voice hoarse with despair, he calls out to Miss Avery, "Are you my lawyer?" His tears are at full stream now as he grips the bars, and I thank God that there are no more cells to pass.

When we reach the interview area, Miss Avery motions for me

186

to sit as she takes her own seat. "Now, I haven't read your case yet. . . ." She looks up to face me and instantly senses that I'm teetering on the ledge. "I'm doing everything possible to get you out of here as fast as I can, Efrain," she says gently as she opens my file. "Just give me two minutes to acquaint myself with the facts of your case." All I can do is nod and wait. She can take an hour. She can take three. She should take as long as I need to stay out of another cell. "Your codefendants Nestor Irizarry and LeRon Bishop . . . Do you know how old they are?"

"Nestor's eighteen. I don't know how old LeRon is."

"Would you happen to know if either has been arrested before?"

"Oh yeah," I say. "Definitely." Then I feel guilty.

Miss Avery jots down notes on her yellow legal pad. "If that's the case, they can forget about YO status because they only give you one shot at that. Now I can get that for you and probably a program, but first I have to move to sever—"

"A program?" I see myself in a dormitory like one of those kids in *Sleepers*. I chase that image away with a milder one of me wearing a fluorescent vest while poking trash along the Bronx River Parkway. It barely makes me feel better. "What kind of program?"

"An alternative to detention," she says.

"Oh," I say. My relief is so profound, it embarrasses me. "Like community service."

"Right," says Miss Avery, eager to put me at ease. "I might be able to get the judge to grant you probation on the stipulation that you attend a weed program for a year."

"But I don't smoke weed." My lawyer smirks at me. "I know everybody must say that to you, but I've never even tried it, Miss Avery, I swear on my mother. I'm, like, the poster child for *Just Say No*."

"That may be true, Efrain, but you're being charged with a drug felony—"

"I know, but it's one thing to cop to something that I did do—"

"A B-level drug felony—"

"I don't want to say I did something that I've never done." Miss Avery clasps her hands under her chin, allowing me to speak my piece. I'm excited now, ready to pull off the gloves and defend myself, no holds barred. "They charged me with intent to sell, Miss Avery, but I never had any drugs on me. Does the police report say they found drugs in my possession?" My lawyer stares at me so intently, I wonder if she actually can see through my polemic—(n.) *an aggressive argument against a specific opinion*—to the opposing emotions colliding within me. One side takes no small pride in my ability to make a strong case for myself, showcasing my lawyerly potential. Meanwhile, the other stands shell-shocked. After all those hours between cells and handcuffs telling myself that I didn't belong there with *them*. I sound exactly like they do, attempting to reason away a guilt that is as precise as it is real.

When I finish, Miss Avery slowly lowers her clasped hands and opens my file. She flips through several pages and then holds up a photocopy of several dollar bills for me to see. "You see these, Efrain?" she says, pointing at the serial numbers on each of the bills. "These are copies of the dollars used by the two undercover officers to purchase the drugs. The serial numbers on this twenty matches the one on the bill found in your pocket at the time of your arrest. Do you understand what this means?"

Now I'm the kid in the paddy wagon after getting head-butted, and no amount of sucking my breath and blinking my eyes can hold back that tear. "Miss Avery, I can't go to jail."

"Efrain, that's what I'm trying to explain to you. Even with a guilty plea, with no prior criminal history and youthful offender status, there's a very good chance that I can keep you out of jail. All you would have to do is agree to attend some kind of program. One, maybe two, meetings per week for a year . . . It'll fly by, and you'll be back to your life before this—"

"I can't do a program and go to college!" I yell. I know the math. Bronx arrest plus Bronx judge equals Bronx program. Then another realization crashes over me like a wave against rocks, launching me to my feet as I imagine my fingerprints scanning through a computer in Albany and triggering alerts on computers in every financial aid office throughout the country. No matter it probably doesn't work like that; the result is the same. If I plead to a felony, I'll no longer be eligible for federal student loans. Neither Harvard nor Hunter will offer me a financial aid package that doesn't include student loans. "My financial aid applications!"

An officer yells, "Hey!"

No sooner had Miss Avery assured him that everything is fine than I sink back into the seat. She looks at me, shaking her head. "Efrain . . ." And with that utterance of my name, she asks all the questions I'd be too ashamed to answer. With that one word, she lets me know that she finally believes me when I insist that I'm not like all the others who have sat at this same table pleading innocence. The problem is, I myself no longer believe that anymore. "You have my word that I'm going to be very proactive on your case, and I will do everything in my power to build a solid preplea report that proves to the court that you're a fine young man who made a mistake you won't repeat. You're not the big fish they want, Efrain, so I think I can get the DA to reduce the charges so you can plead to a misdemeanor with youthful offender treatment."

See, Mrs. Colfax. I'm not a big fish in *any* bowl. "Which means?"

"It means I have a good shot at getting you community

service that you can complete before school begins and eventually get your conviction off your record."

"Expunge," I say. "Verb. To obliterate, eradicate."

Miss Avery sighs, then closes my file. "So you've already applied to college." I just stare at the red marks around my wrists left by the handcuffs. I can't look my lawyer in the eye, instinctually aware that for once my initiative and discipline about the college admission process are not an advantage. "Efrain, the criminal justice system can be slow and unpredictable. You may want to consider withdrawing your applications until your case is resolved."

Incendiary ♦ (*n.*) a person who agitates

When I finish meeting with my public defender, they transfer me to another cell adjacent to the one I just left. I pass the time doing another emotional workout, following an hour of wallowing in self-pity with another hour of kicking myself for getting in this situation. What if the system is as unpredictable as Miss Avery says, and the judge decides to impose bail and send me to Rikers Island? It doesn't matter that the gig is up, and I can tell my mother to go into the shoebox in my closet, where she'll find enough cash to post bond. Until she pays it, I still have to spend some time in a real jail.

The terror of the mere thought must give off an odor. "Them kicks is hot." The gruff voice belongs to a compact body hovering above me. My eyes make a reluctant trek to his face. I eke out *Thanks,* which is all the permission he needs to reach down and grab me by the ankle. I yell and flail, but others just gather to watch, some cheering *Get 'em. get 'em!* He gets off one Jordan, quickly tucks it under his armpit, and snatches for the other, all without letting go of my leg.

Officers burst into the cell. One drags him off of me after harnessing him with a nightstick while the other pulls me up to my bare feet. She points toward a sneaker on the cell floor where the thug dropped it. "Get your shoe." I do as she orders while watching her look for the other one. She finds it in the hands of another detainee, who obviously confused the ruckus for a game of finders keepers. The officer grabs the sneaker out of his hand and gives it to me. Once my kicks are on my feet, she takes me to the tiny cell where I had seen the kid several hours ago. "I'm going to put you in here for your own protection."

Clang! And there I sit for another half hour or so before someone finally calls my name. This officer cuffs me again and takes me through a door and up two flights of steps to the courtroom. When I enter, Miss Avery is already playing verbal badminton with the district attorney and the judge. As the court officer leads me to my lawyer, I scan the gallery looking for my mother. Instead, I spot Claudia in the crowd with her wailing baby. "Face forward," the bailiff barks as he deposits me next to Miss Avery.

"How does the defendant plead?"

"Not guilty," Miss Avery replies on my behalf. For a second, I wonder what she's doing. Then I remember that this is how the process unfolds. If she is going to negotiate a deal where I can plead guilty to a misdemeanor, I can't go on the court record copping to a felony. "Given that the defendant is a minor who has no previous brushes with the law, I ask that he be released into the custody of his father, who is present in the courtroom."

Rubio? Here? Now? I jerk my head around to look for him.

The court officer yells, "Turn around and face the judge!"

Miss Avery puts her arm on my shoulder, which must be like pressing her palm against a block of ice. I stare straight ahead toward the bench. Without taking her eyes off what she is reading, the judge asks, "Is the state in accordance with that?"

The district attorney shrugs as if he were just asked whether he wanted his sandwich on whole wheat or rye. "Fine with me, Your Honor."

"Will Mr. Rodriguez please approach the bench?"

I start to step around the table when Miss Avery pulls me back. "She means your father, Efrain."

My heart boxes my ribs. "What does she want with him?"

"Knowing this judge, she's just going to lecture him on how he's responsible for you now, that he should do a better job minding you than he has been, blah, blah, blah. Maybe even make him go on record pledging to be the second coming of Michael Brady. All you need to worry about is keeping your nose clean and making your next court date, which is six weeks from today."

No, Miss Avery, that's not all I have to worry about.

Abhor ♦ (v.) to hate, detest

As Rubio and I exit the court building and walk down the Grand Concourse toward his car, I sense him glaring at me. We get in his car and drive off in silence. At the first stoplight, Rubio finally barks at me. *"¿Y cuándo te metiste en toda esa baina de drogas?"*

But I don't have any words for the man. Rubio can lecture me, interrogate me, insult me, whatever. I'll save my reasons for *metiéndome* to the parent who actually gives a damn.

"¡Efrain, te 'toy hablando!" I just stare straight ahead at the bumper of the car in front of us. Then bam! Bastard punches me in the left cheek, sending my head banging against the window. When the pain radiates toward my jaw and temple, there's no denying that this was more than a disciplinary backslap. The motherfucker punched me like a man hits another man. I finally turn to look at him. Rubio's eyes blaze, and his chest heaves as if that punch took so much out of him.

It didn't take enough out of me. I spring onto that son of a bitch like a leopard on a gazelle, slamming my fist into his temple and knocking his dome into the headrest. *That,* Mr. Harris, is PE to KE for you. Rubio swings his forearm between us and then slams it into my chest. He knocks some of my wind, and I fall back against my seat. Rubio comes for me, but I muster enough energy to block him with my left and throw a hook with my right. Rubio follows with a cross to my jaw, and it's on. We just go at each other in the front seat of his car, like ultimate fighters in a refrigerator. Drivers pound their horns and curse through their windows, but we won't stop. I can't stop. As I grab a fistful of Rubio's hair, it flashes through my mind: *I'm going to kill him.* Never mind this is the man who gave me life. For giving me this life that hangs in the balance right now, best believe I have it in me to take away his.

I ignore the banging on my window and the muffled yelling in Spanish. Seconds later I feel the rush of cold air, then two hands as they grip my shoulders and yank me out of the car. When I realize what's happening, I throw out my arm to brace myself for the fall against the hard asphalt. I wait for my bones to settle from the crash landing, then slowly draw myself onto my elbow. That's when I see the blood on my knuckles. I don't know whether it belongs to Rubio or me.

"You all right, man?" the man asks. *No, I'm not fucking all right.* "What the hell happened?" *I just gave my father a long-overdue beatdown.*

I stand there in the middle of the street amid all the commotion and stare at Rubio for a minute. Now he has one leg out of the car, the other one still kneeling on the front seat, and two dudes holding him back. *When I'm done with you,* he's cursing at me in Spanish, *you'll never disrespect me again.* I turn my back on him and start to limp away. Rubio demands that I come back and face him like a man. Fuckin' clown. When he's done with me? I'm done with him. I've *been* done with him.

Repudiate ♦ (v.) to reject, refuse to accept

It takes me almost two hours to get from that stoplight on the Grand Concourse to my bus stop at Port Morris. Throughout the entire trip, folks stare at me as if I stepped out of a horror flick. All I want to do is get home, take a hot shower, and sleep forever.

Moms must've been looking out the window for me, because when I reach my floor, she's standing in the open doorway. "Efrain!" She pulls me into the apartment and puts her hand to my bruised face. "Oh my God!" Moms throws her arms around me. "Look what they did to my baby!"

And who is standing behind her but that bastard. He ain't such a pretty boy now with his swollen nose and fat lip. I pull out of my mother's embrace and point to Rubio. *"He* did this to me."

Moms spins around to face him. *"¿Le diste a mi hjio?"*

"¡Claro que sí!" Rubio booms. *"Y lo haría otra vez si se lo busca."*

"¿Si se lo busca?" My mother shakes with fury. "I don't care what Efrain does. Don't you ever hit *my* son again. *Ever!"*

Even though the evidence is all over his grille, I wait for Rubio to admit that I fought back blow-for-blow like a man. And just as if he can read my mind and intends to concede nothing, he says, "I am the man of this house—"

"This is *my* house, César!" yells my mother. "Your house is down the block."

Rubio looms toward my mother. "I'm the head of this family!"

196

He has never raised a hand to my mother, and I'll be damned if he starts tonight. I step around Moms to shield her. "No, you're not. *She* is." I get in his face. "You don't have a family. All you have are obligations you never meet."

"Efrain!" My mother grabs at my arm and yanks me away from Rubio. "Go to your room while I talk to your father."

"Fine." I shoulder Rubio as I shove past him and head to the bathroom. As I turn the corner, I catch Mandy peeking out of her bedroom door. She's crying, and I expect her to run out and throw her arms around me like when Rubio brought me home after hours in the emergency room with food poisoning. Instead, Mandy fumes, then slams her door shut. She turns the lock for good measure. Moms must have told her the truth about where I was. I can't lie. Her reaction hurts, but all I can do is try to explain on our walk to school tomorrow.

I get into the bathroom and look in the mirror to examine the damage. No wonder heads were staring. I still got the best of him, though.

I shower with water as hot as I can stand, washing away the blood, the snot, the dirt, the street, the jail. But even though I lather twice and wash my hair, I just can't strip the weight of what has happened. Sometimes my mother and Rubio's voices rise over the hard spray of the shower. Only when I hear the apartment door slam do I turn off the faucet and pull back the curtain. I towel off, change into the dingy sweats hanging behind the door, slip into my *chancl'as,* and go face my mother.

She stands in the living room staring out of the window. She hears me shuffle into the living room and turns to face me, her eyes swollen with exhaustion and anger. "First things first . . . Did you do it, Efrain? They arrested you for selling cocaine, and I need to hear the truth from you. Are you guilty of the charges?"

I knew this would be a hard conversation, but, man . . . I had no idea how deep it would cut. I don't know what hurts more: the fact that Moms still believes in me enough to grant me the benefit of the doubt or the fact that in the next second I will prove to her that I don't deserve it. "Yes."

And as if that single word gave her a push, my mother reaches for the windowsill to maintain her balance. "How long have you been doing this?" Damn, if she would just scream and curse, or even hit me, I can get through this. I can handle the rage. I want to take it. But I can't carry this kind of weight. If I hurt her any more, it will break me.

"I've only been out there a few times." I drop my head, tears stinging at the corners of my eyes. "And only to make money for college." Moms scoffs. "That's the truth!" I lift up my head because I know if my mother looks me in the eye, she will understand. "Mami, I'm tired. I'm tired of following all the rules and never winning the game. You want to hear the truth? Nice guys finish last, Mami. *No me metí en drogas* to have money for nice clothes or jewelry or anything like that, but why do I have to choose? I'm tired of being the good boy who never has anything to show for it, whether it's a cool pair of jeans or money for school. Doing the right thing is supposed to be its own reward, but that's not enough to pay my tuition. Whatever it takes, remember?" No one should understand better how exhausting it is to do the right thing for its own sake without so much as a rebate. Regardless of what happened tonight, this more than anything proves that I am her son.

But my mother grabs my chin like a vise and yells, "You don't pay tuition when you go to prison!" Moms shoves my head backward as if she wants to snap it off my neck. "And if you get killed, *soy yo la que va tener que pagar.* I pay, Efrain. I'm the one who'll have to pay for your burial plot." She wraps her arms around her body as if trying to contain herself. But within seconds, Moms explodes. "I'm sick of the men in this family taking me for granted! I sacrifice myself day in and day out for years, *¿y pa' qué?* Just for you to decide that it's not good enough and break all the rules and humiliate me, you selfish, insensitive . . ." In all my life, I have never seen my mother so enraged. No matter what he did, she never got this angry at Rubio. The knot of emotions sitting in the pit of my stomach paralyzes me. Moms points at me and says, "I'll be damned if I bury my son or visit him in prison because he's out there running the streets when I'm busting my ass to keep him off them, Efrain Rodriguez. This is not how I raised you, and I won't stand for it."

"*Sí, señora.*" She's had her fill of loving men who lie in her face. I get it.

My mother walks back over to me and reaches up to stroke the bruise on my cheek. Just as I lean into the caress, she snatches back her hand as if she's afraid to be too tender. Moms says, "I want my son back, Efrain." It sounds more like a plea than an order.

"*Sí, señora.*"

Then my mother falls into herself as if diving into her own heart for something deeply buried there. She swallows hard and says, "So I want you to live with your father until you graduate from high school. While you were in the shower, I packed your things in a laundry bag—"

"What?" No way. I can see the reluctance in her eyes and hear the doubt in the spaces between her words. Does Moms really believe that if she puts me out, I'll crawl over to Awilda's like the prodigal son, and Rubio will straighten me out? "No, nope, sorry," I say, throwing myself against the wall and folding my arms across my chest.

"You can't stay here, Efrain. What kind of example is that for your sister? What am I supposed to say to Amanda the day she decides to do God knows what with strange men because she needs to *earn* money for college?"

"Damn, Mami, don't OD!" Ain't no need for my mother to paint that nasty picture in her own mind, never mind mine. "Like that's going to happen."

"If yesterday someone had told me my son was selling drugs, Efrain, I wouldn't have believed it either," says Moms. "And I refuse to hold you to a different moral standard just because you're a few years older than she is, and certainly not because you're a boy."

"But I'm not a boy anymore!" I yell. "That's the problem right there, Mami—"

"I don't know what Nestor *y esos títeres en l'esquina* have told you, Efrain. I don't give a damn either!" my mother interrupts. "Breaking the law and doing time and all that gangster nonsense is not some rite of passage to manhood. Until you understand that, not only are you merely pretending to be your own man, you're not the kind of person who is welcomed in this house. Go, Efrain." My mother's voice wavers. "Before I call the police. It's over to Rubio's or back to jail. The choice is yours."

I come off the wall. "Mami, you can't be serious!"

"Take your shit and leave now!" My mother pushes past me and heads to the apartment door. She grabs the laundry bag and my backpack and flings them out into the hallway. Clothes and cash spill across the dirty tiles, including the leather jacket and Baby Phat handbag I gave her and Mandy for Christmas. The second I rush across the threshold to retrieve them, my mother tosses my jacket into the corridor, then slams and locks the door behind me.

I scoop all the money and clothes back into the laundry bag and then pull my keys out of my jacket pocket. Nothing can stop me from letting myself back in and refusing to go. But when I step to the door with the keys in hand, I can hear Moms wailing as if she were desperate to heave up her blistering heart to make the pain stop. Then I hear the patter of Mandy's feet against the linoleum as she runs from her room to my mother. She cried, too, when my mother finally put out Rubio, but not like this. Nothing like this.

I slip my keys back into my pocket and reach into the laundry bag for a couple of bills. I smooth out each one and slide them under the door. My mother continues to sob, oblivious to my gesture. It's all good. I would hate for her to misinterpret this as a bribe. As smart as I'm supposed to be, I never figured out a way to find a way to funnel some of my earnings her way. When Moms finds a couple of hundred dollars on the floor, will she throw it out because it's from me? I won't be here to take it back, so she might as well get ahead on a few bills.

When I'm done sliding my apologies past the welcome mat, I stand up, grab my bags, and bounce.

Raucous ♦ (*adj.*) loud, boisterous

Marlene answers the door holding an open bottle of soda in her hand. "Hey, Efrain!" She steps aside to let me in as I drag the bag behind me. "What you got in there?" Then Marlene notices my *chancl'as*. "You must be crazy, walking the streets in them sandals in this cold!"

Ignoring her, I ask, "Mind if I wait for Nes in his room?"

Claudia's toddler Joshua races past me on his way from the kitchen to the living room. Seconds later some guy in his late twenties chases behind him. Must be his father. I think his name is Robby. He does a double take and stops in front of me. "Who you?" he says.

"That's Nestor's friend Efrain," volunteers Marlene.

"Efrain?" The guy squints at me, his breath foul with Corona. "I don't know you."

Marlene sucks her teeth and yells, "That's 'cause he's *Nestor's* friend!"

"Shut the hell up, Marlene! I heard you the first time, damn." He starts to say something to me when his cell phone rings. Recognizing the number, Robby flips open the phone and barks into it. "Claudia, where the hell you at?" I take that as my cue to leave. "I know it don't take *that* long to bail nobody outta jail!"

I get to Nestor's door and reach for the knob to find a gaping hole and splinters of wood scattered all over the floor. Someone hacked the knob out of the door. I push it open and find Melo by himself sitting on the floor playing Grand Theft Auto. "Hi, E.!" he says with barely a glance at me. "Where's Nestor?"

It takes me a second to rebound from the question. "He's coming soon." Melo cackles as his game character yanks another out of his car, beats him down with a swift kick to the head for good measure, then roars away in his ride. I grab the box off the bed and read it. *Rated "M" for "mature."* "Melo, aren't you too young to be playing this?"

"My brother bought it for me. Sometimes we play together." Then he makes a face. "But not a lot 'cause Nestor has to work and go out with GiGi." Suddenly Melo gets on his knees and leans forward to open the console under the television. "You wanna play with me?" He's already reaching for another game controller.

I'm not in the mood, but I don't want to hurt his feelings. "Ah, you don't want to play with me," I say. "I don't know how."

"I'll teach you."

"No, you play. I'll learn by watching you, okay?"

Melo falls back on his butt and resumes his game. "Okay."

Not wanting to take the bed should Nestor return, I ease into the lounge chair. All I want is to fall asleep in this chair and awake in my own bed to Mandy's chocolate fingers and my mother's pot banging, the storm in my head subsided and the fault in my belly healed. But with the *pariseo* down the hallway, Melo's exaggerated reactions to his simulated pillage and plunder, and my mother's anguish and rage tearing at my soul, I can forget about sleep any night soon.

Acerbic ◆ (*adj.*) biting, bitter in tone or taste

When I wake the next morning, Nestor is still not home, the Xbox screen saver runs across the television screen, and Melo is passed out across the floor. I haul myself out of the chair to pick him up and carry him to bed. He should be getting ready for school now, but I don't have the heart to wake him. Instead, I head to the bathroom, hoping to find whatever I need to get presentable for school. That's right, I'm going to school. It's all I have left to undo the damage I've caused.

Someone beat me to it, so I lean against the wall and wait. And wait. And wait. I knock on the door, trying to play it off as if I'm concerned. "Hello? Is everything all right in there?" On top of everything, I don't want to be late for Miss Polanco's class.

The bathroom door opens, and a sheet of steam billows out into the hallway. Marlene stands there in a towel that barely covers all that should be covered. "I'm almost finished," she says, running her fingers through her wet hair. "But you can come inside if you want."

I jerk my eyes to the floor. "Just knock on Nestor's door when you're finished." Then I bolt. I feel Marlene's eyes on me, begging for me to turn and peek. And God knows I'm tempted, but not only is she Nestor's little sister, she's only fourteen. I can't go back home too soon.

Then the second I walk into Spanish class, eyes latch onto me while voices downshift into whispers. As I walk to my seat, Marco whispers to Stevie about the bruises on my face, and even Miss Polanco peeks at me from the corner of her eye. When the bell rings, she picks up a stack of booklets off her desk and distributes them to the first person in each row. In Spanish, she announces that we're going to spend the next few days practicing for the Regents exam. The class groans, but I'm all for it. With the Regents almost two weeks away, this focus might keep me off folks' minds and my name out of their mouths. At least in this class anyway.

So we spend the entire period on the writing section of the exam. We have to choose two out of three writing tasks, and each answer has to contain at least one hundred words. The first option says:

> Your Spanish pen pal asked you about cars in America and what kind of cars you like. In Spanish, write a letter to your pen pal discussing cars in America.

Man, the only thing I'm pushing is the subway turnstile. I skip to the next option: create a story based on a cartoon of a guy and a girl sitting on the floor talking while a cat walks by. The Regents doesn't expect Gabriel García Márquez out of an AC senior, so in ten minutes I churn out an inane tale about the couple getting into a big argument about whether cats are better than dogs that ends in their breakup. Only then do I reread the instructions and realize that I was *not* supposed to write dialogue. By the time I finish rewriting my dumb story without the damned dialogue, I have twenty minutes left in the period. If the next question is off the wall, I can write a stupid letter about why the best cars in America actually come from Japan.

In Spanish, write a journal entry describing what you do in a typical day. You may wish to include:

   morning routine
   school activities
   after-school events
   work/household chores
   family activities
   leisure activities (walking, shopping, sports, music, television/movies)
   meals
   evening/bedtime routines

I'm all over it.

Most people use an alarm clock to wake up in the morning. I rely on my worries. Otherwise, I have a typical routine. After I shower, dress, and eat breakfast, I take my little sister to school. Depending on how she feels about me that day, she either talks my ears off or ignores me. Then I walk to school alone because my best friend thinks I'm a criminal and will not associate with me. At school, I learn many interesting things, like although I'm very smart, I'm too Brown and too poor. In other words, I could never be smart enough. On a good day, I spend time with my girlfriend. We study and talk. My girlfriend has some problems, but she stays strong and good, and that is why I admire and respect her. Sometimes I wish I were more like my girlfriend. Every night I take the train to Hunts Point and sell drugs on the street. The people I work with are not bad. They're only criminals. I like them, but I don't know if they are my friends. Sometimes I feel bad about what I do, and sometimes I am proud that I can take care of myself. I would take care of my family, too, but my mother thinks I work as a salesperson in a clothing store. . . .

Scribble, turn, scribble, turn . . . Before I know it, the bell rings, and I'm drowning in a sea of sucking teeth. While everyone else races to finish writing and counting words, I stuff my answer sheets into the exam booklet and take them up to Miss Polanco's desk. She hands me a manila envelope with my name written across the front in her neat cursive. I don't even want to ask what it is. She says, *"¿Y cómo estás, Efrain?"* Her eyes gaze with concern.

I just shrug as I put the envelope in my bag. I don't know how I am. I have seven more periods to go.

Enmity ♦ (*n.*) ill will, hatred, hostility

The second I get into the locker room, Lefty rolls up on me and slaps me on the back as if we were boys now. "What's good, Scout?" My face burns at the sound of my street name echoing through the locker room. Chingy pretends to ignore us while changing into his gym clothes, but I can feel the vapors down the aisle. "I thought you were still on lockdown?"

I say, "Obviously not." Not just to squash Lefty's attempt at chitchat but to send Chingy a message, too. But he slams his locker shut and leaves.

"The cost of doing business, man. Charge it to the game," says Lefty. "Word is that Hinckley posted bail for his soldiers and even got his paid lawyer to rep Julian while Snipes left y'all to fend for yourselves. That's the kind of trifling shit that made me cross the street."

I'd rather charge it to his head, and I almost tell him that I didn't need Snipes to help me. Instead, I hold my tongue and click the padlock on my locker. As I walk toward the gym, Lefty trails me. "Yo, Scout, this school's a large market, and I desperately need to expand operations before my competitors gain share, you feel me?"

I stop dead in my tracks. Dude just got all *Wall Street Journal* on a brother while admitting that he comes to school every day to sell drugs, even though he almost qualifies for Medicare. "What?"

"Rodriguez, Saldaña, fall in!" yells Coach Moretti.

I start toward my spot for attendance, but Lefty blocks my path. "So let's meet after school on the football field, and I'll break you off with—"

"Back up off me, man." My life is enough of a catastrophe. I throw out my arm to pivot past him. "I'm not interested."

"What's going on over there?" Coach Moretti heads toward us intent on knocking heads. A few rubbernecks, including Chingy, follow him.

"Oh, so it's like that?" Lefty backs up to stay in my way. "You want to play me?"

"What the hell are you talking about?" The last thing I need is to get into it with Lefty, but I can't back down. Not with all these eyes on us. Not anymore.

My fleeting attention offends Lefty. He yells, "Oh, so now you don't see me?" Then he steps into my face so that we're chest to chest.

Suddenly Chingy grabs my arm and yanks me backward, coming in between Lefty and me. "Fall back, son," he says with a finger pointed at Lefty's dome. " 'Fore you get your chin checked!"

Coach Moretti yells, "Get security!" That's when Lefty swings. Chingy blocks and prepares to counter when the coach dives in between them. But Chingy and Lefty still lunge and curse at one another, and our classmates jump to keep them apart. When he hears the static from the guard's radio as he nears the gym, Lefty breaks free of the guys who hold him back and bolts through the fire exit. "You two to the assistant principal's office now!" Coach Moretti yells at Chingy and me. "Anybody else who's not in his place within the next ten seconds gets a zero for the day."

"Damn!" Heads race to their places on the floor as we leave

the gym. I shadow Chingy's heels as he bounds down the steps to the lobby and into the AP's office.

The secretary says, "Hello, Rashaan. What brings you here?" Chingy says nothing. He just throws himself onto the bench and folds his arms across his chest. She translates his body language quickly. "You? In trouble? Who sent you?"

"Coach Moretti."

"Oh." The secretary waves her hand as if to say *No big thing*. After all, a little competition gets out of hand during gym class every other week. Then she finally notices me. "Mr. Rodriguez . . . ," she says, as if the sight of me changes her perspective.

I have nothing to say, so I just sit beside Chingy on the bench. He leans his head back against the wall and stares at the clock across the room. I sneak glances for a chance to make eye contact that never comes. Finally, I just say, "Thanks, bro."

Chingy remains stone-faced. Then, as if he can't help himself, he finally says, "Seems like you've had enough beatdowns for a while." With his eyes still fixed on the clock, he asks, "Who stomped you like that?"

Maybe I should fuel the illusion that I had a scuffle in the pen. But I need him to know the truth. This is Chingy. He's fam. "My pops," I say. Although Chingy still refuses to look my way, I see his jaw pulse for a flash. "You think I look bad," I rush to add. "His lip's so fat, he sounds like a Dominican Elmer Fudd." He doesn't laugh, so I try again. "Guess you're going to have to make another adjustment to your admission calculation system." Chingy's eyes slack from something other than amusement, but I still appreciate the reaction.

"Rashaan," the secretary interrupts, "you may go in now to see Mr. Graves."

Chingy nods at her but hesitates to stand. Looking at me from the corner of his eye, he mumbles, "Whatever." Then he stands up and heads into the office.

In my twelve-plus years of school, I have never been called to the principal's office, but to be honest, this beef with Lefty was worth it to get Chingy to speak to me again.

Advocate ♦ (*n.*) a person who argues in favor of someone or something

No matter how much I beg, the assistant principal suspends me for the rest of the day. When I ask if this will go on my record and affect my chances of being valedictorian, Mr. Graves says, "That's something you should've thought about, Mr. Rodriguez, before deciding to follow in Mr. Irizarry's footsteps." It makes me angry to hear him judge Nestor like that and brush me off, but I have to eat it. Instead, I try to argue like a lawyer, saying that I was innocent until proven guilty, that I hadn't yet been convicted of anything, and all that. Homeboy tells me to get out of his office before he suspends me for the rest of the week.

So I reluctantly head back to Nestor's place. God knows in the middle of a weekday, someone will be there. But I lean on the intercom for ten minutes, and no one answers. I even resort to standing under Nestor's bedroom window and hollering at the top of my lungs. If Moms is embarrassed by me now, she'd die where she stood if she saw me acting like *un malcria'o*.

Someone finally leaves the building, and I slip into the lobby. To my surprise, the apartment is silent. I pound on the door, but no one answers. At least I'm out from the cold, so I plant myself on the staircase. I sit there for the longest time, replaying the last few months, from my first night on that corner to the fistfight with Rubio in his car to the argument with my mother last night. The scenes unfurl across my mind, and everyone feels like an actor in one of Nestor's urban legends instead of real people from my own life. I don't recognize anyone, least of all myself. This person is new to me. There are things I like about Scout. He dresses smooth and swaggers in a universe where others don't dare tread. He stays paid. He stands up for himself. That's the Efrain that spoils Candace and checked Rubio.

But I don't think I can trust him.

I need to think about something else. Something I can control. Something I can do now. When I reach into my backpack to break out my SAT workbook, I find the manila envelope that Señorita Polanco gave me. When I open it, I find a photocopy of the Harvard recommendation form with the letter she wrote on my behalf typed across it. According to the date, she wrote and sent it before Christmas, and by giving me a copy, Señorita Polanco defied the common request that recommendations remain anonymous.

To the Admissions Committee:

It is with both great pride and enthusiasm that I write this letter of recommendation for my student Efrain Rodriguez.

Efrain has been my student for over three years. I won't tell you how he performs in my classroom because his grades speak for themselves. I'd much rather tell you what the numbers on his transcript do not convey: Efrain's character makes him more than worthy of being a member of your incoming class. This is a young man with the rare ability to envision beyond his immediate circumstances. Moreover, he already possesses the resourcefulness and discipline to make that vision a reality. Many of my students express an abiding desire to beat the odds stacked against them, but in almost two decades of teaching, I've found that Efrain is the first who refuses to do so by settling for what has been outlined as "good enough" for someone in his position. "Good enough" for a young man like Efrain, for example, might be enlistment in the armed forces, not for any innate proclivity for the military life but simply because there are no other viable options. He is intent on self-determining, making his own decisions among the various (often mixed) messages young men in this community are constantly sent about what they can and should do if they are to be "real" men. Perhaps it is a skill, perhaps it is a gift. Whatever "it" is, Efrain has it, and it will propel him past any gaps in his academic preparation.

This is why I dare to say that it is actually more in Harvard's interest to admit Efrain than it is in Efrain's interest to attend Harvard. This is a young man who will always land on his feet and hit the ground running. If he has one flaw, it is hubris, a flaw that hardly sets him apart from any of the other students who aspire to attend your college. If anything, what sets Efrain apart from your more privileged applicants is that, given the socioeconomic hand that he has been dealt, he has any hubris at all. Because he is a Latino male raised by a single mother in one of the nation's poorest communities, Harvard should not even be in his imagination, never mind his line of sight. Not only will Efrain appreciate and maximize all that your institution has to offer arguably more than those students for whom an Ivy League education has been a foregone conclusion since birth, but he would probably teach his classmates things they otherwise would not (but should) learn by being nothing more than the young man he is.

On a final note, I commend your institution for its new free tuition program for low-income families and have no doubts that Efrain both qualifies for this trailblazing initiative and is precisely the kind of student it aims to support. He is the epitome of all the principles that Harvard professes to value, and I urge you to accept his application for admission. Years from now, I will be proud to say Efrain Rodriguez was a student of mine, and so will you.

Sincerely,

Josefina Polanco

Harvard has a free tuition program?
When did this happen?
Do other elite colleges have programs like this?
Why did no one tell me?
Why did someone have to, kid?
I reread the letter, trying to remember the Efrain Rodriguez that Señorita Polanco describes. My memory of him is hazy, but I

do recall that I like this guy, too. In fact, I like him way more than the other dude floating in my psyche even at his best. The Efrain in Señorita Polanco's letter feels like someone I can trust, and I can't understand how I fell out of touch with him.

I carefully put away the recommendation and see if I can go find him.

Resolute ♦ (*adj.*) firm, determined

Free Tuition for Families Earning under $60K
Families earning less than $60,000 a year
will no longer be expected to contribute
to the cost of their children's tuition,
room, and board at Harvard, school offi-
cials said today. With this announcement, the university jumps to the head of
the pack of elite institutions that are expanding financial aid for undergraduates
from low-income and middle-class families. With this pledge, Harvard has one-
upped such competitors as Princeton and
Stanford, which announced last year that
they, too, would no longer expect . . .

I scan down the Web page on the library's computer monitor, trying not to cry with euphoria. According to the press release, I'd
still need to get a work-study job and take out a student loan, but
it's all good. The only thing I have to do to go to Harvard or
Princeton and Stanford—ain't Ivy League but no school to turn
up my nose at—*is to get in!*

So I spend the next three hours practicing SAT questions.
When I get a wrong answer, and the voice inside me says, *This is
all for nothing,* I visualize running Chingy's admissions software

217

and inputting *2200* all across the *SAT2* line and watching my probability of getting into each school leap by double digits. This works a few times, but reality eventually takes hold. No amount of studying is going to make me bust out a score of 2200 next month. I finally accept it. The best I can hope is that a considerable improvement in my score will make an elite college give me a second look. Maybe all I need is to score 2000. Or just 1800.

That is, if my arrest doesn't impact my application. As much as I dread the answer, I have to find out if it does. There's no other way to silence Scout until I know.

Without bothering to reserve it again, I jump onto a computer and log on to my account on commonapp.org. Using the online Common Application to apply to college is the one piece of good advice that Mrs. Colfax gave me. The problem is that I had finished the main part of the application over Christmas break, and clicking on the Submit button is no different than sealing the envelope and tossing it in the mailbox. I can look at my responses to the questions, but I can't change them. The best I can do is hope that my answer to *that* question is still true. I page through a couple of screens, and there it is:

> Have you ever been convicted of a
> misdemeanor, felony, or other crime?

"Yes!"

The librarian gives me a sharp *Hush!*

"I'm sorry," I say, still a little too loudly. I can't help it. When I completed the application, the answer was no. It's *still* no. I haven't been *convicted* of anything yet. I still have a chance of getting into every college I applied to, including my dream schools.

I smell jawbreaker breath coasting down the back of my neck.

"You finished?" I look up to see a wannabe gangster hovering over me. He wears a Giants cap with the bill to the side and drops an X-Men drawstring bag on the table beside the monitor. "I'm signed up for that computer now." His buddies scurry to the computer stations around me and log on to MySpace.

I shake my head, feeling mad old. For a second, I wish I could turn back the clock five years to when my biggest concern was where to hide my issue of *King*. Then I remember that wasn't my biggest concern then. It just should've been.

"It's all yours, Little Man." I stack up my files, slide them into my backpack, and rush out of the library. I may not have Chingy's admission calculation system to run algorithms for me, but I make some quick calculations on my own as I head back to Nestor's apartment. With or without Rubio's salary, I probably qualify for free tuition. The first order of business is to get admitted. The SAT prep course is making a difference in my performance, and I have stellar recommendations. Miss Avery says she has a good chance of getting my charges reduced and even my record expunged. All I have to do is ace the SAT when I take it again in a few weeks and keep my nose clean.

I go to tell Nestor that I quit.

Inextricable ◆ (*adj.*) hopelessly entangled

I get back to Nestor's apartment to find a new twist on the usual commotion because now the drama is about me.

Marlene throws open the door and hollers over her shoulder, "Here he is, *estúpido*!"

Then, as I step into the apartment, Claudia pushes past me while shaking a few drops of baby formula onto her wrist. She says, "Efrain's home now, Nestor, so you can shut up and give me the baby."

Nestor darts out of the living room, bouncing Claudia's crying baby in his arms. His eyes cut into me as he hands off the baby to his sister. "Where the hell have you been?"

"Who are you?" I ask. "My father?"

We notice Marlene standing beside me, hands on hips, lips all pouty. "Mind your business, Marlene," shouts Nestor. "Go do your homework."

"You ain't my father either, Nestor!"

"That's right, I ain't Papi. And you lucky, too. He would've given you a *galletazo* across that smart mouth of yours by now."

"Whatever."

"E., I need to speak to you in private." Nestor starts down the hallway toward his bedroom, and I follow. He hurls a few curses at the hole where his knob used to be and slams the door behind us. "Where the hell have you been, man?"

"What do you mean where've I been? Where I always am. In school."

Before I can correct myself, Nestor beats me to it. "I heard you got kicked out this morning."

"Not kicked out. Suspended. Yo, who told you that?"

"Never mind who told me. They said you had some beef with stupid-ass Lefty and got thrown out of school around ten o'clock. Where you been all this time?"

"Not that it's any of your business—"

"No, you wrong about that, E. It is my business. It's totally my business."

"—but I came over here first, and nobody answered the door." I feel like an idiot for even telling him that. Since when do I answer to Nestor?

"Bullshit. They finally sprung me about eleven, and I've been here ever since. Not once did I hear the buzzer."

"Well, that's not on me. Maybe you were asleep."

"Damn right I was sleeping. I just spent almost thirty-six hours in jail."

"Oh, and I didn't have to sleep in a cell?"

"At least you got to walk—"

"Walk? This might ruin everything I've been working my whole life for!"

"—without posting no bail. My daddy didn't come rescue me."

I shove him. "Fuck you, Nestor!" Then I punch him in the chest. "At least your father didn't beat the shit out of you. Your mother never put you out in the street. Why the fuck do you think instead of being home with my family, I'm here in the middle of you people and your never-ending bullshit?"

Nestor looks down at his chest and places his hand where I punched him. We just stand there heaving, and the entire apartment is frozen in a rare stillness. Then he walks over to the lounge chair and eases himself into it. "E., I'm sorry I came out of pocket like that, but you gotta understand that this isn't a good look, okay? Not for me, not for you—"

"What the hell are you talking about already?"

My question chases away his momentary calmness because he jumps up and screams again. "I'm talking about you not showing up on the block just hours after we got arrested!" Nestor throws up his hands. "Damn, E., if you're so freakin' smart, why you make me explain every little thing to you? Use your common sense, bro. Do you know how that looks? The cops have all this intel about things getting hot between Snipes and Hinckley, and everyone's wondering who's snitching, and guess who's Suspect Number One?"

"Me?" My stomach does somersaults. "I didn't know a damn thing about Hinckley to be flapping to nobody, let alone the police. Why ain't they looking at Lefty? I ain't down with Snipes like that."

"Wrong again, Efrain. First of all, that shit with Lefty happened a ways back. Second, I'm down with Snipes, and you're down with me. I brought you into this—"

"Don't remind me."

"—because you asked me to!"

I know he's right, but with the stakes at an all-time high, I can't bring myself to just cop to it. "Don't front now like you weren't stressing me." And then all these feelings I had when Nestor tried to recruit Chingy come back to the surface. "You weren't always checking for me like that. You only stepped to me because you figured that when I get to college, I could hook you up with some students, and you could stack more paper and climb the ranks or whatever." It burns so much to say aloud that I expect steam when my words hit the air.

Nestor lowers himself back into the leather recliner and rubs his hands over his face. After a long exhale, he finally looks up at me. "You got it twisted, E. I always wanted you to be down with me. But when Chingy shut me out, I wasn't trying to lose another friend." He breaks eye contact but keeps saying his piece. "I ain't got too many of those left, you know. I mean, bona fide friends who truly got my back 'cause it's *my* back, you feel me? Not because they want something from me or because it's good business. Just you, E. I know that you're down for me whether I'm on the corner slinging or making pizza down the block or whatever. That's why eventually I did step to you. I needed at least one person in all this bullshit that knows me like *that*."

"Nestor, man, I gotta quit." It feels so selfish to break this to him now, but I know this is the right thing to do, and doing the right thing should never wait. "I never meant for this to become my way of life. I only got involved because I needed the money for school, and now the only thing I ever wanted from all this is the very thing that's on the line. I can't risk it."

Nestor exhales again, leaning back in the recliner, folding his arms behind his head and closing his eyes. A minute later, he sits back up and plants his feet on the floor. "I hear you, E. I really do," he says, his voice soft and heavy. "But I don't think you're hearing me. You can't quit right now. Forget about college—"

"Forget about college?"

"There's something way more important at stake, E. Snipes called a meeting tonight in an hour. I know that you didn't know anything about what's going down between Snipes and Hinckley. You didn't need to know. Didn't *want* to know. *I* didn't want you to know for your own protection, but all that's irrelevant. If you don't show your face tonight, you ain't showing it at Harvard in September. You ain't making it out of AC, you hear what I'm telling you? And since I'm the person who brought you into the organization, if you go down, you take me with you." Nestor leans back in the chair, propping an ankle on the opposite knee like a Corleone. "Now, I ain't afraid to die," he says with a quivering voice that betrays his gangster lean. "When I got involved in this, I didn't fool myself into thinking that I'd be some kind of exception to the risks and pitfalls. But you and me, for all our different goals, ambitions, or whatever, we're not that different, least of all now." His eyes travel toward the closed bedroom door, which barely muffles the endless chaos that marks his people. Marlene and Melo arguing over the television remote. Claudia singing along with Rihanna on the radio to her babies. And in a rare appearance, we can even hear their mother yelling in Spanish for all of them to quiet down. Nestor says, "Just like you, the main reason I got into this whole thing is the very thing that's on the line right now."

The weight of the circumstances forces me to lower myself onto the bed. Nestor and I sit there in silence for a few minutes. I finally say, "I'll go to the meeting tonight, but the second the heat is off, I have to quit, Nestor. When the time comes—and it has to be soon—we have to convince Snipes to let me peace out."

Nestor nods. "Good lookin' out. I appreciate that."

"I can't leave you hanging." And in that moment, both Efrains are at a temporary peace with each other. They both know that the decision to attend the meeting is not completely selfish. Both of them take pride in being a good friend. And with the same forcefulness that Nestor came at me when I walked through the door, I announce, "And then the next step is to get you out of this shit, too."

Nestor gives me this smile that for a split second reminds me of Rubio. It takes a moment to place it, but it eventually comes to me. Rubio would give me the same grin whenever I believed in something he knew to be untrue but didn't want to spoil my wishful thinking, like when I found money under my pillow and thought the tooth fairy left it there. Nestor looks at his watch and then lifts himself out of the recliner. "Look, I'm headed to the block."

"When's the meeting?"

"Not until six, but a soldier has to show up on the front, especially since I've been running around for the past two hours looking for your behind." Nestor laughs. "Let's go."

"Nah, man, I'm going to have to meet you at Snipes's."

"C'mon, bro—"

"I'll be there, I swear. Go back to the block and spread the word that Scout'll be in the house," I say. "But I have to head to AC and meet Candace. We haven't spoken since everything went down. I gotta see her."

Nestor is satisfied with that. "I like her for you." He walks to his door. Before leaving, he shouts, "And don't even think about being on time. Be early!"

And just like that, I'm more caught up than ever.

Renunciation ♦ (*n.*) rejection

I wait outside the school until the tutoring program ends. Chingy comes through the door and holds it for someone behind him. Candace. My gut smolders as if I'd swallowed a crust of lava. Candace listens to Chingy with the same intensity that he's speaking. Should I be comforted or bothered by the seriousness of their conversation? Are they discussing me? If they suddenly were to laugh, would I feel better or worse about their closeness?

I catch up to them as they reach the corner and call out Candace's name. They stop and turn. Chingy says something to her and continues on his way. As I near Candace, the fury surges over her cheeks and into her eyes. When I reach for her, she backs up a few steps and tries to storm off. "C'mon, ma, don't be like that." I grab her arm. "I can explain everything."

"What's there to explain?" she yells as she swats at my hand. "You're a drug dealer."

The words slam me in the gut. Even though I always knew I was committing a crime, I still never thought of myself as a criminal. "I've wanted to tell you the truth for the longest, but this is exactly what I was afraid of."

Candace sticks her finger in my face. "You should've been! Just when people in this school have stopped calling me *that K-Ville kid* so close to my back that I actually hear them, my boyfriend gets arrested for selling cocaine on the street. Now the same gossips who never had two words for me are in my face twenty-four/seven asking me questions." She starts to walk away from me. "I'm not doing it, Efrain! I won't go through that again. Not even for you."

I grab her hand. "What are you talking about?" She tries to pull away from me, but I hold tight. "What do you mean you won't go through this again?" I struggle to check my sudden rage at the idea that Candace is making me pay for someone else's mistake. "Sounds like you've got secrets, too, Candace!"

We stand there in the middle of the cold street, fuming at each other. "You're right, Efrain. I do have secrets. Want to hear a secret? Do you remember all those people who broke into stores and stole things after the hurricane? The 'looters'?" Candace sarcastically squeezes quotation marks in the air. "I was one of them. I didn't break the window. I didn't haul off a DVD player or television set. But I stole things. Things that I could. Whatever I could carry to share with other hungry people."

I don't know what hurts more—that Candace didn't tell me this before or that she believed I would judge her for it. I reach out for her hand one more time, and this time she doesn't pull away. "Candace, you did what you needed to survive." I pull her toward me, and she leans into my chest. "Nobody knows what they would do in a situation like that until they're in it." I think about how often people are too busy judging what others in dire straits are doing when they should be giving thanks that they are not in a position to know with absolute certainty that they would not do the same. I say, "I totally understand, ma. Trust me, I do."

Suddenly Candace pushes away from me. "You don't have a clue, Efrain. Lie to yourself if you want to, but there's a big difference between you and me. I didn't steal those groceries because it was the difference between Hunter and Harvard, so don't you dare act like we're peas in a pod, because we're not."

"How are you going to judge me, Candace?" I say. A voice inside of me orders, *Square your shoulders, son, and tell that fickle chick to fall back.* "You know what? I'm not going to argue with you. I'm doing what I have to do because I'm out here on my own." Now I'm the one who starts to back off. "I thought you knew something about that, but I was wrong. I always suspected it, too. That's why I didn't say anything, so forget you."

I brace myself for her to run after me and wild out. I *want* her to. Cuss me. Grab me. Maybe even hit me. Instead, she yells, "No, Efrain. Forget *you*." Even though I don't turn around, I can see Candace standing there, shaking her head at me. "You didn't say anything because you wanted to do what you wanted to do even though you know it was wrong. Just like your father."

In a flash, I'm in Candace's face again. I grab at her, but she sees me coming, and slaps my hands away, her eyes locked on mine. The girl is not the least bit shook. "What you gonna do? Hit me? I'm not scared of you." I reach, Candace blocks. "I stood on the Crescent City Bridge and had the racist-ass Gretna police stick a shotgun in my face to keep me from crossing, so just what do you think you're going to do to me, Efrain?"

I fall back, and for a second, Candace actually looks sorry for me. We are more alike than ever, striving to be something good only because others can be so bad. Candace and me, we're so eager to march forward alone even if we stumble out of bounds. Not for its own sake, though, because pride and independence are virtues. Only because we decided that we cannot rely on anyone to step up for us. It's not a good look.

That true voice says, *Tell her you're sorry for the way your actions affected her.* But it seems trifling. I'm trifling, putting my hands on her like that. So desperate to touch her, knowing all along if she reached out to me, I would push her away. Why hasn't Candace walked away from me? I make it right by doing what she won't.

I walk away, and because we're more alike than she thinks, Candace just watches me go.

Conformist ♦ (n.) one who behaves the same as others

When I hit the block, Nestor says, "Yo, E., LeRon's got something for you." He has a cheesy grin on his face, so I suspect his efforts to salvage my name are working. I walk over to LeRon. "What's up, L.?" I give him a pound and notice the folded sweatshirt draped over his shoulder.

"Yo, Scout, check it." LeRon unzips his parka, and who pops out at me but Frazzle. That's right. Homeboy's wearing a sweatshirt with that Muppet's bushy-eyed grille on it.

"Oh no!" I laugh for the first time in days. "Where'd you get that?"

"My sister made it for me when I told her how y'all be doing me." LeRon starts counting the ways on his fingers. "She says I look like him, talk like him, act like him. . . . Nigga's even afraid of the dentist like me." LeRon is so serious, I crack up some more. "What you laughing at, man? Ain't you ever seen that movie *Marathon Man*?"

"No." I had never even heard of it until now.

"Peep that shit and see if you ever go to the dentist again." Then LeRon tosses the sweatshirt hanging over his shoulder at me. "This one's for you."

I catch the sweatshirt and unfold it. Kermit the Frog. I have to smile. At least, it ain't Elmo. LeRon clowns me. "But Kermy's cool, though," I pretend to argue. "He writes books, does movies. . . . He's, like, a Renaissance frog."

LeRon gives me a look like we're debating capital punishment. "His girlfriend's a pig, yo."

"You don't know my shorty, so keep her out of it." My argument with Candace crashes back into my consciousness. I shouldn't take out my problems with her on LeRon. Least of all now, with all the postraid *chisme* in the crew, but if he volunteers . . .

"Ah!" He points at me. "You were about to wild out, weren't you? Aha!"

I head back to Nestor, yelling over my shoulder, "Yo, Frazzle, one more thing. You need to go see the dentist *before* your teeth start falling out. That be the point." Nestor's cracking up. Guess he knew about Kermit before I did. "It ain't that funny, Elmo."

"Nah, I ain't Elmo, kid."

"Yeah, you are. You're simple, you're ticklish, you're stuck at the age of three. . . ." Nestor unzips his leather jacket. "Yooo . . . it's Fozzie!" I just lose it. "Man, you cats are taking me back. I forgot all about Fozzie."

"Yeah," says Nestor. "Wocka, wocka, nigga." It's a miracle I don't piss myself, I'm laughing so hard. It's insane that I'm laughing at all. An alarm on Nestor's cell phone sounds. "It's time, y'all."

Nestor and I walk down the block, and as we pass the other guys in the crew, they fall in behind us while, across the street, Hinckley's boys sneer. Nestor elbows me and cocks his head in their direction. "The second we're gone, they're going to be all over our side of the street, but that's all right," he says. "For the next hour, we grantin' amnesty, and that'll be the most paper they'll see all month." He holds out his fist, and I give him a pound as I glance over my shoulder. LeRon and a dozen others swagger behind us, blazing mugs across Hunts Point Avenue at the competition. I catch eye with that punk Julian. He spits from the corner of his mouth, but I scoff right back to his face before killing eye contact.

When we reach the office, Trace is outside smoking an L. "How you left the block?" he asks Nestor.

Nestor offers him his hand, and they pull in for mutual back slaps. "It's a lovely day in the neighborhood, bro." Trace laughs, which I've never seen him do. Yeah, Nestor definitely is on the rise in Snipes's operation because Trace doesn't smile for anyone, let alone laugh *with* them.

Trace opens the door, and we all file into the building and into Snipes's office. He has the radio on the quiet storm while he throws darts. The man's pretty good, landing most of them near the bull's eye, although none actually hit. On a table against the wall is a giant submarine hero, some tubs of macaroni and potato salad, paper cups, plates, and whatnot. Beneath the table sits a cooler of sodas and forties on fresh ice.

LeRon points at the hero and yells, "Yo, that's for us?" He ignores the guys who clown him for asking, circling the buffet and praying for consent.

"Go on, Frazzle," says Snipes, and we all laugh. No one thought he knew about that, and I wonder if I got the credit. "Fix yourselves a plate and sit down." Everyone swoops on the hero like pigeons to crumbs. Despite Nestor's grim warnings, the mood is ridiculously light. Snipes turns off the radio and heads to the front of the room and waits for us to settle. Once everyone has their plate and a seat, Snipes begins. "I called y'all here to give you a heads-up. The block is hotter than you think because last week's sweep wasn't on the same old, same old. I got intel that five-oh hosed the av because they heard Hinckley and me are

232

about to declare war over these corners. The po thought *Clean the street,* make both crews worry too much about them to mess with each other."

With a mouth whitened with mayonnaise, LeRon yells, "They was grilling me like a steak, yo. The DT even started volunteering all this scuttle about Hinckley, trying to get a reaction one way or the other." He sinks his Frazzle-like fangs into his hero.

"He tried to play me like that, too," says a dude in the back of the room. "Gossiping like some girl, man. I thought I was back in high school." Some guys snicker. "I told 'im straight up, *Yo, if I cared about that shit, I'd stay home and watch TMZ.*"

Everyone laughs. Then Nestor asks, "But nobody flapped, though, right, Snipes?"

"Everybody in here stood tall." Heads holler *No doubt* and *That's how we do.* "Don't get it twisted," he says, waving for everyone to quiet down. "Just because I appreciate loyalty when it's given doesn't mean I don't expect it or mete out consequences if my expectations aren't met." Now there isn't so much as a gulp on a mouthful of Red Bull, and I suspect I'm not the only one sneaking glances around the room looking for who's missing from this appreciation party. More *No doubt*s and *That's how we do*s but with noticeably less enthusiasm. "Still, I'm happy to see my soldiers staving away the competition and dodging the regulators."

Suddenly Nestor slaps my shoulder and says to the group, "Even the rookie stood tall, and they came at my boy hard." But we never talked about that. Did he find out what happened to me in the holding cell at arraignment? Is he aware of how fast I fell when true thugs came for me? What if that incident made the grapevine? Nestor would've had to spin some yarn on the street to convince the guys that I'm not the one who snitched.

Somebody howls, "Scouut!" Others chime in while Nestor

pats me on the back. A queasy feeling comes over me. I like the props, but I don't deserve them. My night in the pen wasn't my finest hour, even though I didn't flap. The more love Nestor and the boys show me, the harder I have to fight to keep from vomiting.

Snipes looks at me and says, "Scout will tell you that I had my doubts about him from the day I met him. And when Julian stepped to you a while back, it surprised me when you came back the next night."

"Me too," says Trace.

"But let Scout be an example to all of you. Too many of you out here have it in your heads that the only thing you need out there is heart. You be talking sideways about a brother for going to school. You want to talk about gossip? Shit, I'm 'bout to call the Colonel 'cause I know some heads in here be clucking all day, every day." A few of the guys laugh, but most stare at their half-eaten sandwiches. "If you don't have a strong mind, you'd better have mad heart. And if you ain't got no heart, then you'd best be smart. A man needs to have at least one or the other in order to survive. But the man who takes the effort to develop both is the man that thrives."

And heads mumble *Real talk* as if it were the gangsters' amen. It crosses my mind that maybe I should hang back after the meeting and have a man-to-man with Snipes. Be real with him. Tell him that I have to quit and focus on preparing for the next SAT, improving my grade in physics, looking out for Mandy and even Junior, putting Moms at ease, winning back Candace. . . . That as much as his respect means to me, as much as I've grown to like LeRon and the others, as much as the money eases my mind, he was right. These streets are not for me.

Nestor's voice interrupts my fantasy of coasting out of the game as easily as I slid into it. "You dropped this," he says, handing me the Kermit sweatshirt that LeRon asked his sister to make me. I take it from him and dust it off. If I tell Nestor what I'm thinking, he'll insist that it's still too soon to walk away. He doesn't need to say that for me to know that despite all the love, he's right. It's the love that makes Nestor right. Just like these cats to make it so hard to leave now that I need most to go.

Camaraderie ♦ (*n.*) brotherhood

Somehow Melo manages to sleep through Claudia and Robby's latest argument. I lie there in the dark on an inflatable bed wondering if lying in a Ranger grave is what drew Leo to the Marines. He probably gets more sleep in the freezing Iraqi desert in the middle of a war than during one of his sister's nightly battles with her man of the moment.

Then I think of Candace. Lying on that bed, I wonder did she feel the way I do now—alone on a float with no clue where she's going or how to find her family? I feel so close to her now, I force her out of my mind. My immediate worries take up too much space; there's no room for her right now.

"That's it!" Nestor jumps out of the bed, flings open the door, and storms into the living room. Now he and Robby get into it. They play a round of *¿Quien es Mas Macho?* Nestor wins by reminding Robby that he doesn't contribute a dime to this household. *In the few days that my homeboy Efrain has been staying here, he's bought more groceries than in all the months you've been here,* he says at one point. *And he ain't even blood. Ten years younger than you and ten times the man so shut the hell up or step the fuck off!* The apartment door slams as Robby sulks off, and Claudia lights into Nestor for not minding his own business. Nestor takes the high road, enduring his sister's rant without interruption until she chases tearfully after Robby.

When Nestor returns to his bedroom, he slams the door and

clicks the new knob. A startled Melo whimpers, and Nestor rushes over to soothe him. "Shhh, papa." In the darkness, I imagine Nestor stroking his little brother's hair as he coos in his ear. "Everything's okay. Go back to sleep." A few minutes later, the only sound is Melo's deep breathing. Nestor whispers, "E., you up?"

"How can I not be with all that drama going on?" I roll over on the air mattress. "Yo, why you had to put my name in it?" Especially since I haven't given him a cent for staying here, which just makes me feel like an herb.

"For months Claudia's been trying to move that chump in here, and I knew from the jump he was going to try to run shit." Nestor's shadow sits up in the dark. "The night we got knocked, he saw his shot and rushed the crib. Fool hasn't left since. He's the one who broke the knob off my door talking about *Let me get at least one freakin' kid out of my hair*. Sits around all day watching TV, smoking L's, eating up all our food while Claudia waits on him hand and foot. I'm telling you, bro, I need to move the hell up out of this piece!" Nestor throws himself back down on his bed.

"Word to life."

We're quiet for a few minutes. Then Nestor says, "Yo, E., remember that book Baraka had us read? The one about those three guys in Newark who made an oath to go to college and become doctors."

"*The Pact.*"

"Yeah, that's it. When you graduate from AC, let's find a nice apartment somewhere far from these clowns. Be roommates."

The idea appeals to me even though it doesn't fit my dreams. "For me, far from here isn't Brooklyn, kid. When I graduate, I'm kicking rocks all the way to Massachusetts or someplace like that." Only if I'm lucky. Harvard now has the same faded pattern of that yellowing wallpaper in my mother's kitchen.

Nestor is quiet. "You really think you're going to get into Harvard?" He asks as if he wants to know whether I truly believe that much in myself. As if he wonders whether there is enough confidence so he can find some for himself.

But for all my bravado and hustle, I actually don't. Not deep down inside where the truth lives within me. The darkness demands that I face the inevitable. "I can only tell you one thing for sure. I'm not staying here." I hold my next thought, wanting to be sure I only say it if I mean it. "Wherever I land, you can ride with me if you want."

"Can I bring Melo?"

I burst out laughing. "What you think this is, kid?" Then I get uncomfortable. "People are going to think we're gay!"

"No they won't!"

"Shhh! You're going to wake up your brother."

Nestor lowers his voice. "It's gonna be like *Two and a Half Men*. I'ma be Charlie Sheen, and you'll be that other cat. His brother the herb." I grab my pillow and fire it at his shadow. We crack up. "Chill!" Nestor snickers. "Don't wake up Melo."

"Whatever, yo."

Then Nestor gets serious again. "I can't go and leave him here, E. You know that. If I can barely take it . . . ."

"Okay. But y'all can't come with me if you're going to be slinging or anything like that. You need to make your rent legit."

"I know." Silence passes until Nestor yawns. "We don't have to settle everything now. Let's just sleep on it." I hear him kiss Melo on the head, then roll over.

Within minutes, I yawn, roll over, and sleep on it, too.

Contrite ♦ (*adj.*) penitent, eager to be forgiven

A few days later, I get to the corner of St. Ann's and 141st Street fifteen minutes early. I catch the initial break in Chingy's stride at the sight of me, and I expect him to rush past me or even cross to the other side of the street. Instead, he regains his swagger and heads toward me, slowing down to a stop to face me. I speak first. "What's up?"

"S'up." After a few seconds of silence, Chingy continues to walk, and I fall in next to him. "Your moms . . . She be asking for you. I told her that I see you in school every day, but I don't know where you be staying at."

"Tell her I'm at Nestor's."

Chingy shakes his head as if to say *Nah, I can't tell her that.* "Your sister ran up to me the other day crying. Asking if you were dead or in jail."

"Damn."

"I let her know you're all right, but I don't think she believed me."

"I want to come home, but it ain't that easy." Anticipating an argument from Chingy, I rush to defend my position. "With the raid and everything, if I try to bounce now—"

"I know," interrupts Chingy, his voice filled with understanding. "Now you know why I never wanted to get into it."

"Yeah, well, I got in it, so . . ."

239

We walk for a block in silence. Then Chingy asks, "You retake the SAT yet?"

"Nah, not yet. The test is in two weeks, but I don't know if I'm ready." I don't tell Chingy about the recurring nightmares I now have about the test. I log on to the computer to take the SAT, but instead of loading the first screen of exam questions, it flashes Chingy's admission calculation system. The computer demands that I guess what my score will be before it will allow me to take the test. I enter "2200." The screen blinks, and the box where I typed my guess is empty again. This time I put in "1650," and again, it spits the empty box back at me. I panic, typing in one random number after the other as the clock on the wall clicks away minutes as if they were seconds. I say, "My concentration's wrecked these days." I wait for Chingy's sarcastic remark, but he just nods his head as if that's all he needs to hear.

We walk the final block in silence. As we reach the entrance to the school, I say, "Chingy, will you do me a favor?" Finally, he gives me a look as if I have some nerve, and I take that because this is the guy I once knew. I reach into my backpack for the three-page letter I wrote after waking up from that nightmare and not being able to go back to sleep. "When you see Candace at work, will you give this to her for me?"

Chingy stares at the envelope for a second, snatches it from my hand, then runs into the building before I can say thanks. The first bell rings, and I rush toward Señorita Polanco's class. Throughout the day, Chingy no longer gives me those cold stares in class, but he doesn't speak to me either.

Nor does he show at the corner of St. Ann's and 141st Street the next morning either. Or the morning after that. Or the one after that. Not a word from Candace either.

Assail ♦ (v.) to attack

It's almost one in the morning, and I've been out here since seven. With the SAT next weekend, I tried to study for those four hours after school in the library, but my head wasn't in it. Even when the money flows, my heart isn't into this hustle these days either. Every time a car rolls up, I relive the sweep and fall back. But the charges over our heads slow no one's roll but mine, so occasionally I get aggressive with the foot traffic just to keep suspicions at bay.

Hunts Point becomes my escape from the midnight showing of the melodrama du jour at Nestor's apartment. Now Claudia is accusing Robby of messing around with Marlene. Last night I had to listen to Nestor fantasize aloud about actually catching them in the act so he can call the cops on Robby or kill him, depending on how he feels in the heat of that moment. Let me be on the street when that happens. In fact, sometimes I don't mind being out here, and it isn't because of the money. I chop it up with Nestor, LeRon, and the other guys, allowing me to forget that I might have shot the lights out on my future. On the streets, we talk light and laugh hard, never looking any further than when the next blockbuster will hit theaters or Nike will release the latest Jordans.

But now it's time to call it a night. "I'm out," I say. "I'm too through with this cold."

Nestor tightens the strings of his hood. "I'll walk you to the train." We walk to the corner of Bruckner and wait for the light. "So, E., when do you take that test?"

The question throws me. We never discuss college unless I bring it up. "This Saturday." I fake a laugh. "Too soon."

"No matter how you score, you're still going to college, you feel me? Don't forget our pact."

"No doubt." I rub my hands and blow on them. The light changes, and we start across the expressway.

"If you don't get into Harvard, go to Hunter," says Nestor. "Just the other day, I was reading in the *Post* that it's one of the best public colleges in the country."

"Word?" And for some reason, the news actually gives my heavy heart the tiniest lift.

"If you're gonna be the first Hispanic mayor, you have to go to college, man," says Nestor. "No ifs, ands, or buts about it, bro."

He's so adamant, I have to laugh. "If I'm going to be the first Hispanic mayor, I need to quit slinging, kid."

But Nestor is mad serious about this. "No worries, E. I keep telling you, that little arrest ain't going to hurt you none. You're only seventeen. Chances are they'll . . . What do they call that when they throw out your criminal record?"

"Expunge."

"Yeah, they're going to expunge that shit, so forget about it."

"But how do I know that when I'm on the campaign trail, someone like LeRon won't try to blow up my spot?" The dream of becoming the mayor of New York City is so out of reach, I can afford to clown the possibility. "Yeah, he's going to wait until I run to get some payback and put a brother on blast to the New York *Daily News* for calling him Frazzle."

Nestor laughs. "Nah, man, LeRon likes that Frazzle mess. You'd be lucky if he came to you with his hand out. Pay him off and call it a day. It'd be worse if the dude actually wanted you to give him, like, a job!"

I run with that. "I'd hook up LeRon, no doubt. Maybe I give him a job with Children's Services, you know, entertaining the kids in group homes or something." Nestor busts out laughing. "You didn't think I was going to make him the commissioner of something, did you?"

Nestor laughs so hard, he has to lean on me. That gets me started. We stumble a few paces, holding each other up like two drunks. He finally says, "But you'd look out for me, though, right, E.?"

"Yeah, kid, I got you."

"I'm not saying make me a commissioner or anything. But you could hook me up with a little somethin', right? They ain't gonna expunge my record, but you could still grant me a mayoral pardon or whatever."

"Don't count that out, Nestor," I say as I remember something I learned in my criminal law elective last year. "Under certain conditions, you might be able to file a petition in court to have your criminal record expunged even if you're no longer a minor."

Nestor's eyes glow in the beam of the street lamp. "Word?"

"Yeah, but you gotta, like, become a model citizen and whatnot."

"I can do that."

"Yo!"

We stop in our tracks and turn toward the bark. Julian, Lefty, and three more of his boys cross the boulevard on a diagonal. "Go ahead, E.," says Nestor. "I got this."

As much as I want to jet, I can't leave Nestor alone in this situation. "He wants me," I say, the truth burning sour in my dry mouth. "Dude's been trying to get at me for a minute."

243

"Well, tonight's not his night, so go home."

But a mixture of fear and loyalty freezes me in place. Julian and his boys touch down on our curb and slow their swagger. They stop a few yards from us, and as if moving on instinct, Nestor steps in front of me. "What's up, Julian?"

"Fall back, nigga," he says. "This ain't with you."

"Any beef you've got with Scout you got with me," says Nestor.

I come out from behind Nestor to stand beside him. "Why you got beef with anybody is beyond me," I say. My heart pounds as if it wants to leap out of my mouth and scurry for safety. "Ain't nobody knocking your hustle."

Julian steps closer to me, his finger pointing above my head. "Your very presence knocks my hustle, son." Lefty sneers at me, and I just know he's the reason behind the static on street. No matter what Nestor wants to believe, I think he's the police informant, and my arrival on the block made it easy to point everyone's suspicions in my direction. Lefty has it in for Snipes, and I bet anything he isn't even that loyal to Hinckley. I have no idea what game he's running. All I know is that I'm not playing anymore.

I find the courage to say, "Look, bro, I don't know what y'all heard about me, but I think you should question the credibility of your sources." Lefty sucks his teeth, but Julian's eyes flicker. He's actually considering what I'm telling him. "Why do you keep checking for me when I'm not the one jumping back and forth across the street?"

"Real talk," says Nestor.

Lefty yells, "Yo, J., I know you ain't gonna let this Boy Scout son you, man!"

Julian snaps, "I check for you 'cause I don't like the cut of your jib."

Cut of my jib? Dude's been watching too many pirate movies. Charge it to my nerves, but this picture of Julian as Captain Jack Sparrow flashes into my head, and I start to laugh. The harder I try to stop, the more I laugh, and Nestor gets it because he mumbles *Yaaar!* under his breath.

"You see that?" Lefty says to Julian. "That's what I'm talking about right there."

I collect myself barely in time to see Julian reach into the back of his waistband for a chunk of silver metal.

Nestor sees it, too, and before I can yell, he leaps on top of me. A girl's scream from across the street, the *pop-pop-pop* of Julian's gun, the fading thud of his posse's kicks against the pavement—everything that occurs in those seconds lashes into my brain. A burn rips through my side as Nestor's weight slams against my chest. My hip cracks as our bodies hit the cold pavement.

"Yo, E.?" Nestor sounds as if he's the one with a hundred twenty-five pounds pinning him to the ground. "E., you all right?"

"I'm straight," I lie. The pain in my side bustles toward the back of my head, which just bounced off the street. "You?" All I can see is the sooty underpass of the Bruckner Expressway above us.

"I'm good." He tries to laugh, and that's how I know he's lying, too. "But, yo, I think it's time we found another line of work."

This time I let Nestor have his way. "Word is bond," I say.

"Nah, man," says Nestor, more for himself than to me. "Word is *born*." I wait for Nestor to laugh again, but if he does, I can't hear him over the sounds of sirens and screaming. Then I don't hear anything more.

Compunction ♦ (*n.*) distress caused by feeling guilty

I see nothing yet feel everything. When I try to shift my mind off the pain in my side, I realize that my entire back aches. Only pain exists behind the darkness of my eyes, so I make the mistake of opening them.

My mother, her eyes red and swollen, nestled in crow's feet. She realizes that I've come to and sobs out my name and strokes my hair. Rubio appears behind her. That smile—the same one that tells me he knows something I don't—fades onto his face. Then the images fast-forward to Nestor sitting in his leather slice of heaven with the same smile only to settle into slow motion. Four shadows crossing the boulevard. Julian's scowl. A flash of silver. The underpass of the Bruckner Expressway. A flattened wad of gum on the concrete. The darkness again. I flutter my eyes to chase it away.

"Nestor?" I ask. "How is he?"

My mother lets out another sob, and Rubio walks away.

I close my eyes again, yearning for the darkness now. With it comes one of Nestor's urban legends. He and I are on an elevator with Mrs. Colfax. We are men in suits, she an old lady clinging to her purse. I am the mayor of New York, he is my chief of staff, and we laugh at her failure to recognize us. The elevator stops, and Mrs. Colfax flees. We laugh at her some more, Nestor doing his little dance. The elevator stops again, and I step off. I turn around

246

to say something to Nestor, who is still in the car. Suddenly the doors slam shut and the car plunges, Nestor's screams fading as it plummets down the shaft. Even though he is already gone, I lunge for him as if I can still save him. Instead, I fall into the shaft, hanging by one hand for my life, my side tearing, my voice echoing Nestor's name.

I wake up alone in the dark, calling his name and gripping the bloody bandages over my side.

Acquiesce ♦ (*v.*) to agree without protesting

A few days later, they let the kids see me.

First, Awilda comes with Serenity and the baby. As Junior sleeps on the shoulder of my good side, Serenity bombards me with questions about what happened. "Serenity, that's so damn rude," Awilda yells. "You're embarrassing me."

At first, I dodge the questions, patting Junior's back and thinking about Nestor. He was so wrong about what makes a man. Nes wasn't a man because he took care of his family by any means necessary. He was a man because he cared enough about them to come home every night. Being there to soothe Melo's nightmares and not being too macho to kiss him, that's what made Nestor a man. He was a man for blocking men like Robby who would take advantage of his sisters. Only a man could recognize, never mind appreciate, GiGi for being as smart as she was pretty. I hope Nestor realizes he was wrong and is doing his laugh dance all the way to heaven.

I finally tell Serenity one of Nestor's urban legends. She eats it up, at one point yelling, "No! That's not true. You got that from a movie or something." She can't help but giggle, wanting to believe every word I say.

"You're right. I'm making it up," I say. *The truth is worse.* "Still, you don't want to end up like me, so listen to your mother." I don't care if she only did it to gain favor with Rubio, and she will never hold a candle to my mother, but Awilda is here. Not Chingy. Not Candace. Awilda, and she brought Serenity and Junior with her. And as if she can read my mind and wants to prove her sincerity, she says, "We have to go now, Serenity, so give your brother a kiss and tell him that you'll see him tomorrow."

Then Mandy comes. She just bursts into my room and leaps on my bed. "Efrain!"

"Ow, kid!"

Moms appears breathless in the doorway. "Amanda!"

"It's okay, Mami." The first time my mother let me hold her, I was six, my sister about five months. The family kept telling me *You're a big brother now, Efrain. It's your job to look out for your sister.* They put it in my head that I now had some responsibility for Mandy that was different but just as important as my parents, and yet no one would allow me to hold her. I finally complained to my mother, and she called me over and showed me how to hold Mandy, cupping my hand behind her neck to support her soft, tiny head. She felt so heavy in my arms, but the sense of obligation to protect her had been drilled into me. Even though my arm had fallen asleep, my legs were tired, and the small of my back was aching, I refused to put down my sister.

That same feeling comes back to me now as Mandy buries her head into my chest. "You're so stupid, Efrain!" She tightens her grip around me, pressing her forearm against my wound. The pain is excruciating, but I take it. She sobs and repeats, "Why are you so stupid?"

Even as I wince, I reach up to stroke her hair as she cries. "I know, kid." Inside I thank Mandy for sharing my bloodlines, for releasing me from the obligation to put on a brave face, for giving me the permission to break. She keeps calling me stupid as she wails into my chest, and every time I kiss her head, I sob, too. "I know."

Condolence ◆ (*n.*) an expression of sympathy in sorrow

"Hi, Efrain."

GiGi walks into my hospital room. She has on no makeup, and like a true Halle, she doesn't need it. In fact, she looks so much prettier without it. No tight jeans or high heels either. Just a pink sweat suit and simple tennis shoes, all with no brand name I recognize. For the first time, GiGi looks like a girl who is pacing herself toward eighteen rather than racing toward twenty-five. She wears her true age well.

"Hey." She starts to sit down on the chair by the window, but I say, "No, come here." I pat the bed beside my knee. "Just promise not to move around a lot, okay?"

"Okay." She comes over and eases herself onto the bed. "Do you need anything? Water or something?"

"No, I'm good, thanks."

"Man, I'm so rude. I didn't bring a card or flowers or anything." She seems genuinely embarrassed. "I'm so sorry."

"That's all right. I don't need any of that. You're enough." I reach out and pat GiGi's hand as we allow her tears to flow. We sit there for a few seconds, her gentle sniffles occasionally seeping onto the silence. "You and me, we have a lot in common, GiGi. That's why we should be friends. I know there was a time you wanted more, but I don't know . . . You kind of scared me."

"Me?" Her shock surprises me. Don't girls like GiGi know

they're scary? I thought that knowledge fueled all their sway. But then again, if GiGi knew that about herself, she wouldn't have been so hurt when I distanced myself from her. "Why would you be scared of me?"

"I'm not sure, to be honest with you." It seems like one of those things that takes experience to understand, never mind explain to someone else. "On some level, I just knew that Candace was the better girlfriend for me and Nestor was the better boyfriend for you. Not because he was street or anything like that. Just because Nestor, for whatever reason, wasn't afraid of all who you were. I mean, he could appreciate it in a way that I don't think any of us—not me, not Chingy, none of us at school—were grown enough to even see."

But GiGi just looks down at her hands, smiling to herself. She probably understands better than I do. Maybe that's why she came to see me low-key, leaving all the makeup and gear at home. "Nestor loved you like a brother, you know that, right?" Her words switch on my tears, so I just nod. "Before we got together, I had bumped into him at the Hub, you know, and I told him that I had seen y'all on Fulton Street, shopping for clothes or whatever. He said that he lied to you about your boss wanting him to take you to get some new gear. He said, *I just wanted to hang out with E. You know, off the block. When we were all broke, E., Chingy, and me, we'd go to the Hub and look through the windows all the time.*" GiGi giggles. "I told him that was no big deal, but he felt so bad, Efrain. So when he asked me out, I said yes. I figured *He's friends with Efrain, right? He can't be bad.*"

Then she brings her hands to her face and starts to sob. I just lie there, staring at the stained tiles on the ceiling of my room. GiGi eventually wipes her face and clears her throat. "What makes this so hard is that we almost did it, Efrain." I don't think this is something I can stand to hear right now, but I can't stop her.

"Between you and me, I think we could've saved him. Nestor told me about how you guys talked about getting an apartment together once you graduated from AC. He was so excited about that, Efrain. And I said to him, *Well, don't think you're going to move in with E. and still be slinging while he's going to college.* And he said, *I know.* But then Nestor said maybe y'all shouldn't bother 'cause in a year you'd be transferring to another school and moving to Massachusetts or Connecticut or someplace like that. So I said to him, *Maybe if you and me are still together when Efrain moves, I can move in when he transfers. But you know, Nes, we're not going be together if you're still working that corner.* I mean, why go to college if I want to live like that, right?"

"No doubt." I truly had GiGi all wrong. A lot of us guys did, Nestor included. Funny how I judged her in the same ways I never wanted anyone to judge me even when I made the choice to live down to the stereotype. I say, "Thanks for coming to see me, ma."

She squeezes my hand. "That's what friends are for."

Atone ♦ (v.) to repent, make amends

Just when I accept that he's not coming to see me, Chingy shows. He bops into my hospital room as if I lived here. "S'up, son?" Then he tosses a bulky knapsack onto my bed.

I ricochet into a seated position. *"Ow!"*

"That's what you get for almost getting yourself killed."

"What you got in here, kid?"

"Your books, fool."

"Oh." I had hoped that Candace would bring them to me, but she still hasn't so much as called my home to ask my mother about me. "Thanks."

"On top of everything, you're not going to drop out," says Chingy. "Messing up my senior project . . ."

Yeah, I've been lying here thinking about the Rashaan Perry College Admission Probability Calculation System when not agonizing over the fact that Chingy hadn't come to see me. "Well, stick to that 1650 I got on the SAT in October. I was supposed to retake the exam the weekend after I got shot, so . . ." I try to imagine myself back at school. I see the eyes of the other students staring at me in class. I hear their whispers as I limp down the hallway. Before my first crack at the SAT, when I would go to bed at night after studying, I would fall asleep to visions of myself wearing my cap and gown and giving the valedictory speech at graduation. I can't see any of that anymore.

Chingy doesn't know what to say, but I'm not mad at him. He points to the backpack. "There's some other stuff in there, too. Cards and notes and stuff from the teachers and kids at school."

"Yeah? Thanks." I unzip, then reach into the bag. The first thing I pull out is my civil rights textbook. I had used Candace's paper as a bookmark, penciling checks in the margin next to facts I wanted to cite in my own project on the aftermath of Hurricane Katrina. "You've seen Candace around?"

"Just at school."

"How's she holding up?"

Chingy sits on the edge of my bed. "She didn't come to school for a day or two, and I didn't see her at Nestor's funeral." The wound in my side burns at the reminder that I missed my chance to say goodbye. Did Snipes pay for it? I bet LeRon and the others represented even though none of them have come to see me. "Then she came back, and people had a lot of questions, thinking she would have the answers, but they meant well, though. Not like last time, when, you know—"

"I got arrested."

"Yeah. Things did get a little hectic today. Leti was sweating her. *You gotta know something. Your man got shot, and you don't know nothing? Why don't you tell the truth?* GiGi even told Leti *Back up off of Candace already,* and you know Leti's her girl, so . . . Anyway, I've just been hanging out with her. You know, walking with her to school, taking her to class, just to make sure nobody bothers her."

"Leticia's going to start saying that you tried to off me so you could hook up with my girl." I remember seeing Chingy and Candace so cozy after school that day. *Let it go, E. Let it all go.* "Good lookin' out, though."

After a few seconds of silence, he asks, "Have the cops talked to you yet?"

"Yeah. You?"

"Everybody. That's how I found out what happened to you, bro. They just showed up at my place asking questions."

"They probably went over to Candace's, too." No wonder she hasn't come to visit me. Any love the Lamb matriarchs had for me is dead.

"Well, I had nothing to tell 'em, but they didn't believe me. Not that I care what the po think." Chingy pauses, then asks, "They asking you to give up the dude who shot y'all? Do you even know who did it?" I nod. "So . . ." I hesitate to respond. "Man, I know you're not even *thinking* about letting that fool get away with what he did to Nes!"

Chingy's reaction would knock me off my feet if I weren't already laid up in this hospital bed. I expected him to be lackadaisical about it. To say cold things like *Nestor reaped what he sowed*. But here he is telling me to snitch on Julian. "I don't know, man. . . . You know the code of the streets."

"You're not from those streets, and you never were!" he says. "Nestor snatched your life back from those streets." He paces like running water refusing to freeze. "You need to man up and stand tall for our boy, E." Chingy finally stops, and, for the first time since he arrived, he looks me straight in the eye. "Streets or no streets, code or no code, cred or no cred. Nestor would speak up for you. E., please." I realize how much Chingy needs to convince me. Justice for Nestor is atonement for him. But it could mean death for me. He may never have done any time on the streets, but Chingy knows how much this is to ask of me, and yet ask he does.

I knew Nestor. He wouldn't want me to give him up because

of all the trouble it would cause me. Yet Chingy's right. If Julian's bullet had found its target, Nestor'd do it for me. And no one would have stopped him from coming to pay his last respects to me. Not Snipes, not the police, no one. So while I'm happy that it will bring Chingy some peace, I will do this for Nestor. But then I'm going to have to go away for a very long time.

Cultivate ◆ (*v.*) to nurture, improve, refine

It surprises me how often Rubio comes alone to see me. The first time he shows up without my mother, I expect him to try and play father. Lecture me, guilt me for breaking my mother's heart, remind me that I have to be a role model to the other kids, and all that stuff I don't need Rubio to tell me. But, instead, he brings me coffee and *tostada* from a Dominican bakery and a few hip-hop magazines.

"How they treat you here?" he asks. "Good?"

"Yeah."

"You tell me, okay, if they don't treat you good. *Condena'o* HMOs. When you mother pregnant with you sister, they wanna push her out so fast, she almost have Amanda in the rrebolbing door."

I bite my tongue to keep from laughing. I don't want Rubio to think things are settled between us. Laughing might give him permission to abandon me again.

But Rubio returns. In fact, he comes every day, sometimes twice. At first, he tries to talk to me about baseball. I tell him I don't know the first thing about it. He asks me what I'm into. I say basketball. He shakes his head. I don't know if it's because he doesn't follow it or because he's disappointed that I'm not into baseball. "What's wrong with your people anyway?" I say in Spanish. "Living in New York City, then rooting for the Boston Red Sox. Y'all crazy."

That gets Rubio going in a way I never expected. With the

earnestness of someone running for office, he delivers a scouting report on all the great Dominican players on the Boston Red Sox. I pretend I don't want to hear it, and it becomes a game. Rubio swears that Dominicans are going to turn New York City into a three-team town—the Yankees, the Mets, and the Red Sox. Yeah, right, I say. *Dos semanas después de nunca.* Two weeks after never. If you *plátanos* have a problem with the hometown teams, I say, the lot of you can move to Beantown. I expect Rubio to take offense, but, instead, he laughs and laughs. "We can do that," he says, "but then you can forget about ever getting a cab to take you above Ninety-sixth Street."

Finally I laugh. "True." I have to give him that one.

And that's what we always end up talking about when Rubio visits: politics. I should say argue. We don't agree on a damn thing. He says Puerto Ricans should be doing everything in their power to become the fifty-first state. "All that talk about independence?" he chides. "Do they want to end up like the Dominican Republic?" I spit back one of Miss Polanco's nationalistic lectures. It gets to the point that I start to look forward to Rubio's visits just to work his nerves.

The day will come when I will tell Rubio everything that I suppressed all those years when I refused to let him be my father. Things I wouldn't admit to myself. Like how hurt I was that I guarded his secrets to keep him home and yet he still left me. Revelations that come to me at night after each of his visits and I sometimes turn on the television to drown out. I can only handle one loss at time, and Nestor may have been the latest, but now he has to come first. I'm not man enough yet to deal with all that at one time. But one day I will be, and I'll tell my father in a way that he can hear it. Maybe he won't be man enough to *listen,* but I will say it, and it will be enough.

For now it's politics.

Vindicate ♦ (*v.*) to avenge, free from allegations, set free

Two weeks after Nestor saved my life, I run a new marathon. Once the DA gave my parents the date when I had to testify before the grand jury, they booked my flight to Puerto Rico for the same afternoon. Today, I head from the hospital to the courthouse. After I tell the grand jury everything about the night Nestor died, Rubio will drive me straight to Kennedy Airport, where I will board a flight to Ponce. My grandmother will pick me up from Mercedita Airport, and we'll drive another half hour through the mountains to her house in Guavate. I can leave because Miss Avery convinced the DA to drop the charges pending against me in exchange for my testimony. With the evidence the police gathered against Julian after I gave him up, she expects him to cop a plea. And Lefty? I still don't know his exact role in this drama, but he can't outrun justice forever. Whether representing the law or the street, someone will knock on Lefty's door and collect his debt one day. It is what it is.

My mother cries as she helps me pack the few things I have at the hospital. All my other things—except whatever I had at Nestor's apartment, including all that cash—are already in a suitcase in Rubio's trunk. Neither of my parents wants me to testify. They fear for my safety but stand by and respect my decision to do it. As afraid as they are, I know they are both proud of me, and I remember that whenever I have second thoughts about going through with it.

Believe it or not, on most days, I'm not scared at all about what might happen to me after I testify. Maybe it's because I finally had a good dream last night. I dreamt that Chingy, Nestor, and I were walking down St. Ann's Avenue wearing graduation caps and gowns. The funny thing is we were older—college-age—and still heading toward AC. And Chingy and I were giving Nestor daps for realizing his impossible while he did his laugh dance, tickled to be graduating.

I woke up so happy. Even when all the realities settled as my eyes adjusted to the daylight—my leaving indefinitely for Puerto Rico, Chingy heading to Morehouse in ATL in September (after all that happened, he decided that he wanted to be closer to Baraka), and Nestor no longer walking the streets—I felt deeply hopeful for the first time in months. Even though the dream is at once a reminder of both the way things once were and now how they will never be, I truly believe Nestor sent me a message that it doesn't matter that the three of us are headed separately to places we had never planned. Each of us has still graduated to a place that will prove to be better than any other we have ever been.

Dream or no dream, I'm determined to outlast anyone who means me harm because I stood up for Nestor. Why should I live in fear of them? If the statistics hold any water, while I'm attending the University of Puerto Rico, one by one, they will either go to prison or die. Right or wrong, it is what it is. Now I've come too close to both destinies to wish either on any of those brothers, and I felt I had my reasons for doing what I did, so I'm in no position to judge theirs. But I'm mad clear on one thing: how damned lucky I am to have this second chance to beat the game by resisting the temptation to play. All I hope is that if any of them is lucky enough to get one, he is smart enough to take it.

"We got everything, right?" asks my mother as she zips

closed my carry-on bag. Even though we are ready to leave, neither of us moves.

Suddenly I blurt out, "Mami, I'm sorry." I try to squeeze back the tears to no avail. "For everything, Mami." I apologize for so much more than she knows. Things I may never have the heart to tell her, like how for years I knew that Rubio was cheating on her and kept his dirty secrets. That I did so for my own selfish reasons because as much as I hated him for disrespecting my mother, I also still loved him too much to risk losing him. I didn't want him to be angry with me, and I didn't want her to divorce him. Rubio forced a little boy to take sides, and like a little boy, I chose his simply because he was my father even though he was wrong. And he rewarded me for keeping his secrets by leaving instead of fighting for another chance and making things right.

My mother gestures for me to come to her. I limp over and bury my head in her lap. As she strokes my hair, she says, "I'm sorry, too, *m'ijo*. You made some mistakes, but this is not all your fault. We all made mistakes, especially me."

Fervent ♦ (*adj.*) ardent, passionate

I hobble out of the courtroom, and there is Candace sitting with my mother in the hallway. When she sees me, she races toward me and throws her arms around me. Scout would have been angry at her for staying away from me so long, but New Efrain doesn't care. She's here now, and I hold on tight for one last time.

"I wanted to come see you in the hospital, but once the police came to my house, my mother started watching me like a hawk," she sobs into my shoulder. Candace pulls back and I can see her pretty face. She smiles at me. "But you know me. Somehow I was going to find a way to see you."

How could I have ever doubted her? My girl survived a hurricane. I cling to Candace, both ecstatic to see her once more yet scared to death that I won't feel this way about anyone again. "Thanks, ma."

"Your mother tells me you're leaving for Puerto Rico today. When are you coming back?" Candace braces herself for an answer she doesn't want to hear.

"I don't know." Then I have to laugh. "It's funny because all this time you've been wanting to go to college back home, and now here I'm the one returning to the motherland and whatnot."

Candace strokes my cheek. "I'm happy for you." Even though the tears start to fall, I know she means it. "And someone gave me an airline ticket for Christmas, so maybe—"

"Efrain . . . ," my mother calls, pointing at the clock on the wall.

I put my arm around Candace and lean on her as we make our way to the elevator. "Don't think that you're off the hook," I say. "Physics is still kicking my ass, and you promised to help me."

We hold hands on the elevator ride to the lobby. My mother turns to Candace and asks, "Shouldn't you be in school?" Candace casts her eyes toward her sneakers, answering her question. Moms sighs and says, "Since you're here, there's room in the car if you'd like to go with us to the airport."

"Thank you, Mrs. Rodriguez!"

"Thanks, Mami."

My mother shakes her head as if to say *Kids,* but she can't hide her smile. I may look like my father, but I have that smile. From now on, I'm going to do everything I can to maintain that smile on both of us.

Outside the courthouse, Rubio is double-parked across the street, and Mandy sits in the front passenger seat. "How long is the ride to the airport?" asks Candace.

"About forty minutes."

She pouts. "That's not a lot of time."

No, it isn't a lot of time. But it's enough to explain anything that requires understanding, to profess all that we feel should be said, and to hope for everything we dare to want. Because there are no more secrets between Candace and me, forty minutes will do for now.

Acknowledgments

With every book I am blessed to publish, writing acknowledgments becomes increasingly difficult. Not because each book gives me less reason to need or desire support. On the contrary, every book brings new people into my life who—in ways both big and small—enable me to write the next one. Hence, attempting to name all the people I appreciate becomes such a daunting task that I risk not making any attempt at all. Please understand if this time around I focus on the handful of co-creators who played a particular role in developing this novel.

The Gaea Foundation, for the blessing that is the Sea Change residency.

My sister, Elisha Miranda. Thank you for the inspiration that was The Sista Hood: On the Mic (just one of innumerable gifts that you have bestowed upon me).

My literary agent, Jennifer Cayea. I hope you know that your persistent confidence means more than words can say.

My editor, Erin Clarke. Your insightful feedback and endless patience make me so excited to work on *Show-N-Prove*.

Leana Amaez and Vanessa Martir, for the time and expertise you generously lent so I could get certain details just right.

And most importantly, the brothers of the Urban Assembly Academy of History and Citizenship for Young Men, especially Danzel Blash, Devin Dixon, Ravon Morehand, Juan Polanco, and, of course, Chris "Pohetic" Slaughter. Your help improved my ability to tell Efrain's story well.